A KIM BRADY MYSTERY

JUDGMENT

OF

BEASTS

A NOVEL BY

EDWARD J. LEAHY

Black Rose Writing | Texas

ISBN: 978-1-68513-313-9
PUBLISHED BY BLACK ROSE WRITING
www.blackrosewriting.com

Printed in the United States of America
Suggested Retail Price (SRP) $23.95

Judgment of Beasts is printed in Baskerville

*As a planet-friendly publisher, Black Rose Writing does its best to eliminate unnecessary waste to reduce paper usage and energy costs, while never compromising the reading experience. As a result, the final word count vs. page count may not meet common expectations.

ALSO BY EDWARD J. LEAHY

KIM BRADY MYSTERY SERIES

Past Grief
Deceived By Ornament
Proving a Villain

DAN BRADY MYSTERY SERIES

Enemies of All

"O judgment! Thou art fled to brutish beasts,
and men have lost their reason…"
–Marc Antony in Julius Caesar, Act III, Scene 2

JUDGMENT
OF
BEASTS

CHAPTER ONE

Sunday, July 3rd

The enthusiastic crowd that had packed the plaza in front of Brooklyn's Borough Hall held its collective breath. Sabrina Dunn, the former New York City Public Advocate who had once served for a brief time as acting mayor, paused before finishing her speech. "I am running as a third-party candidate for governor because the two major parties have sold us out to the moneyed interests that control this city, this state, and this country. And if I've taken positions in the past that appeared radical, it was only to drag our government kicking and screaming back to the interests of the people rather than the interests of the favored few. I come to Brooklyn, and I ask for your help."

The throng surged forward against the police manning the perimeter in front of the entrance, but one man held back. Dunn's limo was parked on Court Street, and he watched as police forced open a path from the podium to the car.

Just as he'd foreseen.

But he hadn't foreseen the density of the crowd.

An expectant mother cried out, "We love you, Sabrina!"

All it took was a shove that no one saw. "Help! She fainted. We need a doctor."

Those nearby clustered around the fallen woman. In the pandemonium, no one heard her assurances that she was all right.

And his own path to Dunn's limo opened like magic.

No one saw the weapon as he pulled it from under the oversized tee shirt he wore, tucked into the waistband of his cutoffs. The candidate, spooked by the crowd, rushed ahead of her security people to get to the car.

He broke free of the crowd, rushing to help the fallen expectant mother.

Two shots.

Screams.

"Oh, my God," someone yelled. "She's down."

He had a clear path to Court Street.

He turned left onto Joralemon Street, tossing the gun into the shrubbery on the corner, and walked at a brisk pace toward the Borough Hall subway stop. As he reached the stairway, he turned as the rear door opened on a yellow car resembling a cab but without a dome light. He hesitated, surprised to see a fellow employee waiting for him in the back seat.

"Done?"

He exhaled with relief. "Done."

"Are you certain? We can't have any screwups."

"Positive. And the gun is in the shrubbery." He slid into the back seat and pulled off the flesh-colored latex gloves he'd been wearing.

The sudden jab of a needle in his left shoulder startled him, and then...

CHAPTER TWO

Wednesday, July 6th

After nearly two weeks in St. George, Bermuda, Detective Kim Brady no longer jumped at the sudden blare of a car horn from behind as she ran. She moved off the asphalt of Barry Road and onto the grass, slowing her pace both to watch her footing and to take in the ocean view.

The car zoomed past, and she crossed Grenadier Lane and kicked it into high gear as she tackled the last hill leading to the St. Regis Resort. A quick change into one of her new bikinis, and she and her husband, Jake Dudek, would head for the beach for a swim.

This Bermuda trip had been Jake's idea. Coming four months after Kim's third miscarriage in as many years and during an extended personal leave to deal with the depression that was no longer just a passing occurrence, it had been as therapeutic as he'd promised. They'd talked about adopting or fostering; perhaps they'd remain a childless, professional couple, as she'd expected when they'd married, before her experiences on the job had changed her mind. Long walks and ocean swims, and even a return to gentle lovemaking, had all contributed, but nothing had done so much to raise her spirits as returning to running, something she'd stopped when she joined the NYPD twelve years earlier.

She finished hard and was sweating and panting, grateful for the chill of the air-conditioned lobby of the resort. As she crossed to the elevator bank, she spied a familiar face: Justin Cates, a long-time employee of the current mayor of New York City.

As soon as they made eye contact, he sprang from his seat with a big grin. But as he approached, the grin turned sheepish. Four years earlier, when he'd been tailing her as she pieced together bits of evidence linking a serial killer to the death of her grandfather, she'd learned that once he was a friend, he was totally honest.

She extended a sweaty hand. "I suppose it's too much to hope this is a coincidence and you and Rick just flew down for a quick getaway."

He shook her hand, slightly discomfited. Justin could also be finicky. "Can we talk in private?"

Her runner's high evaporated. "No more private place than a crowded room." She forced a laugh. "Sorry. Come on up. Jake will be happy to see you."

Justin's expression suggested he thought otherwise. "Ricky's back in New York. He's just been promoted to executive ADA. We're both ecstatic, but there won't be any getaways for us for the foreseeable future."

"Too bad because they can do wonders, especially in a place like this." As she opened the door to their room, she called out, "We have company."

Jake, wearing shorts and a tee shirt displaying the logo of his employer, the Brooklyn Nets, shook Justin's hand. "Nice to see you."

Kim broke the mood. "So, why has the mayor sent you to Bermuda?"

Justin turned serious. "I take it you haven't been following the news from New York. Sabrina Dunn was shot and killed Sunday night after a rally at Brooklyn Borough Hall."

"So?" She could see what was coming but decided not to make it easy for him.

"Three days earlier, your lieutenant went on medical leave, apparently undergoing a series of tests. I've come down on a private jet loaned to the mayor by one of his generous donors with instructions to bring you back to the city this afternoon. Your hotel bill has already been paid and our jet awaits at the airport."

"And if she refuses?" Jake asked.

Justin's gaze never left Kim. "The mayor personally authorized placing you back on active duty this morning, as he has the utmost confidence in you."

Jake soured. "He also has the hots for her."

Kim finished toweling off. "Confidence or no, he can't force me back against my will. The department hierarchy doesn't know it, but I came here because I was suffering from severe depression. Not suicidal, but close."

"The mayor knows." Justin's voice was a whisper.

"You dug it out for him." She spat the words. "Because you can dig out anything. I suspect you've even discovered what my lieutenant is being tested for."

Justin shrugged. "Not directly, but Lieutenant Adam Bostwick was seen entering Sloan Kettering, so I would conclude it's a cancer."

"Do you have any idea what three mis—" She stopped. Not going there. "I'm not even sure I want to continue with the department."

"That's why he wants to meet with you, to lay everything out for you, and then you can decide what you want to do. Because you're correct, Kim. He can't force you to return to the job, but he can force you to come back to the city."

***

A black Chevy Suburban met the private jet at MacArthur Airport in Ronkonkoma, Long Island, dropping Jake and their luggage at their brownstone apartment on Monroe Place in Brooklyn Heights before taking Justin and Kim to see the mayor.

"I'm sorry about this," Justin said as they crossed the Brooklyn Bridge. He'd said it several times on the plane. She hadn't answered him then, either.

But when the driver took the first ramp off the bridge, the one leading to the FDR Drive, her curiosity got the better of her. "Aren't we going to City Hall?"

"Gracie Mansion." The traditional residence of the mayor of New York. "He thought you'd be more at ease there."

She was certain he'd thought no such thing. Mayor Raymond Brandt did nothing that wasn't the result of careful calculation, and she had to admit that his calculation skills had improved significantly since he'd tried to meddle in a murder investigation four years earlier as a favor to his main political donor. He'd subsequently grown more independent and more moderate in his positions, first winning a special election for the mayoralty, then winning the regular election last year.

Both times defeating Sabrina Dunn, who'd just been murdered.

Justin's mission was making sense.

As soon as they arrived at Gracie Mansion, the mayor dismissed Justin and led Kim to a living room with forest green walls and gestured to two plush chairs facing each other by the fireplace. "I'm sorry for summoning you this way, but circumstances demanded it. I hope you're recovering."

"From the depression you don't officially know about?" Best to set the tone at the start.

Brandt didn't blink. "Such matters shouldn't be taken lightly."

"My husband is a wonderful support for me."

"I'm sure. But you've been through a lot. Your father's suicide, thwarting a plot to firebomb a church, surviving a riot, tracking down your grandfather's killer…"

"Not just tracking down." Four years later, and she still hadn't come to terms with the grim satisfaction she'd felt at the conclusion of that case.

"True, but I need you back, and the city needs you back. Still, I won't push you if you aren't ready."

"Who's running the unit in Lieutenant Bostwick's absence?" The words were out before she could stop them. The mayor couldn't quite suppress his satisfied grin, so she added, "I haven't decided anything, but I'm curious."

"Of course. Bob Nolan is senior, as you know, and he's also the only First Grade detective there, so he's temporarily in charge. Bostwick insists he's only out for some tests and will be back this week." Brandt walked to an antique secretary in the corner of the room, opened it, and pulled out an accordion file, which he handed to her as he returned to his seat. "That's what we have."

Kim glanced through the file. No suspects.

"The conspiracy theories are already flying," Brandt said.

"Well, it was a political assassination any way you slice it." She watched for his reaction.

But he didn't flinch. "Clearly, and there are already commentaries out there suggesting that I may have been behind it. I wasn't, and I will cooperate with the investigation wherever it leads. Speculation also includes Kyle Emory."

The CEO of Emory Equities, a major investment firm whose PAC was a leading Brandt supporter, and whose investments in various gentrification projects around the city had brought harsh attacks from Dunn and others.

"You can investigate him, too," Brandt continued. "You have free rein."

For a moment, she longed to be back on Barry Road, or swimming at St. Catherine Beach.

Brandt brought her back to the present. "Any of us could be next. Whatever you need, you've got. That's a promise."

CHAPTER THREE

Kim's cell buzzed with a text as she approached the Wilson Street head-quarters of Patrol Borough Brooklyn North—PBBN in police parlance—known to its inhabitants as the Castle because its exterior resembled a battlement. It was the home of her post of duty, Brooklyn North Homicide. The text had to be from Jake.

"Welcome back, Detective Kim!" Sergeant Armand Dhillon, manning the desk, grinned from under the NYPD-approved turban, the herald of his Punjabi heritage.

"Did I hear right?" Sergeant Phil Vitello of Brooklyn North's Crime Scene Unit stepped forward. "The former queen bee of the Seven-Three? Welcome back." Kim had relied on him since her days as a rookie cop in the Seventy-Third precinct in the Brownsville section of Brooklyn. His hair was now all gray, and she wondered if he might be considering retirement.

Kim cast a rueful eye at Dhillon. "Thanks, Marshal." His nickname was so obvious that no one could remember who'd coined it.

But Dhillon only grinned. "We've all missed you. There were even rumors you might never come back. Lieutenant Bostwick is not in, expected back next week. The rest of your team is in the field."

"Thanks. Are you doing a double shift?" Dhillon's usual assignment was the night desk.

"No, this is now my permanent assignment. Sergeant Ramos left the department while you were away. This is much better for me, more time with my family."

Vitello gestured to the file tucked under her arm. "I'll bet I know what that is." But then he always had a nose for a hot case.

"I'll bet you do. Let's go upstairs and talk." She remembered the text. "Gotta do something first. I'll meet you in the conference room."

She waited until Vitello walked away. And the text was from Jake. *Took it, didn't you?*

She stepped out onto the street and called him. "I know you think I'm making a mistake. I'm not sure I'm not, but until I give up this badge…"

His voice was soft, just as it had been when she'd lost her baby, which would have been a boy. "I get it, Kim. Not judging you at all. Are they at least going to get you some help?"

"Brandt promised to provide whatever we need. Right now, I'm not sure what that is. I'm on my way to talk to Phil Vitello to find out. Bob Nolan and the others are in the field. I'll meet with them when they get back. Call you later, okay?"

"I'll send you a text when you forget." At least he was chuckling when he said it.

***

To Kim's surprise, her desk was clean. She'd half expected it to become a dumping ground in her absence. She strode past it, into the conference room.

Vitello nodded toward the file. "Mind if I ask where you got yours?"

"Mayor Brandt. He sent one of his people to haul me back."

"His Mr. Cates has been busy, I see. That could be a problem."

In more ways than one. "Right now, let's just focus on what we know, especially what you found at the scene."

Vitello opened his file. "We recovered a Smith and Wesson Governor, a .45 caliber revolver."

"A Governor? Our killer has a warped sense of humor."

"We recovered one slug at the scene, and the Medical Examiner's Office provided a second from the autopsy. Both are .45s. The slug from the scene had penetrated and exited the body before ricocheting off a concrete column in front of Borough Hall and was therefore too mashed for Ballistics to analyze. However, the ME reported two entrance wounds and one exit wound, and the slug recovered from the body matches the Governor…"

"Can we please call it something else?"

Vitello laughed. "Okay, the recovered .45."

"Who's on the case at the Medical Examiner's Office?"

"Dr. Shelton."

Excellent. She'd worked with him on two major cases and several not-so-major ones since coming to Brooklyn North. He wasn't averse to bending the rules to help her out.

"And what valuable information has Hizzoner supplied?" Vitello nodded toward her file.

Before she could answer, there were two sharp knocks on the door and Bob Nolan walked in. "Marshal Dhillon called my cell and gave me the word. Glad to have you back."

Kim stood, and they hugged. Bob had a little more gray encroaching on his temples, but he was keeping trim and fit. His clothes were always somewhat rumpled, but he was still sober, making it five years since he'd fallen off the wagon. "Glad to be back. Where are the others?"

"Here's Cord, now."

Cordell Washington, who had served with Kim in the Internal Affairs Bureau and followed her to Brooklyn North Homicide, had proven to be tough, resourceful, loyal, and reliable. At six-three, the size of an NBA point guard but built like a power forward, he was imposing as he pulled her into an embrace. "Hey, Kim. Great to see you. Spent some quality beach time, I see. I thought you Irish girls char-broiled with too much sun. Keep it up, and you might catch up with my people."

She guffawed. "Not likely. Lots of sunscreen. Besides, I spent more time running than sunning. Did you and Vera get married while I was gone?"

Cord and Vera Koshkin, a stunning petite Russian blonde who was widely considered the sharpest IT tech in the NYPD, had been living together for four years. Kim had tried to match make them when she and Cord were still at IAB, but they had gotten together, anyway.

Cord feigned indignation. "Hey, did I ever hassle you to marry Jake before you were ready?"

The last member of their team, Tim Brogan, joined them. "Sorry I'm late." Another hug.

"Okay, let's settle down," Bob said.

Vitello got up to leave, but Kim gestured for him to stay.

Bob nodded approval. "First, no one in the department knows the lieu is undergoing tests at Sloan-Kettering…."

Kim interrupted. "Not officially, but Brandt knows." She explained how she'd been summoned. "So, we should assume that the commissioner and chief of detectives know."

"Shit." Bob spat the word. "The lieu's a former marine with a lot of fight in him. We may be without him for a while, but he'll make it back. The Chief of Detectives won't act until he knows the lieu's status, but if he's out for any extended period, he's going to want brass at the head of this unit. Kim, did Brandt have anything to say about that?"

"Only that you, as the unit's sole First Grader, were in charge until the lieu returns. So, he's biding his time."

"Meaning," Cord said, "he, not the Chief of Detectives, will make the call. Super."

Bob gestured for calm. "As acting supervising officer, I'm now on the hook for all the lieu's paperwork and meetings. Kim, you're the lead on this case. We don't know much, yet. Witnesses described the shooter as six feet, about one-seventy, white with short, light brown hair and a goatee, wearing blue denim cutoff shorts and a sleeveless camo tee-shirt that was way too big for him. Some said he ran down the subway stairs on Joralemon Street while others were certain he got into a cab parked next to the stairwell."

Brogan spoke up. "I checked the video footage from every camera he could have passed in that station on Sunday night. No one fitting that description appears anywhere."

"And I checked with the cab companies operating in the area," Cord said. "None of their drivers picked up any fares at Borough Hall between the hours of six and nine o'clock that night."

"So, we've ruled out the subway and yellow cab escape routes," Kim said. Which means he must've gotten into a car that looked like a cab. There's a cluster of NYPD video cameras at the corner of Joralemon and Court. They had to catch something."

"Kim, let me know if you need anything else from my folks. Good luck." Vitello left.

Bob turned to her. "You were saying?"

"Cord, Tim, check those cameras through the RTCC." The Real Time Crime Center was the department's database warehouse at One Police Plaza—One-PP for short. It was accessible to anyone with access to the system. "They should show the killer getting into the car, and the car itself. With luck, we might even catch a plate number."

Bob agreed. "I'm sure it'll take time to locate the right view, and Kim, you've had enough for your first day back. A private word, then go home and get some rest. They'll let you know if they find something."

Cord and Tim left. Kim closed the door behind them. "What didn't you want them to hear?"

"Are you okay? Did Brandt pressure you to come back?"

"Yes, and yes. Bermuda did center me, and for now I'll focus on my career as a policewoman. No better way than to get thrown headlong into the deep end on a tough case my first day back. Now, as to my question?"

"First, please tell me what else happened with Brandt."

"Not much. It was the first time in years that he hadn't undressed me with his eyes, so that's something. He mentioned conspiracy theories. He knows he's the top suspect in some quarters."

"How about with you?" Bob was serious.

"The prospect of Sabrina Dunn as governor would have sickened him, but Brandt's a cool political calculator. He knows she had no chance. So, no motive for him. Still, we'll follow this investigation wherever the evidence leads, and he knows that. Which leaves us with a political assassination with what can only be a third-party shooter. Let's get that description to every precinct in the city and get some of the eyewitnesses over to Sheila Gregg in the Artist Unit."

CHAPTER FOUR

Thursday, July 7th

"Something is bothering you," Kim said as she slipped into bed next to Jake. It was nearly two in the morning.

"We never finished talking about the future in Bermuda."

"I thought we were going to wait until we got the results back from all the tests they did." She didn't mention the text she'd gotten from her gynecologist while they were in Bermuda suggesting she schedule an appointment to discuss those results.

"So, you want to put that on hold while you're on this case?"

She snuggled against him. "Please. I can only deal with one major issue at a time."

"I get it. But are you sure you're ready for this?"

"I'm a cop. Cops don't get to choose when they work cases and when they don't."

"But they choose when they come off extended leave, often with professional advice. Shouldn't you at least talk to Alyssa about it?"

Alyssa Walters, the psychologist she'd been seeing since the last miscarriage. "I already agreed to return. I'll be fine. Now, what's been bothering you? Besides me working this case, that is?"

Now he turned sheepish. "I got a call from my boss shortly after you guys dropped me off. He was thrilled to learn I was back from Bermuda and suggested that, as the Nets' Director of Analytics, I should be at the Summer League games in Vegas. And he wants me there for the Overseas Combine, which begins on Monday. I can bring you."

Bermuda would have been cut short, anyway. "I would've liked that, but…"

"I know. The case."

"I'm glad we'll both be busy. We'll talk and text, and you can…"

He propped himself up on one arm. "I don't feel good about this. At least promise me you'll talk to Alyssa."

A chime on her cell signaled a text from Cord. *The RTCC had technical difficulties. They promised to have video from the time frame in question from the camera on Joralemon by 8 this AM.* "I'll think about it. When are you flying out?"

"This afternoon, from JFK. I'll call you when I get there."

***

"You can tell something has happened," Cord said as they stared at the image on the monitor creeping forward frame by frame. "There's a bunch of people running down the subway stairs. And there's the car, a yellow Camry."

Kim downed the rest of her coffee, still not fully alert. Three weeks in Bermuda had robbed her of some of her ability to force-march her way through the day on four hours of sleep. "Freeze it. No dome light and no cab ID. Can you zoom in on the license plate?"

A couple of clicks.

"TLC plates," Cord said, meaning the car was registered with the Taxi and Limousine Commission. "A car service?"

Kim jotted the plate number. "Looks like it. Can we zoom in on the driver?" Wearing sunglasses and a cap with the bill pulled down over his forehead.

"You've gotten great at maneuvering this system," she said.

"Lessons from Vera." Cord squinted and leaned closer to the monitor. "The windshield must be tinted glass. Can't make out any other features."

"Print the image, anyway. Let's resume the slow scan."

A male fitting the description of the shooter pulled open the rear passenger-side door. After a few frames, he was in the back seat.

It looked like he'd hesitated. "Please go back and run that clip at normal speed."

Cord caught it. "What's that dude waiting for?"

"Freeze it and print it." It was a clear shot of the right side of his face. "Okay, continue frame by frame. I want to see if we can tell where he went."

"Looks like he went west on Joralemon."

Where he'd have been certain not to pass any other NYPD cameras. "Okay, send the shot of the suspect to Sheila Gregg and ask her to work up a full-face sketch based on it. Forget the witnesses for now."

Tim Brogan walked in. "Morning, guys. Kim, Bob said he'd be late. Some meeting at One-PP."

Cord laughed. "He's never gonna survive this."

Kim brought Tim up to speed. "You and I will canvass Joralemon west of Borough Hall, checking with anyone with video surveillance for any sign of that Camry. Cord, please run down that plate number in the DMV database. Text me the moment you have something."

CHAPTER FIVE

Joanna Dunbar, the top investigative news reporter for the Independent Television Network, gazed into the camera with confidence as the host of ITN's morning show finished her introduction. "The NYPD says they are making progress, having retrieved the weapon and retraced the gunman's path of escape. A police source also says the gunman may have been caught on video."

The host brightened. "That sounds like progress, Joanna. Have the police established a probable motive? Are there other parties involved?"

"Theories abound," Joanna replied, "but until the identity of the shooter is known, it's all speculation. Mayor Brandt has expressed his outrage at violence in the political realm and has urged the public not to jump to conclusions. Felipe Prinz, the leader of the radical group, Come Home Ernesto, who was recently paroled from prison, is already charging the police with a cover-up of the murder of, in his words, 'the only voice for the common people in the city'. The NYPD has had no further comment."

***

Since winning his office, Mayor Brandt's morning meetings with his biggest contributor, Kyle Emory, had moved from Emory's Fifth Avenue

Apartment to Gracie Mansion. They were less conspicuous, and being on the mayor's home turf provided what the mayor liked to think of as home court advantage.

"Your vision is paying off." It was always good to start with flattery, especially when it was true. "Your projects, from Williamsburg to Long Island City to the South Bronx, are all proving successful. You've proven the critics wrong."

"Thank you. And your suggestion that we provide 'affordable' housing within those projects has proven politically effective, even with the requirement that the residents of the affordable units use a separate entrance. The 'servant's entrance', the Looney Left calls it. They may not like it, but..." Emory ended with a shrug.

"The Looney Left is now minus one loudmouth."

Emory scowled. "With Prinz out of prison, they've exchanged one for another. Is there any truth that he was carrying on with Dunn?"

"How should I know?"

"You seem to know everything these days."

So, his benefactor was still angling for a return to the old micromanaging paradigm. The mayor allowed himself a grin. "Always good for the little people to think I know everything. But my knowledge doesn't extend to who shared Sabrina Dunn's bed. Right now, I'm more interested in finding her killer."

"So you can give him the keys to the city?"

"Don't be dim. You know who the rumormongers think was behind the shooting."

Emory relaxed a little. "Is that why you dragged that poor detective back from Bermuda? Figured she'd clean it up for you?"

"I had nothing to gain from it. You've seen the polls. She had no more chance of winning for governor than she had of beating me in an election. You, however, remained a consistent target of her diatribes."

Emory sipped his coffee. "Then, let's say no more about it."

***

By lunch time, Kim and Brogan had stopped at half a dozen locations on Joralemon and examined video footage from Sunday night, and no sign of the yellow Camry. "Most of the cameras are focused on the sidewalk, not the street. He probably turned onto Clinton Street, and from there he could've gone anywhere."

"Anything from Cord?" Tim asked.

"Not yet." And he should've had something by now. She texted him.

A moment later, she got his answer. *Sorry, I've been doing some digging. The plate number was registered to a car service in Queens for a black Lincoln Town Car that was totaled two years ago. Plates were never surrendered. Owner of the car service says he thinks they were stripped at the scene of the accident. Also, check out Joanna Dunbar on ITN's website this morning.*

Like everyone else in her unit, Cord knew of Kim's friendship with the reporter.

But as she watched the video on her phone, she felt like she'd been sucker-punched. She pulled up Joanna's cell number.

"So, the rumor is true; you're back."

Not the greeting she'd been expecting, but then if Joanna had heard everything else, why not that? "You know better than to leak details of an ongoing investigation."

"Kim, this is a high-profile case. The rules…"

"Are the same. The more you report, the easier it is for the criminals to evade detection. We've been over this ground before."

A long pause. "I need to speak with you in person. Where are you, now?"

"A few blocks from Borough Hall."

"Perfect. I can meet you at the Korean War Veterans Plaza in fifteen minutes."

Kim agreed and ended the call. "Tim, head back to the Castle. I'll be back as soon as possible. Have Cord refer the photo and Sheila's sketch to the Face Recognition Unit to see if they come up with anything."

CHAPTER SIX

As Kim walked through Cadman Plaza Park, memories of the last time she had met Joanna there surged back. The night of the riot, four years earlier. All traces of the fire in the Post Office across the street were gone, but every time Kim passed it, the memories of that night sprang back to life. And now, the architect of that riot, Felipe Prinz, was out of prison.

Joanna had chosen it for a reason. That thought was amplified as the reporter approached from the west along Tillary Street, her face solemn. Despite her anger, Kim embraced her friend. In that place, she could do nothing else.

"Thanks," Joanna said. "Are you okay? Enough to be back on the job?"

Kim swallowed the rebuke she'd prepared. "I'm okay, thanks. But the details you reported this morning could only have come from inside the Castle. No one else knows." But that wasn't true. Brandt knew. Justin Cates knew. The Commissioner and the Chief of Detectives knew, but it was inconceivable they would have leaked it. "Well, almost no one. I can't have this shit leaking to the press."

Joanna remained calm and serious. "People are freaking out about this shooting, even people who hated Sabrina Dunn. Prinz is already ginning up the class war rhetoric, suggesting that someone like Kyle Emory or even Brandt might be behind it."

"The mayor brought me back to lead the investigation. He knows he'll be included. He's giving us everything we need. So, that's a non-starter."

"I didn't say I believed Prinz, Kim. But people are desperate to know you guys are making progress. And you know I can't reveal my source."

"The last time you revealed a source, I was able to prevent a jam-packed church from being firebombed on Palm Sunday." It pulled Joanna up short, as intended.

But the reporter recovered. "This is different."

And now, Kim was glad Joanna had chosen this spot. "Is it? Look around. Think back four years. You know what Prinz can do. And that he's gone this public so soon after his release from prison over a wealthy white liberal pol suggests…"

"They were lovers, Kim. I don't know how long, but at least from before he got sent up. She probably was the one funding his group."

"Hence his outrage." Back to the main issue. "I must know one thing. Is your source within the department or elsewhere?"

"You want to know if he's in the department so you can hunt him down."

"We've always had an understanding, Joanna. I keep you informed, and you respect the needs of the investigation."

"I know. But are you sure you can trust Brandt?"

"That's an odd question, coming from you. Didn't he set you up at ITN after the riot?"

"Yeah, which took a formerly hostile reporter off his ass. I'm not ready to believe Prinz, but I'm not ready to rule Brandt out, either. I'm still a reporter with a job to do. Tell you what, I'll abide by our usual agreement. I won't tell you my source, but I'll let you know whenever he gives me something you don't. Be careful, Kim, because this time I don't think you can trust anybody."

***

Back at the Castle, Kim waved everyone into the conference room and shut the door. Cord had done his usual great job listing everything they had on the marker board, as well as hanging a street map of the area around Borough Hall showing the direction of the escape vehicle. Also hanging on the wall was a printout of the sketch Sheila Gregg had made from the video image and the image itself. "We have a leak."

"You sure it's here?" Bob asked. "Maybe it's Brandt."

Kim repeated Joanna's comment about hunting her source down. "It's here, and it's a guy. Bob, aside from the four of us and the lieu, who has keys to this room?"

Bob thought a moment. "The assistant chief, as commander of the patrol borough; also, the other unit commanders and the three desk sergeants."

"Good. That's a limited group. From now on, this door stays locked. No exceptions." She turned to Cord. "Anything from the Face Recognition Unit?"

"Too soon, but they're on it."

"In the meantime," Bob said, "The department has released both the sketch and the video clip to the media."

The pinging of a cell echoed in the room. Cord pulled his out. "Got a text... Face Recognition Unit... they got a hit on the image. Ivan Koster, did four years at Dannemora for armed robbery, last known address is in Brownsville."

Kim noted it on the board. "Okay, Cord and Tim, go check it out and bring him in if you find him."

Two hard knocks got their attention. It was Marshal Dhillon. "We received a call on a floater in Newtown Creek. Found him on the rocks under the Grand Street Bridge. CSU is already on the scene."

"You go, Kim," Bob said. "Someone has to hold down the fort."

CHAPTER SEVEN

There was nothing worse than a floater, especially one who'd been in the water a long time. But since Kim had an aversion for coincidences, she was sure this one hadn't been there for more than a few days.

She parked on the Brooklyn side of the bridge. The road was blocked off and Vitello's people had already established a perimeter. One look was all it took.

"He had no identification on him," Vitello said. "No wallet, no cash. They picked him clean. But it sure looks like your guy."

"It's Koster. Any ideas on the cause of death?" Kim was trying not to get too close.

Vitello leaned over the body. "Nothing obvious. No signs of gunshot wounds or stabbing. Some signs of nibbling by the creek's inhabitants."

Kim leaned closer, but the stench forced her back. "Pretty bad, considering the longest he could be dead is four days. I have a jar of Vick's in the car…" Years earlier, when she was a rookie cop, Vitello had taught her the police trick of placing a dab of Vick's VapoRub under the nose to screen out the odor of decay.

"Save it, Kim. Leave him to the guys wearing the Tyvek suits. Newtown Creek is one of the most polluted waterways in the state. The

Medical Examiner will get you a cause soon enough." He stared north-west, toward the Kosciuszko Bridge.

She caught it. "Trying to figure where he went in?"

"This far from the East River, the water rises and falls with the tide, but it's pretty much stagnant. He probably went in right here, or nearby. Flood tide Monday morning would have been around one. When the tide went out, he got hung up on the rocks."

Kim stared at the water. "Why would anyone dump a dead body into a stagnant waterway without weighing him down?" It didn't take long for her to answer her own question. "Because they wanted him to be found. See you later, Phil."

***

Joanna grabbed her cell on the second ring. "Dunbar."

"Sabrina Dunn's killer is an ex-con named Ivan Koster. The cops know it and aren't saying anything."

Out of nowhere, she suddenly had the sense that Kim might be in danger. "How do you know this?"

He waited before answering. "Don't you want my information? Or has your pal, Kim Brady, read you the riot act already?"

"I'm a reporter. I have an obligation to check the facts before I report them."

His chuckle chilled her. "How admirable, even upstanding. Perhaps I'd be better off informing some other network, less friendly to Raymond Brandt, less friendly to the police."

Time for a counterthrust. "Perhaps, but then your primary goal wouldn't be realized."

"You don't know my primary goal."

"Don't I? I could make an educated guess. I don't like being used, whatever your name is, but I accept it comes with the territory. Our agreement was that I wouldn't ask your identity, and I'm not, just how you know this latest fact."

Another pause. "Fair enough. I have excellent contacts in the department. Tell you what. Ask your pal, Detective Brady."

***

Kim was updating the board when Cord and Brogan walked in.

"No sign of Koster at his place," Cord said. "Neighbors say they haven't seen him in the past several..." He saw Kim's latest note on the board. "Shit. We sure it's him?"

"Even with the nibbles around his face, yes, I'm sure."

Brogan shuddered. "Christ."

Cord shook his head. "I can't believe anything can live in that cesspool. We got a cause?"

"Not yet. No visible wounds. Vitello thinks he was dead when he went into the water. I've asked Dr. Shelton from the Medical Examiner's office to call me when he has something." She'd met Dr. Lloyd Shelton, very tall and whipcord thin, reminding her of Ichabod Crane, when she was still at Internal Affairs before being transferred to Brooklyn North. Cautious at first, he had grown comfortable enough with her to be considered a friend as well as a source. "He's moved Ivan to the front of the line."

Her cell signaled a text, which had to be from Jake. She'd check it later.

Bob entered the conference room and closed the door. "I just had ten tough minutes with Cirillo." Captain Andrew Cirillo was the commanding officer of all the detective units within Brooklyn North. Rumor had it he was on the fast track for higher command. "The lieu is starting chemotherapy, with radiation to follow. No telling when he'll be back, or even if. The captain has always looked out for him, so he's trying not to replace him, yet. He's assuming command of our unit, but he'll leave me running things and Kim as lead on this and any other cases we catch."

"Did he say what, specifically, the lieu has?" Cord asked.

"Nope. Against department policy. But I think we can all guess." He addressed Kim. "He intends to meet with us both at least once each day, more frequently when we have something urgent."

She pointed at the board. "Ivan's our floater. I'd call that urgent."

The text from Jake would have to wait.

CHAPTER EIGHT

Captain Cirillo, with his black hair, olive skin and compact build, reminded Kim of a fortyish Robert De Niro. He'd come up through the ranks as a tough street cop who knew not to cross the line. He'd made the jump from patrol officer to sergeant to lieutenant in ten years, the minimum possible under NYPD regulations, but it had taken several years to make captain. Given his feel for departmental politics, Kim had to assume it had been his choice. Cirillo regarded them both, now, with raised eyebrows. "Back so soon, Nolan?"

"Kim has a development."

She laid out everything they had on Ivan Koster.

"Sounds like a dead end." Cirillo wasn't trying to be funny.

Kim continued. "Dunn was a third-party shooting. Koster was hired by someone else and then killed. Assassinate the assassin. His sole motive was money. That there were no outward signs of attack suggests he was likely either poisoned or drugged. The autopsy might tell us more, possibly not."

"A dead end."

He would not put her off. "That's what the individual who planned this wants us to think. They've made it easy for us if we look no further than Koster. We got the guy. Great. Except the real criminal is the one who paid him. And that criminal likely has a political agenda."

Cirillo rolled his eyes. "I see your experiences have failed to dull your nose for politics."

Bob jumped in. "In fairness, Captain, Kim didn't go looking for this case."

No, Bob, we're not getting into Brandt's summons. "I picked neither the crime nor the target. But now that I'm here, I intend to go wherever the evidence leads. Unless you want to take me off the case."

A cool grin. "You know I couldn't even if I wanted to. The mayor's orders to both the Chief of Detectives and me were explicit."

So much for not getting into the mayoral summons.

Cirillo leaned forward. "You'll understand how Brandt hand-picking the lead detective investigating an assassination from which he stood to gain, and with such insistence, might make my nose twitch."

So much for an aversion to politics. "Mine too, even with his assurance that he understands we'll look at him. Then again, pollsters gave Sabrina Dunn no chance of winning the election. And Brandt defeated her by huge margins both times he faced her for the mayoralty. So, I can't see Brandt with a motive. If anything, he benefited from her opposition."

"So, you don't suspect him?" Again, the arched brows.

"I said I don't see a motive. Yet. I'm still gathering facts. Koster was the shooter. He got into a car that resembled a taxi, with stolen TLC plates. His body was left where we'd be sure to find it. Dr. Shelton will get back to me as soon as he has a cause. In the meantime, there's the matter of Felipe Prinz."

Cirillo's face hardened. "What about him?"

"He's doing his best to agitate the masses. I only just learned that he and Dunn were lovers. I'd like permission to reach out to my FBI contacts to see if they have anything on it."

"Where'd you hear about him and Dunn?"

Shit. No choice but to tell him. "Joanna Dunbar."

The captain's eyes narrowed. "Was that in return for all the details she's been reporting?"

She exchanged glances with Bob, who shrugged. "No, someone's been leaking stuff to her, possibly someone inside."

"It can't be anyone within the unit," Bob said. "But we think it's within PBBN."

"Find it and plug it."

***

The text wasn't from Jake. *Ivan Koster?* Joanna.

Kim texted her back. *When did you hear from your guy?*

Joanna's response was immediate. *Just before I texted you.*

Bob was making a note on the board about Koster's death.

"No, Bob. Nothing on the board about it. No talk outside of closed doors about it."

"Aren't you being a little paranoid?"

Maybe the leak wasn't from within. Maybe the mastermind was having the details leaked. They had to know which it was. "Yes. But if anything about his death leaks to the media, we'll know it wasn't from inside."

He considered it. "Worth a shot. Where will you keep the details until then?"

She held up her cell. "Here."

Back to Joanna. *Can you keep a lid on it?*

If I do, he'll leak it to another network, one not committed to police safety.

And then Kim would lose whatever control she currently had. *Okay. Go ahead.*

She walked to the board. Under Koster's name, she added, "Believed to have fled the jurisdiction."

Bob chuckled. "Well, I suppose that's kinda true."

"Change of plan. Leave the door closed but unlocked. But nothing else gets posted until we figure this out."

CHAPTER NINE

Friday, July 8th

The apartment already felt empty with Jake gone, so she hoped that running would help fill the void. It was just 5:15 when she walked out the front door in her shorts, singlet, and surf-colored Brooks Ghost 14 running shoes. The sun wouldn't be up for another fifteen minutes, and the temperature was a mild seventy-two. She broke into an easy jog to warm up as she turned down Monroe Place. At Pierrepont Street she cut over to Henry Street and turned left. The streets were empty at this hour, which allowed her to run on asphalt and give her knees a break.

By the time she turned onto Union Street, about a mile into her run, she had begun to perspire, her breathing had evened out, and she picked up speed. Union was narrow, and now there was a bit of traffic, so she kept to the sidewalk. She passed the 76th Precinct and wondered how Jake was doing. When she reached Columbia Street, she turned right and began her favorite leg of this route, the one that gave her a panoramic view of Manhattan across the river.

As she drew near to the Brooklyn Bridge Park piers, she was seized by a sense of being followed. Without breaking pace, she glanced around, scanning right and left. A few other early morning joggers and walkers were out, and the sun was now up, but nothing unusual. Still, the idea someone was following her persisted.

She turned off the street and onto the greenway, keeping to the path closest to the river to enjoy both the view and the breeze. Passing the Pier One Playground, she glanced back over her shoulder to glimpse the Statue of Liberty in the distance before following the trail's loop around the playground and heading back toward home. As she did, she caught sight of a man, slim and muscular, perhaps about forty, running several yards behind her. Picking up the pace felt good until she heard footfalls behind her.

They grew closer.

Don't look back but be ready.

Fists clenched.

On her left was a path leading out to Furman Street. As she turned onto it, the male runner glided past her, not even glancing her way.

Annoyed at her paranoia, she maintained a fast pace all the way home.

***

Kim was grateful the summons from Dr. Shelton had come to her cell and not through the Castle. It was still early when she entered the Brooklyn Medical Examiner's Office, but then her meetings with Shelton were usually in the early morning with no one else around.

"Great seeing you back." He shook her hand. "I have good news and bad news."

"And you know I'm a bad-news-first person, so let's have it."

"No sign of trauma, no obvious cause of death. We'll have to wait for the tox screen to come back. I've asked them to put a rush on it."

"Not surprised. The good news?"

He flipped on a light and pointed to a photo on the corkboard. "That's an enlarged photo of Koster's left shoulder."

"Looks like a needle mark."

"Detective, you have the basic instincts required for forensic medicine." He pointed to another photo showing Koster's neck and left shoulder and arm. "It would've been almost impossible for him to inject himself in that location…"

"And since the video shows he got into the car from the passenger side, someone must have been waiting for him in the car with the needle."

"Then again, you're already a brilliant detective. I'll call you the moment I get the tox screen results."

***

"I was hoping you might explain this to me," the mayor said. He and Justin Cates had just watched a recorded segment of Joanna Dunbar's report from the previous evening announcing to the world the name of the assassin.

"There may be a leak from within the Castle. Do you want me to question Ms. Dunbar?"

The mayor stared at the paused screen. Kim Brady should have called if she suspected a leak, and she's too smart to not have suspected. Which could only mean that she had not ruled out the possibility that he was the leak. "No, Justin, thank you. That could only raise suspicions."

Cates' eyes narrowed. "Why would that be a concern?"

Et tu, Justin? "Appearances matter, especially for the mayor. I summoned Detective Brady because I have the utmost confidence in her ability."

"Should I speak to her?"

That would raise even more suspicions. "No, I'll leave it to her judgment."

***

Kim's next stop was Federal Plaza in Manhattan. Agent Ken Taylor, with whom she'd worked on two major cases, including the one involving her grandfather's killer, still had the same office. Only the size of his desktop monitors had changed. Any larger and he'd need a bigger desk.

"Good to see you're back," he said as she took a seat. "Don't tell me, let me guess. Ivan Koster."

"If you have anything on him, especially known associates, that would be great. But I came about Felipe Prinz."

"Another old acquaintance. You think he was involved in the Dunn shooting?"

"Is it true he had something going on with her?"

Taylor laughed. "Oh, yeah, both carnal and financial. Which is odd because Sabrina Dunn, while hailing from an old, moneyed family, didn't have all that much on her own. The family didn't appreciate her class treason, so there was no continuing cash source."

"You think she was fronting for another source?"

"A definite possibility. We know she had an account at a bank in the Cayman Islands, initially funded with money from a trust for her, but we can't get any records on it. What we can do is look at her American bank records for deposits, but that could be made harder if she had accounts under other identities."

"I haven't interviewed the family, yet. Perhaps they can shed some light."

Taylor looked doubtful. "She may have been the black sheep, but she was still theirs. I'd step lightly. Richmond Dunn and his wife are neighbors of former mayor Mike Bloomberg on East 79th Street. They're old money, having originally made it in manufacturing. They're very private people. Don't go directly there. Call Dunn Holdings and go through channels."

Great, more game playing. "Anything else?"

A deep sigh. "A suggestion. When you go, soften your look as much as possible. I suggest a dress and heels if you can stand it."

She'd only worn a dress and heels on the job once, when she'd learned of a serial murder while she and Jake were out to dinner. It wasn't an experience she wanted to repeat.

***

By late afternoon, she'd made it through a labyrinth of phone transfers and obtained the address of the townhouse on East 79th Street and an appointment for the following morning.

"Been tracking the media all day," Bob said. "Nothing about Koster leaving the country."

A text to Joanna had confirmed she'd heard nothing new. "Too early to say for sure it's not from within; not dispositive, as the lawyers like to say." She shot him a glare. "And don't say I should've gone to law school." Which is what Dad had often said.

She received a text from Joanna. *My old station,* City News, *just reported Koster's body was found under the Grand Street Bridge. WTF!!*

Kim replied. *Meet me at the Korean War Veteran's Plaza.*

***

"Sorry Kim," Joanna said as she met her getting off the B38 bus at Cadman Plaza.

"Your guy didn't call you with this, first?" Kim gestured for Joanna to follow her as she turned for home. "What happened?"

"I pressed him a little when he gave me Koster, and he threatened to go to another outlet if I didn't trust him. I tried to reassure him, but he did it anyway. Since he never told me who he was, there was no downside for him."

"He must have told you something for credibility." And that might give us a clue.

"He dropped a lot of names. You, Bob Nolan, Lieutenant Bostwick, Washington, and Brogan. He told me the initial facts of the case. Was the report on *City News* true?"

"Yeah. I need the number he called from."

Joanna handed her a slip of paper. "Numbers."

Burner phones. That figured.

CHAPTER TEN

Saturday, July 16th

A Latino woman answered the door of the East 79th Street townhouse and scowled. "Yes?"

Kim showed her badge. "Detective Brady, New York City Police. I have an appointment with…"

"You are expected."

Kim followed her through the massive foyer and sat in a chair on one side, as directed. Presently, a white-haired man wearing khaki slacks and a dark blue shirt came down the ornate stairs. "Detective, I'm Richmond Dunn."

Kim stood and showed her badge. Dunn looked her up and down with a mild expression of disapproval. Kim had decided not to follow Ken Taylor's advice on the dress and heels, opting instead for tailored slacks, a light blazer, and dress flats.

"My wife is waiting upstairs in the family room. She's still quite upset." They started upstairs.

"I'm sure she is. So sorry to disturb you at such a painful time."

"We're surprised you didn't come sooner. Our daughter was murdered nearly a week ago."

Her instincts told her to step lightly. "In a murder investigation, we get as much direct evidence as we can, first. Then we go looking for suspects. It doesn't happen as quickly as they show on TV crime shows."

He stopped at the top of the stairs. "Do I take it that my wife and I are suspects?"

"Not at all. But you might provide some insight as to who may have wanted your daughter dead."

"I should think that would be obvious."

She tried a small grin. "There is no such thing as an obvious fact."

He softened. "Sherlock Holmes." He gestured to a door on their right, a comfortable looking room furnished in soft earth tones and plush furniture. A woman a few years younger than Mr. Dunn sat on a camel-colored loveseat in a black dress, dabbing her eyes with a tissue. "My wife, Monica Dunn."

Kim extended her hand. "I'm so sorry for your loss."

The woman glared. "Are you? I would think the police would be dancing in the streets."

Don't blow up at her. "I'm a homicide detective, Ms. Dunn. I…"

"Mrs. Dunn, if you please."

No wonder Ken suggested a dress. "My apologies. Mrs. Dunn. I take any homicide, whoever the victim and whatever the motive, as a personal attack. I didn't agree with your daughter's politics, and I didn't vote for her. But I…"

Mrs. Dunn cried out. "You can't know what it's like to lose your only child."

Kim choked the sudden pain back down and took a deep breath. "I have a better idea than you realize. And I want those responsible for her death arrested, tried, and imprisoned."

"Isn't the man responsible for her death already dead?" Mr. Dunn asked.

"The shooter is, yes. But we're certain he was not acting alone."

Mrs. Dunn sobbed. "Why don't you start with Raymond Brandt?"

Before Kim could respond, Mr. Dunn said, "My dear, let's please hear what the detective has to say."

"You never should have cut her off. I told you so. It only stoked her anger."

"Monica, please!"

Kim kept her tone soft, calm, and reasonable. "Let's start with this. Has anyone threatened either of you recently?"

"No," Mrs. Dunn replied. "Of course not."

Mr. Dunn said nothing. Kim turned to him. "Have you had any disagreements or conflicts that could have mushroomed into something worse?"

"I'm a businessman. I have contentious dealings all the time. They don't result in murder."

"I understand you built your wealth in manufacturing," Kim said. "But you are currently the chairman of the board of a company with large real estate holdings. That's a hot business in this city, but one that's been rocked with uncertainty since the Covid pandemic struck."

"What's your point, Detective?"

"I'm just wondering if that could lead to contentious dealings turning violent. Is there anyone with whom you've had contentious dealings recently? Or anyone who might look to force their way into your business?"

"No to both," Mr. Dunn replied.

"Anyone who would have seen your daughter's political views as a threat?"

"They all did," Mrs. Dunn said.

Kim turned to her. "Who?"

"You'll have to forgive my wife. As you can see, she's quite upset. My dear, why don't you go rest and the detective and I can continue this conversation?"

Kim was about to ask that Mrs. Dunn remain, but the woman turned angry. "You will not shut me up, Rich. I told you cutting her off was a mistake, and it was. You did it to mollify your business cronies, who were afraid of her, just like you were. I told you it would make her more radical, and it did. But you allowed your emotions to rule your judgment."

"My dear, please…"

Kim broke in. "I'm sorry, but what do you mean, cut her off?"

"We had placed Sabrina's fortune, an inheritance from her grandfather, in a trust. My husband is the trustee, and the trust was to terminate upon his death. He'd been approving her requests for withdrawals from the trust for years, but when she became involved with that... that gutter rat..."

"Felipe Prinz?" Kim asked.

"Yes." The woman spat the word. "When she did that, parading him all over town and making no secret that she was sleeping with him, he cut her off, saying he'd only provide her with fifty thousand dollars per year to live on. She'd have to work for the rest. That's when she ran for Public Advocate."

Kim did the math. "That was nine years ago. Do you mean her relationship with Prinz goes back that far?"

"Probably further," Mr. Dunn replied. "They'd already been together a while when we learned of it."

Time to press. "You must have gotten some rather strong negative reactions from your business associates."

Mrs. Dunn answered. "Certainly, he did."

Mr. Dunn rallied. "Yes, but nothing to suggest they'd become violent."

"Anyone else who might?"

"No." He stood. "I'll walk you to the door."

Kim knelt next to Mrs. Dunn. "I am truly sorry for your loss, and I will do everything I can to bring her killers to justice."

The woman finally met her gaze. "Yes, I believe you will. Thank you."

Walking down the stairs, Mr. Dunn again apologized. "She still hasn't recovered from the shock."

"But you have."

He paused. "You don't understand. All of Sabrina's anger was directed at me. Her actions were deliberate and were intended to make my business positions untenable. You've dealt with Prinz; you know he's a terrorist. I couldn't have her using the fortune my father built to fund efforts to tear it all down. Believe me, if there had been any other way, I'd have taken it." He resumed their walk down the stairs.

"What happened after you cut her off? In your relationship, I mean."

"It ended. We've had no contact with her since."

She stopped at the door. "Who is the executor of her estate?" When he hesitated, she added, "She must have a will."

His manner became guarded. "Yes, of course. But I don't know who the executor is, nor do I know who drew it up. A will was drafted by our family attorney when she was twenty-one, but I believe she has another."

"One more question. What happened to the balance of her trust upon her death?"

An excellent question with an interesting answer.

CHAPTER ELEVEN

"Welcome to *City News Saturday Morning.* Our lead story: According to a reliable source, the police department has evidence linking Mayor Raymond Brandt to the assassination of gubernatorial candidate Sabrina Dunn. The assassin, Ivan Koster, once worked as a messenger at the law firm of Cappelli and Lidster, the same firm that hired Brandt just out of law school. Cappelli and Lidster represented Koster when he was tried for armed robbery, a charge on which he was ultimate convicted in 2003. Mr. Koster was released from prison in 2007."

***

The Deputy Commissioner for Public Information sat facing the mayor across what had once been Fiorello LaGuardia's desk. "Of course, I'm going to release a statement about it. But not before I nail down a few things. You can help. First, did you ever know Ivan Koster?"

He couldn't believe this was happening. "No."

"You didn't work on his armed robbery case?"

"I've never even met the man, let alone worked on a case for him."

The deputy commissioner leaned forward. "Wasn't he a messenger at Cappelli? Wasn't that the reason the firm represented him?"

"I don't know if he was or not. I don't recall anyone by that name at the firm."

"So, you're saying the firm employed no one by that name?"

"They may have, but I was a junior associate and not there very long. The name isn't familiar to me at all." He didn't like the way the deputy commissioner was glaring at him.

"That's not exactly a denial." The deputy commissioner stood. "But I understand. We'll release a statement saying the department has nothing linking you to Koster, and, to the best of our knowledge, the *City News* report is false."

"That's waffling. You need to say that there is no link between the mayor and Koster and the report is false."

"Mr. Mayor, I can't say that because you didn't say it. You said you don't remember Koster. I can't risk someone popping up later with an additional fact that makes it look like the department is covering for you. I suggest you make your own statement. Now, if you'll excuse me…" And he left.

After fuming for a minute, he buzzed for his assistant. "Get Cates."

***

Meet me at Millie's Cuban Kitchen. Lunch is on me. The text from Rick Conti came as a pleasant surprise and a welcome diversion after she'd watched the DCPI's tepid denial and the mayor's thundering one.

Kim had first worked with Rick when she was still with Internal Affairs, investigating a murder that had been committed by someone impersonating a police officer. After a shaky start, he'd become both a friend and an ally. But as she walked to Millie's, two blocks down Wilson Avenue, pleasant surprise turned to suspicion. Rick's partner in a relationship that had somehow remained private was Justin Cates. The timing smelled like week-old fish.

Rick rose from his seat as she entered. "Good to have you back, Kim. Bermuda did you a world of good."

"Thanks. Too bad it was cut short."

"Yes. Someday, when we've both retired, perhaps we can co-author a book about it." He turned serious as they sat. "But I'm very glad you're back. Justin tells me you've gotten into running."

"Yes, although I'm already struggling to keep to it as faithfully as I did in Bermuda. What else did Justin tell you? Today, I mean."

"That you're still as direct as always. Did you see the two news conferences this morning?"

Kim's Cuban sandwich arrived with a side order of *tostoñes*.

Rick smirked. "No *croquetas*?"

"With an uncertain running schedule, I watch my diet. Stop stalling."

A shrug. "I was curious what you thought of the two statements."

"Until we know more, it's the best DCPI can do. But it was weak. Brandt's denial should've been heavier on facts, lighter on bombast. What does Justin say?"

"That Brandt really doesn't remember. I checked the file on Koster's armed robbery case. Cappelli and Lidster represented him, so that much is true. We need to find what else is true."

"We'll need the employment records to verify that Koster was there at the same time as Brandt and the case file to see if Brandt worked on it. And it'll take a subpoena for either."

Conti's face twisted into a scowl. "There's no way the DA will approve applying for a subpoena. The firm will move to quash it, and regardless of whether they win, they'll make us look like we're part of the Brandt defense team."

"I'm not looking to defend him. If it's true, perhaps we should look at him." She mentioned Brandt saying he knew he'd be a suspect. "I thought he meant he'd be suspected in a broader, political context. Now, I'm not so sure."

"You think he might have been behind this?"

"We can't eliminate him, not yet. I need the subpoena, and I'm requesting it." She received a text from Dr. Shelton. *Got the tox screen. Need to talk FTF.* "Gotta go. In the meantime, there's something else you can do for me. Find out who's the executor of Sabrina Dunn's estate."

CHAPTER TWELVE

Joanna responded immediately to the summons from Ed Lyons, the owner of the Independent Television Network, her employer. Everyone had seen the two press conferences. And she never forgot that Lyons had hired her at the recommendation of Raymond Brandt, then a state senator and mayoral candidate, after she'd been fired by *City News* after her coverage of a riot four years earlier.

She'd been known as a reporter with a left-leaning agenda, so landing at a right-of-center network had raised a lot of eyebrows. But she enjoyed working at ITN because editorial never interfered with reportage. She wondered now if that was about to change.

"You never got this information about Brandt and Koster, did you?" Lyons asked.

"No. In fact I haven't heard from my source since he gave me Koster." She recounted her last conversation with him.

Lyons scowled. "So he went to your former employer. How would you feel about doing an interview with Mayor Brandt?"

"I can't imagine he'd have anything more to say than he did this morning."

"What's your opinion, having heard the initial report and his response to it? Do you believe him?"

"Honestly? I'd have expected a much stronger statement from both the mayor and the department."

"And I suspect that by this time tomorrow, he may wish he had. Because the rest of the New York media will not be kind to him today."

A deep breath. "I'm not sure we should be, either."

***

Dr. Shelton remained quiet until they were alone in an examining room. Koster's body was gone, but the wall was lined with photos taken during the autopsy. He handed Kim the tox screen report. "Massive fentanyl overdose. Well beyond what would be administered even for prolonged surgery, when a patient would also be ventilated. He was injected after he got into the car, and death would have followed at once, turning him blue because the flow of oxygen to the brain was cut off." He pointed to the photos. "But his four days in the water eliminated that, as well as any other evidence."

"And you're certain this couldn't have been self-administered?"

Shelton looked like he might snap at her but relented. "I know, you're just doing your job. It's not impossible, but it would have been extremely difficult. An addict wouldn't have gone to the trouble. He'd have injected as addicts usually do—in the arm."

"Anything else I should know?" Best to get all the bad news in one shot.

"I found some signs of scarring from prior injected drug use."

"How long prior?"

"Hard to tell. Some scarring can last up to five years. These appear somewhat faded. My guess would be they're a year or two old."

A guess wouldn't cut it. "Can you at least absolutely rule out that none of them were from this lethal dose?"

"The mark on the shoulder is fresh."

"That's not what I asked."

"I know, Kim. It's not possible to determine what drug entered the body through each wound. But I can say with certainty that the shoulder mark is the newest and therefore the likely source of the lethal dose."

That would have to suffice.

***

As she passed the main desk at the Castle, Bob waved her over. "What's this about a subpoena? Cirillo's got his shorts in a knot."

"You mean we got it?" Sounded too good to be true.

"No, Cirillo got a call complaining about you. What's going on?"

Kim recapped her chat with Rick Conti.

Bob sighed. "Well, the captain is waiting for both of us."

They were waved into his office right away.

Captain Cirillo glared at Kim over his glasses. "So?"

She recapped her interview with Sabrina Dunn's parents. "Lots of friction there, but the main takeaway for me was that the remainder of her trust went to Richmond Dunn upon her demise."

"Could be a helluva motive," Bob said.

"Have you told DCPI?" Cirillo asked.

"Of course not. Her father despised her politics and cut her off. She found funding from other sources that lasted nearly a decade. That pissed him off even more. And yes, he profited by her death. It doesn't make a case against him, at least not yet."

"In your best judgment." Cirillo relaxed. "So, your reason for requesting this subpoena was not to establish Brandt's innocence?"

"No. For all I know, it could verify the *City News* story."

"Which," Bob said, "would make him a suspect."

But Kim needed something more immediate. "Captain, if we didn't get the subpoena, what was the reason?"

"As the Brooklyn District Attorney explained to me, that the known killer may have at one time worked at the same firm as another person does not constitute probable cause for that other person."

"Bryce Mitchell called you himself? Or one of his ADAs?"

"It was Mr. Mitchell himself. He also wondered if you ever stuck to the facts of a case you were investigating, or did you always go off on wild goose chases?"

"Maybe he should check my record." It was out before she could stop herself.

"I doubt he has the time." Cirillo didn't crack a smile. "Mitchell also mentioned that Brandt left Cappelli and Lidster on bad terms. A senior member of the firm might talk without a subpoena. Give it a shot."

Not a bad idea.

He opened a drawer and extracted an index card. "You mentioned Sabrina Dunn's will was drawn up by the family attorney. That would be Wilfred Renwyck. Here's his office address and phone number."

CHAPTER THIRTEEN

Kim heard the familiar voice the moment she left Cirillo's office. Felipe Prinz was on the wide-screen TV mounted on the wall. "Those responsible for the death of Sabrina Dunn will be brought to justice, no matter how highly placed, no matter how powerful. And if Raymond Brandt and the police who do his bidding will not do so, then the masses will rise and finish the job."

"Doing what he does best," Bob said. "Pouring gasoline on the fire."

She returned to her desk and called Ken Taylor at the FBI. "I assume you guys are keeping tabs on Prinz. Where can I find him?"

"I doubt he's going to help you," Taylor replied. "He'll assume he's a suspect."

"Everybody's a suspect at this point. The one we want may well have been gunning for Sabrina for a while. If Prinz knows, he'd have ample reason to tell me who."

"Worth a shot, I guess. You going to ask him to make nice in the meantime?"

"I'll ask, but he won't. At least I might slow him down a little." She took the contact information and thanked him.

"What about Renwyck?" Bob asked.

"A detour. Richmond Dunn told me the first will was replaced by another, and I told Conti. So, either Rick didn't repeat it to Mitchell, or Mitchell threw us a curve ball."

"Why would he do that?"

"No idea. And I don't care, yet. But Renwyck won't be in his office until Monday morning, and with luck we'll catch Prinz tonight. He might very well know who the executor of Sabrina's estate is. At the very least, he'll know who drew up the second will."

***

Kim and Bob found Prinz at the apartment he'd shared with Sabrina in a spanking new building on Norfolk Street on the Lower East Side.

His eyes narrowed as recognition dawned. "I remember you."

"And I remember you," she replied. "May we come in?"

"You have a warrant?"

She had already asked Bob to let her handle this. "No, and there's no need for one. You are not a suspect. You said earlier today that you want Sabrina's killer brought to justice. I assume you meant it. It's our job, so perhaps we can work together to see justice done."

"How do I know you're not fishing on behalf of the FBI so they can throw me in jail again?"

Kim shrugged. "Did you have Sabrina killed?"

"Of course not."

"Didn't think so. Do you want her killers caught?"

Prinz flared. "What the fuck…"

"Relax, it was a rhetorical question. This is not: now, may we come in?"

He stood aside and let them in. The interior was clean, the furnishings ultra-modern. Kim imagined in the daylight the glass walls made the place painfully bright.

Bob glanced around. "Not very proletarian."

"What can I say?" Prinz replied. "Sabrina's politics were pure, but she struggled with shedding her capital class lifestyle."

"So," Bob said, "you suffered through."

Kim broke in. "Did you know Ivan Koster?"

"No. I thought you said I wasn't a suspect."

"You're not. I wondered if he had ever approached you. No? Okay. Did anyone else threaten her or harass her?"

"Yeah. Privately, her oligarch father, and publicly, his lackey, the mayor."

No way around it, she'd be forced to wade through his rhetoric. "Did either of them, to your knowledge, threaten her with violence?"

"With violence, no. But she was getting calls over the past few weeks that she didn't talk about. I think someone was pressuring her to get her to drop out of the gubernatorial race."

Kim pulled up her Notes app. "Did she get the calls on her cell or a landline?"

Prinz snorted. "Landline? Are you shitting me?"

"I have to ask. Did she have more than one cell?"

"No."

"Do you still have it?"

Prinz hesitated. "Yeah, but I'm not giving it to you."

"You want this murder solved or not?" Bob asked.

"I want it solved, but I'm not handing you the keys to our movement to do it. I give you that phone, you turn it over to the FBI, and nasty shit happens to good people."

Before Bob could respond, Kim said, "If anyone sent her threatening texts, the only way we'll know is that phone."

"And you'll also see shit she wouldn't have wanted you to see. Sorry. And, no, I won't tell you anything about sources of funding, bank accounts, or who else we were working with. Looking for someone with a motive? Look at the people in power and the people who pay good money to keep them there. Check out Brandt and his patrons. Yeah, that'll happen."

She remained cool. "I'm looking at anyone who stood to gain from her death."

"Try her father," Prinz replied. "He gets the balance of her trust."

"Yes, I know. Who inherits her estate?" At least he'd given her an opening to ask.

Prinz scowled. "I just told you…"

"That's the trust, which isn't part of her estate unless the trust agreement says so, which in this case it doesn't. I'm talking about everything else she owned—real estate, personal property, bank accounts…"

"I don't know. We never talked about it." He appeared baffled.

"You're not the executor? Do you know who is?"

"No."

"Do you know who might have drawn up her will?"

Prinz just shook his head, dismayed.

Kim received a text. It was from Ken Taylor. *I'm in the office. Turned up something of interest.*

"All right. Do us a favor; lay off the inflammatory public statements. Ivan Koster probably wasn't working alone. Finding whoever hired him will take time." Kim gave him her card. "If you want to know how the investigation is going, you can call me. But public exhortations do not help the process."

He grew indignant. "They do if people in power are thwarting the process. No, Detective, I will make whatever public statements I feel are necessary because I don't believe for one minute that you will ever discover who had Sabrina killed."

CHAPTER FOURTEEN

"So," Taylor said as Kim and Bob took seats in his office, "Mr. Prinz was both grief-stricken and prickly. I shouldn't wonder. The IRS has been watching Ms. Dunn's foreign banking activity. They've identified an off-shore account in Grand Cayman, from which she has received funds in the past two years. She also transferred funds into it, presumably proceeds from the trust."

"Suggesting she could have an alternative funding source?" Kim asked.

"Perhaps, although it could also be a money-laundering vehicle."

Kim thought back to Joanna Dunbar's investigation of Brandt in his first run for mayor, in which he was getting donations under the table from Kyle Emory. It had never been made public. "Or a tool for dodging the campaign finance reporting rules."

Taylor nodded. "Another possibility. The problem is, we can only monitor transactions at this end. There's a reason people choose Cayman Islands banks for this sort of thing. I've printed out the transaction history from her New York bank for the past two years." He patted a file folder on his desk.

"What's the catch?" Because he hadn't given her the file.

"I have to ask," Taylor replied. "Do you have a leak in your shop?"

"I thought we did, because the information Joanna Dunbar got would most likely have come from PBBN. But no one in our shop knew about Koster having worked with Brandt." She recounted Joanna's description of her last conversation with the source.

"Sounds like someone connected to the murder wants to throw blame on Brandt." Taylor thought a moment. "Or someone on Brandt's staff is doing the leaking."

Kim grinned at him. "Welcome to my world."

But Taylor remained grim. "Are you certain there is no leak in PBBN?"

She exchanged a quick glance with Bob. "I can't completely rule it out, no. Because I don't know for certain that Joanna's source was also the source for the *City News* story."

Taylor picked up the file. "How will you keep this completely secure?"

She turned to Bob. "We'll work at my apartment. When we're not working, I'll keep it locked in the safe where I store my Glock and Chief's Special."

Taylor's grin broke the tension. "The one that belonged to your granddad?"

The lightweight Smith and Wesson long nose .38 revolver with a five-round chamber, which her grandfather had used on the job from 1950 until his death in 1963, had been a gift from Dad when she graduated from the Academy. It was her second piece. "Yes. So, does my protocol satisfy?"

He handed over the file. "I've given it the once-over, but I'll be interested to know what you think."

***

Joanna had just left the ITN studio at Columbus Circle and was walking down the subway stairs when a familiar figure approached. "Good evening, Mr. Cates. A little far uptown for you, isn't it?"

"I wander near and far in my work. Got a minute?"

"Down here?" They weren't even at track level, and the heat was already stifling, as only the subway in the summer could be.

Cates already had beads of sweat on his forehead. "I wouldn't be op-posed to a walk in Central Park. Plenty of daylight left."

Back up the stairs. Still hot, but at least a slight breeze.

He waited until they'd passed the USS Maine memorial and had en-tered the park. There were a few strollers. "That was quite a smear your former network laid on the mayor this morning."

"So, it wasn't true?"

"It wasn't true."

"And now he wants to go on a friendly station to tell his side of the story?" She'd been expecting this ever since her talk with Ed Lyons.

"No, he wants to know the source."

"I can't tell you what I don't know. My source never gave me this piece of information, and if he's the *City News* source, he doesn't wish to be identified."

"You must know someone over there who could tell you."

She drew back. "No, I don't. As you may recall, I did not leave there on friendly terms. I severed all ties."

"You could re-establish them."

He had to be joking. "Sure. A reporter from a rival station, one with an opposing editorial view, asking them about their source for an exclu-sive story. What have you been smoking?"

But Cates remained serious. "I will remind you the mayor helped you when you needed help the most."

"And he reaped a handsome reward when I did that interview with him just before the special election. The public saw it as us kissing and making up and it legitimized his leap to the political center."

"He needs your help now, Joanna."

"Are you threatening me? Is he? Because that's not the way to go, here."

Cates flashed a disarming smile. "No threats, Joanna. Just a request."

"I'd love to help him, but I can't." A sudden thought. "Besides, what if it's true?"

CHAPTER FIFTEEN

Sunday, July 17ᵗʰ

The phone call came late in the afternoon, after Kim had spent hours plowing through the RTCC databases and examining Sabrina Dunn's phone and bank records. She'd found many transfers from the Cayman account. She'd also found a payment to a Brooklyn Law firm, Danson and Rhinebeck, from five years earlier. The phone calls were too voluminous to be examined all at once. She'd ask Cord and Tim to get on it in the morning.

The call was from Joanna. "I had the most uncomfortable conversation with our Mr. Cates last evening." She repeated it to Kim. "He claimed it wasn't a threat, but it sure felt like one."

"Did you tell Ed Lyons?"

"No, if I did that, he might turn around and tell Brandt to back off. I don't want him to think I'm a wimp. Besides, if Brandt goes to Lyons to complain, it'll suggest he really has something to hide."

Kim took a moment to digest that possibility. "When Brandt brought me back, he assured me he knew he'd be looked at and he welcomed it. Now this."

"Did you talk to Prinz?"

"Yes. Angry and grieving, but not enough to cooperate. Wouldn't even give me her cell phone."

"So much for grief."

Kim thought back on the encounter. "I think the grief is real. He knew nothing about her estate, or even if she had a will. They were together a long time, and it looks like it was more than just mutual convenience."

"So, we're back to Brandt?" When Kim said nothing, she added, "We have a deal, you know."

"Yes, we do. I'm looking at Brandt, but my gut tells me he's not the guy. Why bring me back to run the investigation? He knows I'd never cover for a murderer." She kept her concerns about Richmond Dunn to herself.

"Maybe Brandt's counting on you thinking that way, and not looking at him as closely as you might."

CHAPTER SIXTEEN

Monday, July 18th

"The demonstration, which took place in front of Brooklyn Borough Hall, the site of the shooting, was organized by the leftist group, Come Home Ernesto. The group's leader, Felipe Prinz, repeated his charge that the police are dragging their feet in their investigation." Clip of Prinz: "What is Mayor Brandt hiding? What is his ulterior motive? Does he know more about who committed this heinous crime than he is saying?"

The image froze, and the report continued. "Mr. Prinz was recently paroled after serving a prison term for his role in a riot that resulted in the shooting death of a New York City firefighter. Joanna Dunbar, ITN."

***

Having assigned Cord and Tim the task of finishing plowing through Sabrina Dunn's phone records, Kim asked Bob to join her in her law firm tour.

Wilfred Renwyck was short, portly, and balding. He ushered them into his office, which looked like it was straight out of a movie set, spacious, complete with a mahogany desk and credenza, black leather chairs, a round, glass-topped conference table, and a wall lined with photos of him with politicians, actors, and sports figures. "I understand this is regarding the Sabrina Dunn murder. A terrible tragedy. Such a lovely girl."

So, Richmond had alerted him she was coming. "Yes. I understand from her father that you drew up her will."

"Her first will. She had a replacement drawn up several years ago by a different attorney."

"Why?" Bob asked.

Renwyck's face remained impassive. "I assume she wanted to change the terms."

But Bob persisted. "No, I mean why did she change attorneys? Aren't you the family attorney for the Dunns?"

"I am. As such, I am paid by her father. I suspect she wanted the advice of an attorney with a different perspective."

Kim took over. "Do you know which attorney she consulted?"

"I couldn't say."

Interesting word choice. "Does that mean you know but won't say? I believe the identity of someone's attorney is not privileged information. And this is a criminal investigation."

"She never informed me."

Another dodge. "Which is not the same as saying you don't know, so you do. Tell me. I already know about the bad blood between Sabrina and her father, as well as her political activities. You have no interest to protect here, and each bob and weave by you makes me wonder if we should investigate you."

Renwyck held up both hands. "My apologies. I only meant to imply…"

"Last chance. Who drew up her new will?"

"A Brooklyn attorney named Alec Danson. Community activism and all that. Good day, Detective."

***

Danson kept them waiting for twenty minutes, but when the door to his Livingston Street office opened, no one was inside but him. "I can't help you. The contents of Ms. Dunn's will can only be revealed by the executor. Once the will is probated, it will be a matter of public record."

Kim had no time to argue. "Very well who is the executor?"

"I don't believe it's in his interests for me to tell you."

Kim replied before Bob could say anything. "That's not your call. You are one step away from obstruction, Mr. Danson."

"Very well. It's Felipe Prinz."

CHAPTER SEVENTEEN

Kyle Emory sat back from his half-eaten omelet and fixed his glare on his host, the mayor. "I see Mr. Prinz has re-emerged as a public figure."

The mayor covered his annoyance by taking a sip of coffee. "He has, as have his most fervent followers. And what better way to implant the idea of his innocence than accusing the police of inaction?"

Emory looked askance. "You suspect he was behind it?"

"He doth protest too much."

"And what would have been his motive?"

Mayor Brandt allowed himself another sip. "Who knows? She could have been throwing him over. More likely he saw her poll numbers tanking and realized her star was fading. Whatever. I'll leave that to the police."

"Ah, yes. Your hand-picked detective, Ms. Brady. What does she think?"

"I haven't spoken with her since the day she returned." Because he hadn't been prepared for the old desires to flare back up, as they had.

"Probably wise. So, you think Prinz is responsible?" Emory's voice dripped with skepticism.

"It's possible."

"Because Dunn's poll numbers were dropping. I suppose that makes sense." Emory slipped into deep thought. "I only see one problem with your theory. The last Quinnipiac poll showed a jump in her support of seven percentage points."

***

As soon as they left Danson's office, Kim texted the news about Prinz to Ken Taylor. His response was immediate. *I'm not surprised he hid that from you, although he had to know you'd find out. Between that and his escapade last night, we are intensifying our watch on him. Will keep you informed.*

Captain Cirillo was waiting for Kim and Bob when they returned to the Castle and waved them into his office. "I heard from Lieutenant Bostwick's wife this morning. He's been diagnosed with Stage Three Hodgkin's, and he'll be undergoing radiation and chemotherapy. He wanted to continue working through treatment, but his doctor warned him the chemo would significantly impair his immune system."

"Not a good idea around here," Kim said. "Especially with Covid variants still lurking about. How long will he be out?"

"That depends on how his body responds to treatment. Could be six to eight months."

Bob whistled. "He'll never be able to stand it that long."

"His wife will make him stand it," Kim replied. She then briefed Cirillo on the latest developments on the case. "Cord and Tim are plowing through Sabrina's phone records, identifying every caller from the past six months. The FBI has experts searching for clues as to who owns the second Cayman account from which funds were periodically transferred to her New York account. I've verified that she paid the maintenance on her apartment herself. The Smith and Wesson .45 recovered at the scene is unregistered."

"So," Bob said, "we can assume it came up the Iron Pipeline." Police slang for Interstate 95, the route usually taken by gun runners.

"We can, but it means we can't trace it." Kim faced Cirillo. "Ken Taylor's guys are bird-dogging Prinz. In the meantime, Bob and I will interview Sabrina's campaign manager."

"No," Cirillo said with a growl. "Bob and I have a CompStat meeting at One-PP."

***

Kim had been chagrined to learn that Sabrina Dunn's campaign manager was Evelyn Burke, an attorney she'd come to know while investigating the murder of a community activist that was part of an anti-immigrant terror campaign. Burke was the founder of Citizens for Immigration Justice, which had been infiltrated by Felipe Prinz's group, Come Home Ernesto. CHE had turned CIJ's protests into violent confrontations with police.

Evelyn's greeting was warm. "Come in, Kim. How are you? I heard you've had some health issues."

"I'm fine." Provided she kept moving on this case. "I'm back on the job, investigating Sabrina Dunn's murder. I understand you were her campaign manager." Her tone left no doubt that she thought it odd.

Evelyn gestured for them to sit. "Sabrina and I became friends after Felipe went to prison. She was more distraught over that than losing the special election. I convinced her she still had a role in New York politics, but she needed to reign in her anti-police rhetoric. You probably noticed she no longer spoke of 'defunding' the police."

Kim allowed herself a small smile. "I assumed she could read election results."

"That, she could. And it was working. Her poll numbers were improving. Our internal polling showed she had a chance of catching the governor."

"Winning the election?"

"No, but allowing the governor's other opponent, Leonard Zoloff, to win. And he would've been a much easier target in four years. Sabrina was young enough to wait." A sudden frown. "I already miss her. She spent three years convincing Felipe to moderate his rhetoric. But any hope of that was lost when she was killed."

It pulled Kim up short. "So, someone who supported Zoloff would've wanted Sabrina to stay in the race?"

"Without question. Unless they feared she might win the whole thing. It all depends on what data they were seeing and how they were reading it."

"Did Sabrina ever receive any threats that you know of? Did you?"

"I never did," Burke replied. "And Sabrina never told me of any. Why?"

Kim repeated what Prinz had said about potential threats. "My guys are analyzing her phone records now, but threats can be delivered in other ways."

"You're assuming her murder was politically motivated?"

"I'm assuming nothing, just allowing for the possibility."

"You don't want to hear this, but I wouldn't rule out the current resident of Gracie Mansion."

"I haven't."

Evelyn studied her for a moment. "Didn't he summon you back from your leave to head this investigation?"

"How do you know that?" It was out before Kim could stop it.

A shrug. "People talk. I won't repeat it."

Kim returned to her question. "Who stood to lose the most if Sabrina had won? Aside from the other candidates?"

"The usual suspects." Evelyn gave Kim some pieces of campaign literature.

Kim read through them. A guarantee of affordable housing units within every new residential or mixed-use development project in the state; a mandate for every business with at least 100 employees to be unionized; state-provided day care for working families with young children; a provision for Universal Basic Income; residential and employment support for the homeless; an increase of the tax rates for anyone earning more than $100,000; a wealth tax; allowing non-citizens to vote; a universal green energy mandate.

"Something to offend almost everyone." Kim folded them and tucked them into her jacket pocket.

"I'm sorry you feel that way. Because…"

Kim hadn't come for a campaign speech. "If your poll numbers were accurate, this had to scare some powerful people shitless. If you think of anyone specific, please contact me." Kim patted her jacket. "I wouldn't have voted for Sabrina, but we can't tolerate gunning people down just because we disagree with them. I will solve this case."

As she left Evelyn's office, she received a new text from Cord. *Checked the employment records at Cappelli and Lidster. They only go back ten years, and Brandt was gone by then. Old man Cappelli remembers Brandt and thinks he may have worked on Koster's case, but he isn't sure.*

CHAPTER EIGHTEEN

Tuesday, July 19th

After a few runs, Kim had refined her pattern. Running to Joralemon Street and then over toward the river made it almost exactly a half mile to Brooklyn Bridge Park. Picking up the path there and turning south to Pier 6 and looping along the greenway up to Pier 1 and back to Joralemon Street was another two miles, and the half mile home made it three. The three-block stretch on Joralemon where the roadway was Belgian block was the only tricky part, and she stuck to the sidewalk.

She tried not to flinch as she passed 58 Joralemon Street, which looked like an ordinary brownstone but was in fact a ventilation station and emergency exit for the subway lines running nine stories below. Inside, she and her grandfather's killer had had their ultimate confrontation.

She shook the memory away as she passed it again on her way home. Three miles had been her daily distance until today, when she had run an additional half-loop in the park, turning back at the little beach at Pier 4. As she cruised home on her first four-miler, she felt like she could do a few more. Her euphoria lasted until she approached home.

Justin Cates was sitting on her front steps. "Another Molly Seidel."

Kim chuckled at the reference to the young American who had competed in the Tokyo Summer Olympics. "Sorry, I don't plan on running marathons. Although I admire her a lot." Time to get serious. "What's wrong?"

"I wish I could keep up with you but running killed my knees."

Translation: not out here. "Come on in."

Once in the apartment, Kim grabbed a bottle of water from the freezer. "I put it in just before I head out. By the time I return, it's semi-frozen." She took several gulps. "Four miles in thirty-five minutes."

Justin whistled. "Sub-nine-minute miles. Nice. What's your goal?"

"Build up distance. Hoping to do a five-miler on Sunday." Another few gulps, then she plugged in the coffee pot that she'd set up the night before. "It'll be ready in a few minutes if you'd like some. Now, a repeat: what's wrong?"

"Why do you think..."

"Because you're back to bird-dogging me, which you know I hate. And since we're friends, it must be for a reason other than just collecting intel for your boss."

"I'm not collecting intel," he said. "I'm watching your back. You're doing a lot of work without a partner. Whoever had Dunn killed won't flinch at knocking off a detective who gets too close to the truth."

"Sounds like someone's been watching too much film noir. Besides, you're not qualified to watch my back. You could get us both killed." But there was no missing the worry in his face. "What aren't you telling me?"

"The mayor knows Brogan and Washington were at the law firm yesterday. He and Cappelli didn't part on the best of terms."

"Hold it right there. We will not discuss this investigation. Whatever I hear about the mayor, I will be double-checking, just as I do with anyone else. Please tell him that sending you to spin every negative news item that comes out about him is not in his best interest."

"Okay. But he is worried about you, Kim, and so am I."

"Fine, then tell him to have another detective assigned to our unit until Lieutenant Bostwick returns from medical leave so we're back at full strength. Now, please excuse me while I take a shower. Help yourself to some coffee. There's milk in the fridge and sugar on the counter if you take either."

But when she came out of the shower, he was gone.

***

Mayor Brandt braced himself as Justin left and Kyle Emory was shown in. Two breakfast visits in as many days signaled something unpleasant was in the wind. That Emory was here two hours before his usual time underlined it. "Shall I order you breakfast?"

Emory sat across from the mayor. "No, thank you. I have a breakfast meeting with some business associates later this morning. We're discussing a redevelopment proposal for the Brownsville section of Brooklyn."

"What redevelopment project? I've heard nothing about it."

A wintry smile. "Not yet. We're only discussing its viability. You'll be informed in due course."

"I'd prefer to be consulted, and now."

Emory's tone remained reasonable. "We're just in the brainstorming stage."

"Good, I love to brainstorm, especially when it involves the city."

"I'm not even certain my potential partners are interested."

"I'm already interested, and it sounds like you'll be asking for the city's approval and cooperation. That becomes far less likely if I think you're holding out on me now."

"The city doesn't count your first three years in office since you won a special election to finish your predecessor's term. I assume you want to run for re-election in three years."

The mayor disliked this conversation more with each passing minute. "A reasonable assumption. But your unstated project is already unpalatable on two counts—one, that you're hemming and hawing, and two, that it comes preceded by a threat."

Emory sat back. "Not a threat, merely an observation. Very well. We are looking into the possibility of a project that would entail a private consortium purchasing the City Housing complex in Brownsville. The consortium would then redevelop the property in stages, demolishing the current six-story buildings and replacing them with high-rises…"

"How high?"

"Between eighteen and twenty floors. The new buildings would retain so-called affordable housing units of approximately the same number the current buildings hold, and the rest would be a gentrified development. The purchase price would be a windfall for the city, which would be useful given the current budget difficulties."

It sounded like a pipe dream. "How much of a windfall?"

"That remains to be determined. Would you be interested in the concept?"

"I might. What happens to the current residents of each building as it's demolished until the new high-rise is built?"

Emory shrugged. "I'm sure the city can find temporary lodgings for them. Perhaps you can use the motels your predecessor wanted to convert to homeless shelters."

The mayor cringed. "I'm sure the neighborhoods would find temporary housing projects as objectionable as they found homeless shelters."

"The heartlessness of some people."

But the mayor saw another problem. "Those motels are scattered around the city. Families would be uprooted. Kids moved to different schools…"

"A small price for exchanging life in a city-run rat-hole for a luxury high-rise. Any other concerns?"

One was obvious. "You're talking about tripling the population in a four-square-block area surrounded by other high-density housing. We're already struggling with mass transit over there."

"Good point. Perhaps the city can use part of its windfall to build a subway spur along Sutter Avenue off the Two and Three lines. It could run to Pennsylvania Avenue."

"Sutter Avenue is only three blocks from Livonia, where those two lines run now."

"Three blocks can be a long walk late at night through a dangerous neighborhood. Although, a police substation of the local precinct would also help."

The mayor couldn't help but laugh. "Who else is in on this?"

"At the moment, there are two other potential partners, Fredrick Hammond and Conrad Vinson. There could well be a fourth, but I'm not certain enough to give you a name."

Hammond was a familiar name. His son had been mixed up with the CHE group and was now serving a twenty-five-to-life sentence for killing a firefighter during a riot. Vinson's plane had fetched Kim Brady back from Bermuda at Emory's suggestion. "You have delusions of grandeur."

"That's what brainstorming is all about."

"But you didn't show up unannounced at my doorstep at 8:00 in the morning to brainstorm."

Emory finally turned serious. "No. Earlier this year, someone in the city council introduced a bill requiring all development and redevelopment projects in the city to be contracted either to minority-owned contractors or contractors with a fully unionized workforce. That is blatant discrimination against non-minority small contractors."

"I agree. But then, that's not your real objection. It's the union bit."

"I object to both. My contractors often subcontract smaller jobs to local contractors. It helps reduce the overall cost of the job. They don't check on skin color of the locals and I don't think they should. The only way to end discrimination is to end all discrimination. I know this bill was one of Sabrina Dunn's pet causes, but with her gone, the city council will listen to you."

CHAPTER NINETEEN

Bob Nolan had been resisting using Lieutenant Bostwick's office, but finally succumbed. "There's just too much bureaucratic bullshit for my desk. Goddamn it, there's a reason I never took the lieutenant's test."

Kim had to laugh. "This, too, will pass." She turned serious and told of her encounter earlier that morning with Justin Cates.

"Do you think he'll relay your request to the mayor?"

"Yes, and Brandt will be put out because I didn't ask him myself. But I'm not about to do that."

Bob grinned. "Out of respect for the command structure, no doubt."

"Yes, but I also don't want to get into the habit of asking favors from him. I suspect there's a huge price tag at the end of that road."

"Think he still has the hots for you?"

"I can't rule it out. And then there's the possibility he might be the guilty one."

Bob said nothing, but his glare demanded an explanation.

"He expected we'd look at him, but when anything makes him look bad, he freaks out."

"He doesn't enjoy being falsely accused." Bob shook his head. "Everyone in this thing has a fucking agenda." He answered his ringing phone and listened, his eyes going wide. "Yes, Chief. Thanks."

"What?"

"That was the Chief of Detectives. Remember Martin Stransky?"

"Sure." He'd been in Kim's unit in Internal Affairs and had done some key undercover work in the terrorist case.

"We've got him on temporary assignment until the lieu returns."

Cates had relayed her request to the mayor, and he'd complied. Now, that price tag was more than just a figure of speech.

***

Stransky arrived at the Castle shortly after ten. "I got here as fast as I could." He looked the same—not too tall, slightly muscular, blue eyes and blond hair. "Great to see you, Kim. Bob."

Kim shook his hand. "Great to see you. Bob's temporary supervising officer. How's Marisa?" Marisa Fuentes, who'd been another member of their unit at IAB, had married Martin three years earlier, shortly after her stint at IAB had ended.

"She's moved over to the Manhattan South Special Victim's Unit," Stransky replied. "Her experience on that terrorist case had a lot to do with it."

Cord and Tim joined them as Kim finished bringing Martin up to speed on the case. "Martin will be with me. Cord and Tim, I need you guys to finish with Sabrina's phone call log. Who the callers are and what they do."

Bob spoke up. "What do you want to do about the will?"

"Why not wait for it to be probated?" Tim asked.

Kim shook her head. "Prinz is the executor, and both he and Danson know we're interested. I'm guessing Danson will delay probating for as long as Prinz can stand it. Let's subpoena Danson for it."

"Why not Prinz?" Cord asked. "It would give us the chance to press him about it."

"He'd just deny he had a copy," Kim replied. "Danson can't. Legal ethics requires him to keep client records until the matter is settled."

Stransky laughed. "You should have been a..."

Kim gritted her teeth. "Don't say it."

***

"Dunbar." She was just leaving City Hall following a press conference by the mayor at which he announced his opposition to the Construction Industry Fair Employment Bill being debated in the City Council. She didn't recognize the number.

"Good morning, Ms. Intrepid Reporter." The informant.

"I didn't think I'd be hearing from you again."

He laughed. "Oh, no. It's just that the mayor's connection to Koster played better on a station that's itching to bring him down. Judging by their commentary in the aftermath, I believe my judgment was vindicated."

It certainly had been. The Righteous Indignation Factor over at *City News* had been off the meter ever since. "So, what do you have for me today?"

"I assume you were at the mayor's press conference?"

"Yes."

"What's your take?"

"That Kyle Emory must have some enormous project up his sleeve and doesn't want to pay union wages to build it."

He snickered. "See, that's why I enjoy talking to you. You cut to the chase."

So, she did. "Where does all this lead?"

"You know that Sabrina Dunn championed this bill in her campaign. Mr. Emory met with the mayor early this morning and pressed him to oppose it. They agreed it would be easier to do with her out of the picture."

"I know you won't like this, but I have to ask…"

"How do I know this? You know I can't reveal that. But Justin Cates can verify it."

"He was there?"

"Ask him." The call dropped.

CHAPTER TWENTY

"This is outrageous." Danson shoved the subpoena back at Kim. "A blatant attempt by the government to pry into the private dealings of a political dissident when she's no longer here to defend herself."

Kim had no time for this. "Interesting argument, Counselor, but a subpoena is a subpoena. If you refuse, you can be held in contempt."

"Not if the judge grants my motion to quash it."

Once outside, Martin turned to Kim. "Now what?"

"We head over to see Rick Conti. I'll call to let him know we're coming."

***

"You're a hard man to reach these days," Joanna said when Justin Cates finally answered his cell.

"Sorry, it's been a busy morning. What's up?"

"I need to ask you something, but without telling you why."

He laughed. "Yeah, I know how that goes. Shoot."

"Did the mayor meet with Kyle Emory this morning?"

"Why do you think I'd know?"

A dodge. Almost a confirmation, but not quite. "I'll take that as a yes."

"Please answer my question. You're not just fishing; you're looking to confirm something you've been told."

No choice. "Yes, because I don't know the identity of my source."

"I could ask if it's the same source that leaked the details of Ivan Koster, but I won't put you on the spot. Yes, they met this morning. The mayor often has breakfast meetings with Mr. Emory."

"Did they discuss the Construction bill?"

"I wasn't there."

That pulled her up short. In all the time she'd known Cates, she'd seen traits of his she didn't like, but he wasn't a liar. "Did you speak to the mayor afterward?"

Silence.

Suspicion confirmed. "Another yes. And you spoke about the bill?"

"The mayor has been opposed to the bill from the beginning. Whatever Emory said this morning, it had no impact on his stance. It discriminates against small non-minority construction firms."

"Did they speak about a new major project?"

Another silence.

It was making her skin crawl. "Is that still another yes?"

"Sorry, Joanna, I have to go." The call dropped.

She called Kim Brady. When the call went right to voicemail, she left a message recounting the two conversations.

***

Kim heard the beep but ignored it. She was already on a call with Rick Conti.

"Yes, I know," he said. "Danson already moved to quash. Meet me at the courthouse in an hour."

She and Stransky were heading to Lower Manhattan to meet with Ken Taylor. "I'm in the field. You can't defend your own subpoena?"

"I need you there to explain the details of your investigation to the judge."

She was about to agree when her inner alarm went off. "Why is that even relevant? We're looking to see who might have had a motive." No answer. "Rick, who's the judge?"

"Vickers."

Judge Ronald C. Vickers, also known as Let 'em Run Ron. Rick often said Kim was the only member of the NYPD who'd ever challenged Vickers to his face. When Raymond Brandt had won re-election a year ago, she'd hoped that Vickers would finally be voted out. But he'd survived the voters' anti-progressive outrage by a slim margin.

"I doubt my presence will help," she said at last.

"You can speak to the facts better than I can. See you in an hour."

Kim checked her voicemail, expecting a message from Joanna. But there was a second message, one from her gynecologist, instead. "Please make an appointment to review your test results, and do it soon."

CHAPTER TWENTY-ONE

"Good afternoon, Mr. Conti," Judge Vickers said as he entered. "I see you brought your entourage. Mr. Danson, I hope you don't feel outnumbered." He turned to face Kim. "Detective Brady, we meet again."

In their prior encounter, Kim had launched into the attack. She decided against that here. "This is Detective Martin Stransky, who's on temporary assignment to our unit."

Vickers nodded. "Let's all be seated. Mr. Danson, it's your motion."

"Your honor," Danson said, "the People are seeking access to a will that has not yet been probated. I have not yet discussed its contents with the executor of Ms. Dunn's estate, and application to probate hasn't even begun. Given that the executor is Felipe Prinz, who has been and remains targeted by the government, People's subpoena is a bald-faced attempt to pierce the inner workings of a dissident group to harass its supporters."

"Your honor," Rick replied, "as a probated will becomes a public record, the government will ultimately have access, anyway."

"In which case," Vickers said, "why the subpoena? Why not just wait for probate?"

"I've asked Detective Brady to join us to speak to that very point." Rick gestured to Kim.

"I'm leading the investigation of the murder of Sabrina Dunn..."

Vickers interrupted. "Didn't your people fish her killer out of Newtown Creek the other day?"

"Who himself had been murdered. Someone arranged for Ivan Koster to murder Sabrina Dunn. The longer we wait to identify potential suspects, the more difficult it will be to make a case against them."

"The probate process takes several weeks," Rick said. "And counsel has already admitted the process has not even begun."

"Your honor," Danson said, "their investigation is a fig leaf for government intrusion into a dissident group whom they have already persecuted."

Rick interrupted. "Prosecuted, your honor."

"Noted," Vickers replied. "Detective Brady, I'm concerned that you would first look to Ms. Dunn's estate for suspects to her murder."

"Greed is a common motive, your honor."

Danson spluttered. "You see? She's already decided Felipe Prinz is a suspect."

"Have you?" Vickers asked.

"I've interviewed him, your honor. His grief and outrage appear genuine, so I don't consider him a suspect. But I also can't rule him out."

"Who else haven't you ruled out?" Danson asked.

Vickers glared at him. "If you don't mind, Counselor, I'll ask the questions. Detective, whom do you suspect?"

"When I interviewed Mr. Prinz, I asked him if Sabrina had received any threats recently. He told me that something had been bothering her, but she hadn't said what. I requested her cell phone so we could search for any threatening texts or calls she might have received, but he refused."

"Obviously," Danson said with a snort. "More government snooping, your honor."

"You sound like a broken record, Alec," Rick said.

Kim continued. "That was his reasoning. But then he lied about the will, claiming he didn't know who the executor was, when he was."

"He didn't know because Sabrina never told him," Danson replied. "She was afraid talk of a will would upset him."

Vickers sat back to consider matters. "Detective, your sole interest in the will is to search for a greed motive?"

She didn't want to say it, but she needed to be transparent. "That, plus any enumerated assets."

Danson exploded. "Hah! Looking for funding sources!"

Vickers leaned forward. "Calm yourself, Counselor. Detective, why would you need funding sources?"

Shit. "We must allow for the possibility that Sabrina might have been threatened by someone who had been supporting her and perhaps was angry at some position she took. We must look at every possibility."

"And from there it goes straight to the FBI," Danson said with a growl.

"Your honor," Kim replied, "I'd be willing to agree not to share the contents of the will with any other agency."

"You can't trust them, your honor. They'll say anything to get their hands on that will." Danson sat back in disgust.

"Your honor," Rick said, "the People will stipulate to Detective Brady's terms as a condition of granting the subpoena."

Vickers leaned forward and stared at Kim. "I'm going to deny Mr. Danson's motion to quash, Detective, with the requirement that the terms of the will not be divulged outside the confines of the NYPD. If anyone leaks it for any reason, I will hold you, personally, in contempt."

She nodded. "Thank you, your honor."

Vickers turned to Danson. "Provide Detective Brady with a photocopy of the will today."

Danson reached into his briefcase and withdrew a copy, handing it to Kim. As she took it, her cell buzzed with a text.

It was from Joanna. *My source has returned. Here's the number he used today.*

CHAPTER TWENTY-TWO

"The Mayor's threat to veto the Construction Industry Fair Employment Bill, which had been championed by the late Sabrina Dunn, reportedly came after a meeting with Kyle Emory, a staunch supporter of the mayor and a major contributor to his campaign. Mr. Emory has financed several redevelopment projects around the city, and an as-yet unsubstantiated report claims that a major new project may be in the works. When asked about the mayor's veto threat, Felipe Prinz of CHE said, 'Now we know why they wanted Sabrina out of the way.' Police have identified no suspects in their investigation. Joanna Dunbar reporting."

***

Kim paused to listen to Joanna's report as she made her way to the unit's conference room at the Castle, where she gathered the guys. "The leak isn't here."

"Maybe it's Cates," Bob said.

Kim reviewed her notes. "No, and on two counts. First, we hadn't reported the details about Koster's death to the mayor at the time they were reported. Second, Cates is thoroughly loyal to Brandt. And Joanna knows him. She would've recognized his voice."

Cord was the first to speak up. "Could it be someone else within the mayor's office?"

"Possibly. But someone with an ax to grind, and someone who knew Koster had worked for Brandt's first law firm. That's an arcane bit of knowledge."

"I did some digging at the firm," Brogan said. "Koster worked there when Brandt did, and Brandt did some grunt work on the armed robbery case. Apparently, he missed a step, and it hurt Koster's defense. It was the reason he left the firm."

"Good catch, Tim." But Kim's inner alarm sounded. Brandt had lied. "Go over the mayor's staff. Everybody. Make a note of any holdovers from the previous administration."

"Think he's being done down from the inside?" Bob asked.

"It's the only explanation if the leak is from his shop." She paused a moment. "Which I doubt. I'll also chat with Cates the next time I see him."

Cord shot her a look. "You expect to see him soon?"

"Quite likely. He's bird-dogging me again."

Bob's head snapped up. "Whoa. What's that shit about?"

"Oh, I've told him to stop. But if I know him, he won't, especially if he's under Brandt's orders."

"You think Brandt could be behind Dunn's killing after all?" Tim asked.

Kim's inner alarm was still blaring. "He could be, or else someone is going to great lengths to make him appear guilty."

"He ain't helping himself in that regard," Cord said.

"No." A pause. "And he lied about knowing Koster." If she talked to Cates before she talked to Brandt, Cates would tell him, tipping him off. "I'll see Brandt tonight if I can. Then I'll have a better idea of what to ask Cates. In the meantime, Cord, please get the tower-ping history of this latest cell of Joanna's informant and see if we have a pattern. I'll go through the will."

***

Joanna wasn't surprised when Ed Lyons called her into his office. She hadn't given him an early warning about her latest report, as she usually did. He glared at her as she took her seat but said nothing, giving her an opening. "I take it the mayor has called to voice his displeasure."

"He has, and he said you spoke to Cates to verify the story, and he didn't."

"He verified Brandt met with Emory this morning, whose support for the mayor and history of major projects are both well-documented. I clearly said that the report of a new project was unsubstantiated…"

"Which means you shouldn't have mentioned it at all." Lyons was fuming.

"It's the only thing that explains the tone and timing of the veto threat."

But Lyons wasn't finished. "You also said the construction bill was championed by Dunn. You made it sound like a motive for Brandt to have her killed, and then you included the quote from Prinz that underlined it. If you're going to bring out that kind of heavy artillery, you'd better have more than a rumor from an unidentified informant to go on."

She considered it. He was right. And yet… "What if Brandt was behind it?"

Lyons was thunderstruck. "You don't believe that."

"What I believe doesn't matter. Only the facts matter. He didn't need to threaten a veto. That bill isn't likely to pass the City Council, and even if it does, they won't have enough to override the veto."

"I'm not following you."

"He met with Emory this morning. Emory has good reason to be torqued up about that bill, so he sends Brandt to drop a nuclear bomb on it. He also had to be scared shitless by the prospect of Sabrina Dunn as governor."

"So, you think he told Brandt to have her killed? That's rather far-fetched."

"All I know is that Brandt has been acting awfully guilty."

Lyons nodded. "I can't argue with you there. Would you be willing to do an interview with him so he could clear his name?"

"Did he ask for that?"

"No, I just thought of it."

She didn't believe that. "Sure, if he'll go for it."

CHAPTER TWENTY-THREE

The mayor had been reluctant at first to meet with Kim, but then had reversed course and invited her to dine at Gracie Mansion. She'd declined dinner and suggested they meet after five at City Hall.

She half-expected Justin Cates to be with him when she was shown into the mayor's office, but it would be just the two of them. "Thank you for seeing me on short notice, Mr. Mayor."

"Am I now a suspect?"

Not the question she was expecting. "Should you be?"

A humorless laugh. "I should've known, always a cop."

"You haven't answered my question."

"Answer mine, first."

Fair enough. "You lied to me about not knowing Ivan Koster. You lied about Sabrina Dunn's poll numbers. Justin Cates is back to tailing me, which I've repeatedly asked him not to do. And your statements to the press have been way out of line with your usual demeanor. In short, you've been acting guilty."

"I have the right to remain silent."

She remained serious. "If you want to lawyer up, that is your legal right."

"Good grief! I was only joking."

Enough. "You haven't been straight with me since you dragged me back up here to work this case. If you think I'm going to shield you, you're mistaken."

He gestured surrender. "Okay, okay. Ask me whatever you want."

"Was Joanna Dunbar correct this afternoon? Is there a major new project in the works?"

"Every redevelopment project is on the public record. There is nothing in progress that hasn't been reported."

In progress. "What about in the discussion stage?"

"There are lots of projects in the discussion stage. Most never get beyond it. The few that do must submit formal proposals to the city planning commission and file environmental impact studies, all of which become part of the public record."

"You met with Kyle Emory this morning, true?"

"I meet with him often, usually over breakfast at Gracie Mansion. He dislikes the hubbub of City Hall."

"What did you discuss?" It was like pulling teeth.

"The construction bill. It would be a nightmare for future projects. He asked me to make a firm statement in opposition, and I did so."

"Did you discuss anything else?"

"Not that I recall."

"You mean the way you didn't recall working on Ivan Koster's case?"

He sat back and sighed. "Okay, I guess I earned that."

"Why the lie?"

"Because it was an embarrassing episode from my past. I'd missed a recent case on Search and Seizure, and we couldn't get evidence excluded. I was asked to leave the firm. Plus, I was concerned it would lead you down a false trail."

"Did you ever have any contact with Koster after you left the firm?"

"No. Never."

"Did anyone on your staff?"

"Not to my knowledge. I don't even know what he did after getting out of prison."

Time for another tack. "Why did you pretend Dunn was still trailing badly in the polls? She'd made substantial gains."

"Different pollsters yield differing results. Election polling has been in flux since the 2016 election. My polling sources disagreed."

"Isn't Quinnipiac the gold standard in New York polls?"

"Perhaps, but there's a first time for everything."

It all added up to plausible deniability. She took no comfort from it.

He had one for her that took her breath away. "Find anything interesting in her will?" When she looked stunned, he added, "I understand you got one over on Judge Vickers. Congratulations."

"He denied Danson's motion to quash provided I not disclose the contents to anyone outside the department." The contents hadn't been earth-shaking, just a list of assets and a few bequests aside from the bulk of the estate going to Prinz. Martin was checking on the location of two other properties Sabrina had owned.

"And?"

"You're not in the department. Even Rick Conti didn't get a copy. Now, you can do something for me: keep Justin Cates off my tail. He can only get in the way."

"And you don't want him leaking information."

Another odd thing to say. "No, I don't."

"I'll speak to him about it. Thank you for coming, Detective." And then the expression she hadn't seen in so long returned.

Desire.

Shit.

CHAPTER TWENTY-FOUR

Wednesday, July 20th

Kim was too keyed up to take her usual day off from running.

She'd told Jake the night before about her interview with the mayor.

"Did he hit on you?" Jake asked.

"No, but I suspect he wanted to. I could see it in his eyes."

"Most pols can't keep it in their pants, and they can't stand rejection. Please watch yourself."

"I will. How was the overseas combine?"

"Spotted a couple of prospects. And our young guys look good so far in the Summer League games. I just wish you could be here."

"Me, too."

He'd laughed. "Liar. Anything else new?"

Brandt's ogling had shaken her. "The gynecologist's office has been calling asking me to schedule a consultation. But I want to wait until you're back."

As she now made her way along the Brooklyn Bridge Park greenway, she admitted he was right. This was where she belonged, in the middle of a big case. At the end of the loop near Pier One, the same runner she'd seen on her first run after returning to Brooklyn, and a few mornings since, passed her, running hard.

Must be on the same schedule.

As she approached the brownstone on Monroe Place, she was taken aback to see Justin Cates waiting for her again. "I spoke to your boss about this last night."

"He told me."

"But you came, anyway. Please don't make me go up the chain of command on this."

He remained silent and nodded toward the front door.

"Getting pushy, I see." But she let him in rather than cause a scene.

Once inside the apartment, he said, "Brandt had nothing to do with Sabrina Dunn's murder."

"So, he sent you to proclaim his innocence?"

Justin flopped onto the sofa. "No, he told me to stay out of your way and let you do your job."

"So, why don't you?"

"Because I've been doing some digging on my own, and you need to know what I've learned."

She grabbed a water bottle from the freezer and offered him one from the refrigerator. When he declined, she opened hers and took several gulps before sitting in the easy chair across from him. "Listen, this is not some cozy mystery, where the amateur sleuth solves the crime. This business of tailing me ends now."

"You must trust me, Kim. If I thought the mayor was behind this shooting, I'd help you in every way I could to nail him. But I know for a fact he wasn't."

Despite him not agreeing to back off, she gestured for him to continue.

"Emory was in yesterday morning to complain about the construction bill. But I've since learned that the tip Joanna got was correct. There is something big afoot, so big that Emory can't bankroll it himself. He's got at least two partners, possibly more, all of them bringing big money to the table. One of them is Fredrick Hammond."

A blast from the past. "Not the mayor's biggest booster." The mayor had still been a state senator when Hammond's son was a fugitive from justice. Brandt had pressured him to have his son turn himself in.

Hammond had been furious when his son could not satisfy the authorities with evidence on Prinz and was convicted of murder. "Nor of Sabrina Dunn, either. How do you know this?"

"I can't say just yet. I'm just trying to give you some direction. But the project would involve privatizing one of the city's major public housing projects. You can imagine what Sabrina would have thought of that, with or without her construction bill."

"Did she know about it?"

"Not likely. Even I'm not supposed to know about it."

"Stop. Tell me how you know. I need to be sure it's…"

He laughed. "No, not by illegal means. That's all I can say. I've confirmed it in my own way. If you find the right person, I'll help you connect the dots." He started for the door. "Oh, as for the bird-dogging, as you call it, I won't interfere with you, but I have to do what I have to do."

"Justin, I'll be forced to go back to the mayor."

"Please don't. If I'm right, he's got enough problems as it is."

∎∎∎

As soon as Kim entered the Castle, Sergeant Dhillon beckoned her. "Captain Cirillo wants to see you in his office right away. Bob, too."

She stopped by Bob's office.

"Ken Taylor's up there," Bob said. "He's got a burr up his ass about something."

Her partnership with Taylor went back to her days in Internal Affairs. When she'd been transferred out before the end of her two-year tour at IAB, Ken had promised the FBI would always have her back.

Cirillo looked pissed as she and Bob entered his office.

Taylor didn't wait for niceties. "Is it true you have a copy of Sabrina Dunn's will?"

Kim took an empty seat. "Where did you hear that?"

"Don't fuck with me. We need that as much as you do."

She turned to Cirillo. "You didn't explain it to him?"

Cirillo spread his hands. "I thought it best for you to tell him, yourself."

Thanks, Captain, you're a real mensch. "Yes, I have Dunn's will. But the judge would only agree not to quash the subpoena on the condition that it not be shared outside the NYPD. I didn't like it, but I wouldn't get a hold of the will without it until it's probated."

"Which it likely won't be until the cows come home," Taylor said. "Can you at least confirm Prinz is the executor?"

"Yes. But that's all I can tell you. Anything else, and I can be charged with contempt. No, thank you." She turned to Cirillo. "Are we done?"

"For now."

She stormed out with Bob close behind. When they were back in his office, she closed the door. "How the fuck did he find out?" If it had been Justin, that would put him and the mayor in a whole new light.

A knock on the door.

"Come in," Bob said.

Martin Stransky joined them. "I just saw Ken Taylor leave. He looked pissed. What happened?"

"Someone leaked to him we have Dunn's will, and he wanted me to share the contents, which I can't." She threw up her hands. "Another leak. This case is a fucking sieve."

Martin turned sheepish. "This one's my fault. I told Ken about the will."

"You did what?"

"I'm sorry, Kim. I knew the G was eager to get hold of it, and I figured he'd be glad to know that once our investigation was solved, he'd be able to get it."

Bob interrupted before Kim could roast Martin. "Except the judge's condition won't end with the termination of our case. The feds will need to get their own subpoena." He softened his voice Kim. "Do us all a favor. Go see Taylor and put things right with him."

"I'll think about it. In the meantime, what was that shit with Cirillo? He knows Vickers' condition as well as we do."

"Maybe he was pissed you didn't tell Taylor up front."

"Maybe he should drag his ass down off Mt. Olympus once in a while and talk to us."

Two sharp knocks. It was Sergeant Dhillon. "I think you guys need to see this."

They followed him out to the wide-screen TV. "… say that the affair between Mayor Brandt and the detective began when he was a state senator. Once again, a well-placed source has informed *City News* that the detective hand-picked by the mayor to lead the investigation into the assassination of Sabrina Dunn is a woman with whom he has been carrying on an extramarital affair for several years…"

CHAPTER TWENTY-FIVE

Two minutes later, Captain Cirillo appeared. "Conference room. Now. The entire unit." He closed the door. No one sat.

Kim was trying to figure a way to slow down events.

"Brady, you're off the case." Cirillo held up a hand to forestall protest. "We have no choice. It now looks like the deck is stacked. We've got to make sure the public retains trust in the department."

So much for slowing down events. "Gee, Captain, I thought you might be interested in the facts."

"In the public arena, perception trumps facts every time. It's about time you learned that." Cirillo turned to Bob. "Who's senior in the unit after you?"

"Tim Brogan."

"Okay, Brogan, you're leading. And your chief suspect is the mayor." When Kim laughed, he wheeled on her. "You find this amusing?"

"Yes, in a sick sort of way." She recalled what Justin had said about Brandt having problems. "Don't you see? You're doing exactly what they want."

"Who?" Cirillo asked.

"Whoever is behind this. You never asked me if the affair story is true."

"I don't care if it's true."

"Well, you should. This may be my last day with the NYPD, so sit down and shut up and listen. All of you."

Cirillo was so stunned, he sat. So did the others.

Slow it down. Think it through. She let a couple of minutes go by to gather her thoughts. "Thank you. Like most rumors, this one has a thread of truth to it. Brandt had a thing for me a few years ago. Nothing happened. End of story. When he summoned me from Bermuda, he was friendly but nothing else. However, several people around here knew of his interest, right Bob?" No way would she mention that his interest was ongoing.

"I'd say it was common knowledge, even joke material."

Kim allowed herself a small grin. "No doubt. My husband knew all about it. In fact, he sensed Brandt's interest in me before I did. But station-house gossip usually remains confined to the station-house. We've been worrying about a leak…"

Cirillo shifted in his seat. "We're back to that?"

"We are. I'm sorry if this is tedious, but investigative work often is."

"Don't you lecture me, Brady."

"You need a lecture. Deal with it. We first thought the leak might be here but ruled that out when information was leaked that we didn't have."

"But now you think the leak is here?" Cirillo asked.

Kim put her hands on her hips. "Were you this disruptive in school?"

"Captain," Bob said, "please let her talk."

"Thank you, Bob. No, Captain, Joanna Dunbar's informant isn't here. But this latest tidbit suggests that he might have worked here at some point. If I were still on the case, I would ask Marshal Dhillon to provide a list of everyone who was here four years ago but has since left the department. I would pay particular interest to anyone who left on bad terms. I would then investigate to see if they had any connection with someone who stands to gain by both Sabrina Dunn's death and Raymond Brandt's removal from office. Because it's now apparent that their goal is to cast as much suspicion on Brandt for the assassination as possible. Getting me off the case is just a bonus."

"And who might that someone be?" Cirillo asked.

She considered revealing the project Justin Cates had mentioned but decided against it. "Anyone with means who wants something both Dunn and Brandt opposed."

"Kim," Bob said, "if the person is no longer here, how would they have gotten the information about our investigation?"

"When you see who left on bad terms, you should be able to figure that out."

Cord spoke up. "Kim, what was that about this being your last day?"

"I was shit on once before by the department, when I was hustled out of IAB a year before my tour was up. I'm not putting up with it a second time. Captain, I am going back out on personal leave, effective immediately. When I've exhausted my time, I will resign from the department."

CHAPTER TWENTY-SIX

Two hours after a rival station had reported on an alleged extramarital affair between the mayor and, Joanna assumed, Kim Brady, the mayor still hadn't called a press conference or issued an angry denial. She went right to Ed Lyons. "It makes no sense."

"It certainly isn't like him. You say you know the detective the report mentioned?"

"He was interested in her at one point. She wasn't interested, and still isn't. From what she tells me, he's cooled his jets since then."

Lyons frowned. "But the fact that he was even interested is likely what's preventing him from saying anything. Still, it makes him look guilty. Even I'm wondering, and I've known him for twenty years."

"Why don't I invite him on for an interview? One-on-one is a lot better than a press conference."

"What if he denies it, but she claims he hit on her?"

A good question. Joanna had called Kim three times and texted her twice, with no response. "I don't think she will. She's a very private person. Besides, if this is an attempt to make Brandt look like he's obstructing the investigation, he deserves to tell his side. And if he really is a lecherous bastard, that should come out, too. But a whispering campaign doesn't do anyone any good."

"Okay, give it a shot."

***

When the bell rang, Kim was certain it was Bob or Cord.

But when she opened the door, it was Joanna. "I know it sucks. But don't shut me out. I'm not the one who reported it. Seems to me you need a friend."

"I've got one. Unfortunately, he's in Las Vegas right now." Kim realized that was cold. "Sorry. Come on in."

"Does he know?"

"Yes, I called Jake when I got home. He was totally understanding. The one good part of an otherwise shitty day. They already took me off the case." The moment she said it, Kim wondered if she'd said too much.

"That's the worst thing they could've done."

"Did you get any hint of this?"

Joanna looked stunned. "Are you serious? You don't think I would've given you a heads-up if I knew?"

Okay, she was letting her emotions run away from her. "Sorry, Joanna. I'm just confirming a suspicion. The informant is playing ITN and *City News* off against each other. He doesn't go to both at once."

"So far, yes. But after tonight, I may not hear from him again. I've invited the mayor on for an interview."

"And he accepted?"

"Not yet. My boss is talking to him to convince him to do it. If he accepts, he will deny there was ever anything between you. But I'll have to ask him if he even ever approached you. I already know he was interested."

Yes, he was. But he'd never asked, never blatantly came on to her. There was only the gray area. The desire. The hunger in his eyes. "Ask him."

"If I do, some other network will probably come after you for confirmation."

Kim sighed. "It is what it is. In the meantime, please keep me informed of anything you learn from other sources about the case."

"I thought you said you were off the case."

"The department took me off. I'm now on leave, and no one tells me what to do on my own time."

***

Bob Nolan shuffled through the pile of paper on his desk, not absorbing anything. He was at once proud of Kim and furious at her. It wasn't like her to give up.

He forced himself back into the jumble of notes on the case. But all he could think about was how much he hated being shut up in Lt. Bostwick's office, cut off from the banter outside.

Cord knocked. "Bob, I got the list from Marshal Dhillon."

"What list?"

"The one Kim suggested, everyone from the Castle who's left the department in the past four years. Most were transfers, and some retirements. No terminations for cause. There were five resignations, but there's no way to tell which were on bad terms, if any."

Bob gave a humorless laugh. "I thought desk sergeants knew everything."

"Most do. But some folks around here still hold back with Dhillon. You can guess why."

That, he could. Old prejudices die hard. Then again, Cord might know a thing or two about that. "Kim thinks he's the best desk sergeant she's seen."

"She would. Thing is, what do I do with this list? I'm not sure how she planned to proceed."

Bob sat back. "I could suggest that you take that list over to her and find out. But if you did, she might slam the door in your face. I've never seen her like she was this afternoon."

"That strip she tore off the captain was probably the biggest whuppin' he's had since grade school. In an alternate universe, she'd be running this department."

Bob laughed. "An alien universe. She's like her old man was, doing things her own way with no tolerance for political bullshit. Ask around. See if any of those names ring a bell with anyone. We need a break." After a pause, he added, "We need a fucking miracle."

CHAPTER TWENTY-SEVEN

Thursday, July 21st

The forecast was for temperature to be in the high nineties by mid-afternoon, and even at dawn, Kim was sweating heavily as she ran. This time, she'd done two loops around the greenway, five miles, her longest run yet. She was standing on her front steps stretching and cooling down when she saw the familiar runner sprint by.

So, he lives in the neighborhood, too.

A moment later, Justin got out of a car parked across the street from her apartment on Monroe Place. He watched the other runner go, then crossed. "Here I am, as requested." He climbed the steps to her door.

She'd texted him the night before. "No sign of your boss on the news stations last night. Is he waiting to see what develops from our chat this morning?"

Justin said nothing until they were inside. "He doesn't know about it, Kim. You asked me not to tell him, and I didn't." He flashed a grin. "I thought you'd trust me by now."

"You know what Ronald Reagan said: trust but verify."

"Didn't think you'd have been a fan of his."

"He was before my time, but my dad liked that quote. I figure it's cards-on-table time. You're continuing to poke around on the case despite my objections, and I'm continuing to work the case despite the department's objections. Let's at least keep each other informed, so long as it's just between us."

He flopped onto the sofa. "Shit. He's gonna be pissed when he finds out you're off."

"He doesn't know? They didn't tell him?"

"Not that I know of. And I'm certain he would've told me."

She told him how she'd reacted.

He took a deep breath. "I'm sure it felt great to say it, but you can't go through with it. Police work is in your blood. And I can prove it to you."

"Yeah? How?"

"You're still working this case."

The bell rang. She glanced out the front window. It was Cordell Washington and Vera Koshkin. She buzzed them in and met them at the apartment door.

"Good morning, brilliant American lady detective." Vera's wide grin vanished when she saw Justin.

"Well," Cord said, "this is awkward."

"At least I know you three didn't plan it this way." Kim invited them in.

"Just back from a run?" Cord asked.

"Yes. I can't trust you three not to plot while I take a shower, but the air conditioning in here is making me cold. Give me a minute to change into dry clothes."

The only chatter she overheard was Cord introducing Vera and Justin. Then Vera slipped into the bedroom and closed the door. "Cord told me about yesterday. I worry about you ever since."

"Thanks, Vera. Nothing to worry about."

"We see. Come."

Back in the living room, Vera and Cord took the sofa, Justin the easy chair, and Kim grabbed a dining area chair. "Cord, does Bob or anyone else in the unit know you're here?"

"No." Cord recounted his conversation with Bob. "No one knows what to do, next. We traced the informant's calls to Joanna Dunbar and the number at *City News*. He used a different phone each time he called

Dunbar but didn't change off when he called the other guys. Five calls, three phones. No other calls from any of those phones. A different tower ping for each call, scattered between lower Manhattan and Brooklyn."

"So, no obvious origin," Kim noted.

"Right. Also got the list of people who've left, but nothing jumps out." He explained Kim's ideas about finding the informant.

Kim took over. "The informant must be working for whoever wanted Sabrina killed. I was hoping one of the terminated people might develop into a lead. Let me see the list." She scanned it. "Sergeant Ramos quit? I thought they just put him on a different shift."

"They did," Cord replied. "He worked it for a week and then quit. I asked why they moved him, but no one seems to know."

Kim's nose was twitching. "I wish I still had access to the department's systems."

"You're on leave," Vera said. "You still have access."

Kim powered up her laptop and found she could log on. "Wow. Thanks, Vera. Nice to know I didn't completely shoot myself in the foot yesterday." She turned to Justin. "Where were we before Cord and Vera arrived?"

"We were about to put our cards on the table."

She remembered. "Right. Someone has been working damned hard to both frustrate our investigation and make the mayor look guilty."

"So far, they've succeeded," Justin said. "The latest polls show a five point drop in his approval ratings from two weeks ago."

"Fuck polls," she replied. "And you can tell him I said so. Whoever is behind all this wants him removed as a roadblock as much as Sabrina. Justin, you mentioned some enormous project in the works. Brandt denied anything specific. I think he was running scared, and that you know more than you've already told me. I forgive you. Tell me now."

He hesitated. "I'm still not sure."

"Noted. Tell me what you think you know."

Justin summarized the privatization idea. "The mayor is resisting because it's radical, plus there's too much infrastructure that would need upgrading."

Cord spoke first. "Gentrifying a housing project? Isn't that an oxymoron?"

"They want to use the same technique as that high-rise in Manhattan, with both lower income and upper income housing."

"With a servant's entrance for the lower income residents." Cord spat the words.

"I guess. With the Williamsburg redevelopment nearly done and income rolling in, Emory and Hammond are ready for the next big thing."

"Emory has backed Brandt all along," Kim said. "Don't tell me he's looking to bail."

Justin shook his head. "No, but he's pushing hard for this project."

Kim turned her attention back to her laptop. "Vera, remember on the serial killer case, you were able to access the HR files?

"*Da.* Is easy."

"Can you look up Sergeant Miguel Ramos' file from here?"

"*Da.* Log out from the system and I log in." Vera took over the laptop, signed in, and did a search. "Come see."

Kim studied the record. "Hmmm. Just after I went on personal leave, Ramos was reprimanded."

"That was about the same time he left the department," Cord said. "Does it say what the reprimand was for?"

Kim checked. There was no link. "No. Just the notation. Then the termination date. See if Bob can find out from Cirillo what the reprimand was about. Pull the phone records for any numbers you find for him. Justin, you mentioned Emory pushing the mayor for this project. Is it possible the other money men are pushing Emory to push harder?"

Justin appeared helpless. "I know nothing else about it."

"Cord, have someone pull Emory's phone records. See if anyone interesting pops up."

"Yes, ma'am. And what will you be doing on your personal leave?"

"I can think of two people who might have some idea of who's involved." Although she didn't relish talking to either of them.

CHAPTER TWENTY-EIGHT

Kim dressed as if on the job, a decision she regretted after ten minutes on the R train. The air conditioning wasn't working, and it was a relief when she got off at City Hall. Walking the two blocks to the FBI offices at Federal Plaza did little for the sweat stains under her arms.

The door to Ken Taylor's office was open, and he was alone.

"What the fuck do you want?"

She sat without waiting for an invitation, then she reached back and closed the door. "You're pissed I got the will and wouldn't give you a copy. I'm pissed that you went over my head rather than talking to me about it, like the colleague you're supposed to be. I have way more to be pissed at than you do, but that's beside the point. You may have information I need…"

"And you definitely have information I need."

"We've been over that. I was forbidden to share the provisions of the will by a judge who's had me in his crosshairs for four years. He knew you'd pressure me, probably wants you to, and for me to give in so he can throw my ass in jail."

"I hear you've been taken off the Dunn case."

Well, wasn't that just peachy? "No doubt the mastermind of the assassination knows, too."

"I doubt it. Captain Cirillo called to tell me. He said you took a leave of absence, so you're off."

"Fascinating. No, it's the other way around. He pulled me off, then I went out on leave. I'm considering my options."

Taylor leaned forward. "Meaning what?"

"That's irrelevant. I'm working this case on my own time, beyond the reach of Cirillo's meddling. Tell me, did he offer to provide you with the contents of Sabrina's will?"

"No."

"Didn't think so. See, he doesn't want to get cited for contempt any more than I do. If it helps, I saw nothing in her will that jumped out at me as a lead."

"I might spot something you wouldn't."

"True. Perhaps you can request a subpoena from a federal judge. I'm surprised you haven't, already. In the meantime, Justin Cates tells me that there's some major redevelopment project in the works to privatize public housing."

"Doesn't sound criminal," Taylor said.

"Some might disagree. Sabrina certainly would. And Brandt's resistance suggests he might have agreed with her."

"Providing a motive for someone to murder her and blame him." Taylor's tone suggested he thought it unlikely.

"Yes. According to Mr. Cates, Emory is looking to team up with Fredrick Hammond and some other unidentified investors on this project. Would you have any idea who they might be?"

Taylor turned to his desktop. "We established a file on Hammond four years ago, but our interest ended when his son was apprehended." He brought up a file that Kim couldn't read from where she sat. "No, sorry, nothing on business associates other than Emory, so… wait a minute."

"Something else?"

"The Justice Department set up a separate file on Hammond nine months ago. I don't have access, so I'll have to make an inquiry."

Kim already had her phone out and her Notes app open. "Any idea what it might be about?"

"Doesn't say. But if I had to guess, I'd say it's taxes, financial dealings, or foreign dealings. I'll check it out and get back to you."

Kim stood. "Thanks, Ken."

"Don't mention it. And I'm sorry about the blowup. Just don't do anything rash."

"Haven't you heard? I'm a loose cannon, like my father was."

***

Bob Nolan came out of his office and was surprised to see Brogan, Washington, and Stransky all hunched over their laptops and whispering over their shoulders at one another. "What's going on?"

Brogan's head popped up. "Just checking a few leads."

"What leads? About what?"

All three cleared their screens, and Brogan suddenly looked like a deer caught in the headlights.

"In the conference room. Now." Bob led the way, noting there was no new information posted on the marker board. He also saw Brogan and Washington whispering to one another as they came in. He closed the door. "Okay. Something's up, and I want to know what it is. Right now. Brogan?"

But it was Washington who spoke up. "What's with the surnames? What happened to Tim, Cord, and Martin?"

It hadn't been a conscious decision, but he'd slipped into it once he'd moved into the lieu's office.

Cord turned to Tim. "Must be a command thing. Maybe we should call him 'Acting Lieutenant Nolan, sir' and tug the forelock."

Bob had to laugh. "Knock it off."

"Maybe the lieu's office is possessed," Tim added.

Bob turned serious. "Tim, you're supposed to be leading. What's going on?"

Tim turned to Cord. "Maybe you'd better explain."

Cord didn't look pleased. "We got a new angle on the Dunn murder. A source within City Hall says that the rumor about some mega-redevelopment deal is true—Emory, Hammond, the usual suspects—but the mayor is resisting."

Tim spoke up. "It's likely someone in that group planned the assassination and they're now looking to pin it on Brandt."

"Hold it," Bob said. "Who told you this, Tim, and when and where did they tell you?"

"I told him," Cord said. "The source told me. And I can't reveal..."

Bob's voice dropped to a growl. "There are no secrets within this unit. Even Kim kept her cards on the... Wait a minute. She's behind this, isn't she?"

Tim said nothing but turned to Cord.

Cord hesitated. "Not exactly. I went over to her place this morning. Vera and I. When we got there, Justin Cates was already there. Apparently, he's been checking in with her. He was the source for the information on the project. But we came up with something else." He recounted what they'd learned about Sergeant Ramos. "Do you know why he was reprimanded?"

Bob was taken aback. "I didn't know he was. She thinks he's the informant?"

"She doesn't know, but if the informant is a former Member of Service who left disgruntled, he might fill the bill. And the timing of his departure fits."

"No, it doesn't," Bob replied. "He was already gone when Kim came back from Bermuda. How would he know she was on the case?"

"I'm sure he still has friends here," Tim replied. "We're checking his phone records for some clues regarding his activities, but it would help if you could find out what he did to earn the reprimand."

"It should say in his file," Bob replied.

"It doesn't," Cord said. "Vera checked the HR file. It only says he received a reprimand, and then that he resigned his position a few days later. Looks to me like he had a move in his hip pocket, ready to go."

Bob heaved a sigh. "Let's just step it back a moment. Is it my imagination, or is Kim Brady still running this investigation?" Silence. "That's what I thought. Look, guys, I like Kim as much as you all do. We all know she's got brass onions. But if she keeps on, she'll be out on her ear. She's already pissed off Cirillo and the FBI."

"I'd withhold judgment on the feds just yet," Cord said. "She went over to see Taylor this morning. She texted me they've kissed and made up. Now, about Ramos' reprimand?"

Cirillo would have the same questions about it, and if Kim's name came up, there'd be hell to pay. "Let me see what I can figure out."

CHAPTER TWENTY-NINE

Kim was surprised to find Felipe Prinz at the condo on Norfolk Street. He sported a scraggly beard and the neatness of the apartment had declined by a factor of three.

He scoffed when he saw it was Kim. "Shouldn't you be over at City Hall, goin' down on Brandt?"

"Don't believe everything you hear." She sniffed the air. A faint hint of weed. "You straight enough to have a serious conversation?"

"I thought you'd be off the case by now."

"That's what they want."

"Who?"

"That's what I want to talk about. If you're not too out of it to be coherent."

He hesitated. "It's legal, now, you know."

Unfortunately. Something else to make the job harder. "Some other time, then." She turned to go.

"Wait. What did you mean, it's what they want?"

She gestured to the apartment.

He relented. "Yeah, come in."

"I meant," she said once they were inside, "that whoever is behind Sabrina's death will do anything to disrupt the investigation. Hence the leaks and the rumor, which of course isn't true."

He snorted. "Of course. So, why did he pick you to head the investigation if not to make sure he didn't get nailed?"

"He respects my work. So should you, even if you haven't liked the results in the past."

He stared at her. "So, now you don't think I did it?"

"I never considered you a likely suspect, although I had a momentary doubt when you lied to me about the will. You thought I wanted to establish a motive for you. Well, that's not the case. I needed to learn as much about Sabrina's contacts as possible."

"I'm still not giving you her cell. You agreed not to turn the will over to the feds, but you'd turn over the phone. Don't bullshit me."

She tried a smile. "No, I wouldn't do that. And I didn't come for the phone. There's a rumor floating around about a redevelopment plan being pushed that would involve privatizing a major city housing project. Have you heard anything about it?"

"I'm the last person they'd tell."

Now, she laughed. "Oh, yeah. But you have ears on the street, sources of information. And, no, I'm not asking who they are. I'm asking if you ever heard about this privatization project."

He lapsed into silence. So, he knew.

"Felipe, do you want Sabrina's killer caught? Koster was a hired gun. The actual killer is the one who hired him."

"Word is it's somewhere in Brooklyn," he said at last. "Huge money behind it. Huge money behind Brandt. So, it's gonna happen."

"If Brandt was going to approve it, why would they be trying to smear him with this rumor about me?" She let that sink in. "It's important to know who's behind the project."

"I don't know, and that's the truth."

"Did Sabrina know about it?"

"Of course, she did. She was going to raise the issue once…" He froze.

"Once she got more facts. Felipe, I promised not to ask for her phone. But you can help me. Please go through her phone log and note every call and text from anyone not in her contacts list, or that looks out of place."

"What do you mean, out of place?"

"You know what I mean. If you want this case solved, you must help me." She waited.

"Okay."

She took out a card and wrote on it. "This is my cell number. Text me the list when you have it. Make a note of repeat calls you didn't know about. Get it to me the moment you complete it, but be thorough, please."

CHAPTER THIRTY

"Nolan, I need you in my office, on the double." Cirillo's tone left no doubt that Bob was in deep shit.

He stopped to check on Brogan and the guys.

"Still diggin'," Brogan said.

"Sounds like someone tattled," Cord added.

And Bob had only asked two people about Ramos. Then again, everyone at the Castle was on edge. "Any further word from Kim?"

"No." Brogan looked concerned. "I wonder what kind of reception she got from Prinz?"

Bob glanced around. "Don't even mention that out loud."

Cord gestured to the clock on the wall. "You'd better get up there. His eminence is waiting."

Bob was still debating with himself how to handle the interrogation he was certain to face when he entered Cirillo's office.

"What's this I hear about you sniffing around about Sergeant Ramos?" Cirillo asked without preamble.

"Just following up on a theory, Captain. The thing about Kim Brady and the mayor was a joke around here a few years back..."

"Which means it could have come from anyone. Your job is to find whoever hired Koster, not to rehab the reputation of Detective Brady. Answer me straight, Nolan. Did she put you up to this?"

"No. But…"

"Good. It stops here."

"I think it's a good lead, Captain. Kim Brady has a lot of friends here. Admirers, even. The only person who'd leak this kind of shit would be someone with a grudge. Sergeant Ramos appears to have been reprimanded before he resigned. That sounds like he might hold a grudge."

"Which has nothing to do with the murder."

"How do you know that?"

Cirillo's eyes narrowed to burning slits. "Watch yourself, Detective."

But enough was enough. "No, wait. First, you yank Kim off the case at the first sign of trouble, then when we have a lead on the leak that's been plaguing this investigation, you haul me in on the carpet to cut us off. Okay, if you're so sure Ramos is clean, tell me: what was the reprimand for?"

"I don't know and neither do you."

"Right. The difference is, I'm not afraid to find out." He turned to leave.

"Get back here, Nolan. If Brady is gumshoeing around the city, pretending she's still on the case, I can't stop her. But if you or anyone in the unit is communicating with her about this case, you'll all face disciplinary action."

Somehow, the knowledge he'd just stepped in it didn't bother him. Instead, he returned to the unit.

"Still in one piece, I see," Cord said. "If not especially pleased."

"No," Bob replied. "Someone tattled, I don't know who. Cirillo realizes we're working with Kim."

Brogan groaned. "Shit. What now?"

"We keep doing what we're doing. It's not without risk. Cirillo already threatened me. But his reaction over Ramos was off the charts. Something stinks, and we need to find out what it is. Cord, the lieutenant you guys served under over at Internal Affairs—what was his name?"

"Colangelo. Steve Colangelo."

Bob remembered the name. "Call him, brief him, and ask him for anything he can give us on Ramos' reprimand. And let me know when we hear from Kim."

***

Evelyn Burke took Kim's hand. "Didn't expect you back so soon."

"But you expected me back?"

Evelyn turned serious. "What's wrong?"

"How close were you and Sabrina?"

"In what way?"

Fencing. Not a good start. "In any way. The last time we spoke, you suggested you were more than just her campaign manager; almost like a mentor."

"I'd prefer to say a trusted advisor. Yes, that's true."

"So, she might have discussed matters in greater depth with you than, say, Felipe Prinz?"

"She might. Why?"

Still cautious. "Are you aware of a proposal by a consortium of investors to privatize a vast housing project?"

Evelyn pondered it. "If I tell you, you will no doubt ask my source. But if I ask you where you heard about it, you'll refuse to tell me yours."

"I'm sure you can guess." When Evelyn's eyes went wide, Kim added, "A reasonable guess."

"Sorry. One can't help oneself these days. I still can't tell you my source, but you might be able to guess as well."

"Right now, I just need to know if I'm on the right track."

"Yes, there is a group that wants to privatize one of the city projects in Brooklyn, replacing the existing buildings with high-rises. Force feeding the great unwashed into gentrification."

"I take it Sabrina knew?"

Evelyn nodded. "I told her. She wanted to make an issue of it in her campaign, but I suggested we wait until we knew more about it. It took me quite a while to calm her down. Next, you'll ask if I know who's involved. I don't, but I suspect Kyle Emory has to be in there."

"He is. Also, Fredrick Hammond, plus at least one other whose name I don't know. I was hoping you would. Do you know if Sabrina was getting threats? Felipe said he suspected something, but she denied it."

"She said nothing to me about any threats. But she seemed distracted that last week."

CHAPTER THIRTY-ONE

Friday, July 22nd

Kim knew she should take a rest day from running, that she was inviting an overuse injury, but it was the only way to deal with the tension. Her loop run was truncated when she saw Justin waiting for her at the turn on Pier One. "You're ambushing me on my run, now?"

"I was afraid we might become too conspicuous if we continue to meet on your front steps."

"When did you become paranoid?"

"When my boss got elected mayor. Mind if I walk with you?"

She looked him up and down. Not yet 6:30 in the morning, and he was dressed in a cream linen suit and a teal tie. All that was missing was the Panama hat. "I don't suppose I could get you to jog?"

He snapped his fingers. "Damn, I left my running shoes in the car."

"Where did you leave your car?"

"At your place. Besides, this is your fourth straight day of running. You'll hurt yourself if you're not careful."

"Okay, okay." She led the way onto Furman Street, then left onto Old Fulton Street. "It's about a mile walk from here."

He'd turned serious. "Good. Lots of time to chat. The mayor just learned late last night about your situation. He's not happy."

"Who told him?"

Justin looked like he'd been caught with his hand in the cookie jar.

"Justin, I thought we'd agreed not to tell him. If he demands I be put back on the case, it'll make things terrible for me."

"I explained that to him, and he understands. His concern is that you're operating without backup."

"I thought you were my backup, with or without my permission."

"I am. But he now shares your concerns about me. He wants to know how he can help."

That was easy. "Tell you everything he knows about who's behind that redevelopment proposal so you can tell me."

They stopped for the light at Front Street.

"That's what I told him."

"And...?"

His hesitation told her everything. "He said he'd already told me everything."

"Bullshit."

He cracked a small smile. "I didn't say that. But I thought it."

They walked in silence until they made the right turn at the head of Henry Street. Justin broke it. "Talk to him, Kim. If he hears it from you, he'll realize he has no choice but to tell you."

"I can't be seen anywhere near either City Hall or Gracie Mansion. And if someone inside the department is in on this, which I can't rule out, we don't dare risk a phone call."

Neither said a word until they'd crossed Pineapple Street.

"What about a burner?" he asked. "I could buy it for him, and he could call you. In fact, I can buy two and give you one. Wiretap-proof."

She had to laugh. "You may have a future in undercover work."

"You don't get it. I've been doing it for years." He stopped at his parked car. "I'll be in touch."

***

Bob was glad to see Cord already there when he arrived at the Castle. But his hopes were dashed when Cord said, "Colangelo knew nothing about it. He also asked why Kim hadn't called."

"Did you tell him?"

"Yeah. He wasn't surprised. He'd seen the report and guessed what it meant. But..."

"You think there's more?"

"Yeah. Or, rather, Colangelo does. He said he'd do some digging on his own." Cord checked his watch.

"You have somewhere to go?"

"Vera's been working on phone records for me. And I've been digging through the bank stuff. We're gonna meet over at Kim's this morning and compare notes."

Bob suppressed a snort. "I didn't hear that."

***

Kim's legs felt like lead as she climbed the steps to the brownstone. She froze outside the apartment door. Inside, the television was on.

She pulled the Chief's Special. As this case became more entangled, she had taken to tucking it in the waistband of her running shorts at the small of her back.

With the pistol in her left hand, she tried the knob to her apartment door with her right.

Locked.

Whoever was inside must have broken in.

But who broke into an apartment and turned on the television?

She knocked twice, then stepped back into a two-handed stance.

"Who is it?"

Oh, for God's sake. She stuffed the weapon back in her shorts. "Me."

Jake opened the door, and she flew into his arms. "What are you doing home?"

He planted a long, sweet kiss before answering. "After the combine, I stuck around for some of the summer league games, but my staff can handle that. You sounded more and more down, so I thought I'd surprise you." He stepped back and looked her up and down. "You had your piece out until you realized it was me, didn't you?"

She stepped past him, into the apartment. "Don't be silly."

"Right. What did the gynecologist say?" When she turned away, he added, "I thought so. Kim, you need to make that appointment. I'll go with you. Whatever it is, we'll face it together."

CHAPTER THIRTY-TWO

Mayor Brandt wasn't sure he'd heard right. "You want me to do what?"

But Cates didn't back down. "Kim is right. You two can't be seen together. And phone calls can be traced. But a call from one prepaid cell to another can't be unless someone knows about it in advance. And she needs to talk to you directly."

The mayor tried not to think back on that night years ago when, just by chance, he'd run into Kim and her husband at a restaurant. She'd looked more lovely than he'd ever dreamed. It had taken ages to tamp down the desire that flared in him that evening.

He'd thought it was long past until the day he summoned her from Bermuda, looking tanned and fit, dressed casually in white shorts and a yellow top, her hair clipped back in a casual bun. Keeping his manner professional had been easy at first because he was asking her to come back before she was ready, knowing she needed to recover, and a businesslike demeanor masked his realization that he was a heel. But watching her go, the sway of her hips, desire had thundered back.

"I don't see any other way," Cates said.

The mayor's attention snapped back to the present. "I'm not about to skulk around with burner phones like some back-alley drug dealer. What progress has she made so far?"

"No answers, just a lot of questions."

The mayor's personal assistant entered his office. "Sir, both have confirmed. Dinner at Gracie Mansion, cocktails at six."

He thanked her, and she left. Cates gave him a quizzical look.

"Just politics. Keep an eye on her. Have you seen any indications of a threat?"

After a momentary hesitation, Cates shook his head. "Nah."

"You're holding back something, Justin."

"Welcome to the club." He walked out.

***

Jake had left before Cord and Vera arrived. Before long, the dining table was buried in printouts of Sabrina Dunn's phone records.

Vera picked up one sheet. "Here is list of calls made from one number. Three calls in all. First one was a month before the shooting. The second was a week before. The last was not a call, but a text, and it was received two days before."

Kim did the math. "Sixteen days ago."

"Right," Cord said. "No way the cell carrier would still have the text."

"And even if they did," Vera added, "it would be encrypted, and they couldn't decrypt it. Only the sending or receiving cell could provide that."

Shit. "Prinz won't turn over her cell."

"Couldn't we get a subpoena?" Cord asked.

"Perhaps," Kim replied, "but Prinz would find an excuse not to comply, or just toss it in the river. And we'd lose whatever cooperation we might otherwise get from him." Not that she'd gotten any. "Fuck it. Ask Rick Conti for the subpoena. It's worth a shot."

Ken Taylor sent a text. *Think you can drop by this morning? I have something that may interest you.*

***

Bob Nolan poured himself a cup of rancid coffee in the break room. While he debated with himself whether three sugars would do it or if he needed a fourth, Therese Vargas, Captain Cirillo's administrative assistant, a civilian employee of the department, walked in. "Hi, Bob. How can you stand to drink that stuff? The Firehouse Deli is just across the street, and their coffee is fine."

The timing was perfect. He'd heard rumors she'd been involved with Sergeant Ramos. "I never know when your boss is going to call me in for a roasting."

She giggled. "His bark is worse than his bite."

"The tooth marks I carry tell a different story."

She giggled again. "That's what Miguel used to say."

"You mean the captain got on his case, too?"

"All the time."

"I don't get it. I always thought Sergeant Ramos was a good man."

She turned serious. "He is. You're a good man, too. It's the captain who has the problem."

Bob gestured for her to sit with him at the table, and she did. "What was his problem with Miguel?"

"They were fine for a long time. But then, Miguel had to leave early one day. Not too early, maybe a half hour. He asked me to sign out for him. It was one time, and he made up the time two days later, staying on after he'd signed out. Captain Cirillo found out and wrote him up for falsifying attendance. He said as a desk sergeant, Miguel should know better, and he switched him to the night desk. Miguel's pride was hurt, and he quit."

"Do you still see him?"

She turned to make sure the door was closed. "No. He had to make things right with his wife. I understand. He has two young boys. But it was nice while it lasted, and we're still friends. We talk on the phone from time to time."

So, the rumors were true. "What's he doing these days?"

"He's head of security for a bank, I think."

Bob drained the last of his coffee and winced. "You're right, I should stick with the deli. Enjoy the rest of your day."

CHAPTER THIRTY-THREE

Kim held up her hands as she entered Ken Taylor's office. "I come in peace."

"That's what they all say. It's okay, I invited you, remember? My contact at Justice says the IRS is auditing a US multinational corporation, in which Hammond holds a controlling interest, with foreign subsidiaries."

Kim shrugged. "Taking advantage of cheap foreign labor."

"Taking advantage of a major tax loophole. Income from foreign subsidiaries isn't taxable until the sub pays the parent a dividend. So, multinationals have devised schemes to move money that doesn't look like it's from the foreign sub. In Hammond's company's case, it's an arrangement between a sub based in the Channel Islands and a British company with a joint venture in the Netherlands. The IRS is working with the UK on the audit."

"Ken, there's a reason I didn't major in finance."

"Then, let me cut to the chase. The Channel Islands sub made three payments to Hammond's company through the Dutch joint venture." He handed her a printout. "But a fourth, for $125,000, was made directly to this account in the Caymans on May 27th."

Kim stared at it. "That's the account you identified as Sabrina Dunn's, the one funded from her trust."

"Correct."

Kim examined the printout further. "Ken, that payment was reversed on June 3rd."

"Yes."

"So, it was probably a mistake."

"A distinct possibility." But he clearly didn't believe it.

Neither did she.

****

"Welcome to 'New York at Noon' on *City News.* The advocacy group Come Home Ernesto held a rally this morning in front of City Hall denouncing a rumored project that would privatize that property, demolish it, and replace it with high-rises. Felipe Prinz, CHE's leader, charged Mayor Brandt with selling out to wealthy real estate interests."

Prinz appeared on screen. "Gentrifying private property isn't enough for this mayor. Now, he wants to squeeze out the last bit of affordable housing in this city. Wealthy interests are running amok, with no end in sight. Now we know why Sabrina Dunn was assassinated, and why the mayor has hobbled the police investigation by putting his mistress in charge of it."

****

Mayor Brandt pounded Fiorello LaGuardia's desk. Enough was enough. He buzzed his secretary.

"Yes, Mr. Mayor?"

"Call the police commissioner. Tell him I want to see him, the Chief of Detectives, Captain Cirillo, and Detective Nolan here in my office at two o'clock, sharp, or heads will roll. Then call Ed Lyons at ITN and tell him

I've accepted Ms. Dunbar's offer of an interview. Tell him tonight at 8:00 will be fine."

***

By the time Kim caught up with Prinz entering the Norfolk Street condo, she had seen the clip. It was time for hardball. "You're either an asshole or my prime suspect."

He snorted. "Typical. Lock up anyone with a dissenting voice. Don't blame me because your sleazy affair leaked out."

"That's bullshit and you know it." She shoved a photocopy of Sabrina's bank statement under his nose. A transaction from the Caymans account was highlighted. "In May, that account received a wire transfer of $125,000 from a Channel Islands company. You and Sabrina doing a little money laundering?"

Prinz looked like he'd been slapped. "How would you know about activity in a Caymans bank? They have secrecy laws." His expression hardened. "Oh. Right. I forgot. You're working with your pals at the FBI. Well, you're barking up the wrong tree. That was an error, and the transaction was reversed when we discovered it."

She waited until she saw the "oh, shit" look on his face. "So, you were aware of her Caymans account, as well as her other assets. Good. Explain, please, why an erroneous transfer took a week to reverse."

"I told you, we returned it once we saw it."

"More bullshit." She handed him the printout from the Channel Islands company Ken Taylor had provided. "Wire transfer errors are caught and corrected right away. And when they are, the money is redirected to the correct account. As you see, once the $125,000 was returned, it was never redirected elsewhere."

"Where did your FBI friends get this?" His bravado was gone.

Kim shrugged. "Not for me to say. But that company is involved in a series of transactions with Fredrick Hammond. You understand my interest, now."

Prinz lapsed into silence.

"It's put up or shut up time. You haven't given me the list I requested, so give me the phone. If there was something going on between Hammond and Sabrina, tell me. Because, if you don't, you go right to the top of my suspect list."

CHAPTER THIRTY-FOUR

Bob Nolan scrunched up his toes as he sank into the sofa in the mayor's office at City Hall.

"I would like someone to explain why Detective Brady was taken off the case." The mayor glared at the commissioner. "It certainly wasn't my idea."

The commissioner turned to the Chief of Detectives, who turned to Cirillo.

Cirillo didn't hesitate. "It was mine, Mr. Mayor. Knowing this would be a troublesome case, it seemed best not to have any distractions."

"Did you consult with your commanding officer?" the mayor asked.

"No. It was my call."

The mayor leaned forward. "No, it wasn't. I appointed Detective Brady to this case because she is the best homicide detective on the force." He turned to Bob. "No slight intended."

Bob snapped to attention. "None taken, sir. I agree."

The mayor turned his glare on the commissioner. "I want Detective Brady reinstated. Today."

But it was Cirillo who responded. "She's on personal leave."

"I'm certain she will be glad to return." The mayor turned to Bob. "Would you agree, Detective?"

"No question, sir. She's never really left the case." When Cirillo glared at him, he shrugged. "She told you she wouldn't."

The mayor appeared amused. "I'm not surprised. But I have a question. Where did this rumor of an affair between me and Detective Brady come from? It was never true."

"You think it came from the department?" the commissioner asked.

"I don't know. That's why I'm asking."

"We're looking into it, sir," Bob said.

Cirillo's glare grew angrier. "And why haven't I heard about this?"

"Because it's just one of many things we're looking at. You probably would've told me not to, but whoever leaked this intended it as a roadblock."

Cirillo turned red in the face, but the mayor forestalled him. "Let him talk, Captain, because I want to hear this. Please proceed, Detective."

Well, a mayor outranked a captain. "Sir, the leaks of details of the investigation have been so specific and on target, they could only have originated in the department. You may recall at a Cadman Plaza riot four years ago, you made a statement on television praising Detective Brady. It became an item for gossip around the water cooler, all in fun, of course."

The mayor grunted. "Of course."

"Nolan," Cirillo said, "there must have been half a million viewers saw that clip. It could have been any of them."

"No, Captain," Bob replied. "A casual viewer would not have known about the added resources then-State Senator Brandt was providing the department, specifically in assuring crime lab results were expedited to us, or that they came to us because of conversations between him and Detective Brady."

The mayor made sure he asked the next question. "Have you turned up any leads on this leak?"

Not here, for the mayor and the brass to hear. "Anything I say now would be pure speculation, Mr. Mayor. The leaker, whoever it is, may not be directly linked to the assassination, but could lead us to someone who is."

"Either you have someone in mind, or you've just spun some king-sized speculation." The mayor chuckled. "But I'll leave you to sort it out. I agree with your approach. Captain Cirillo, please make sure Detective Brady is officially back on the case today. Detective Nolan, has she been working the case full time since going on leave?"

"Yes, sir."

The mayor turned to the commissioner. "Then please see she is not charged for any personal days she's taken. Captain, you will keep the chief and me informed of the developments on this case as they happen. Am I clear?"

CHAPTER THIRTY-FIVE

Cirillo didn't say a word all the way back to the Castle, and that put Bob even more ill-at-ease. The captain would take his questions about Ramos as second-guessing, and he'd be furious at Bob having discussed personal matters with Therese Vargas. He'd been tempted to bring it all up when they were with the mayor, but that would have been disastrous.

They'd just made the left onto Flushing Avenue from Broadway when Cirillo finally broke his silence. "What was all that about speculation?"

"Cops may gossip among themselves, but they adhere to the adage about what you hear here stays here. And a cop would have to be incredibly sick or pissed off to torpedo an ongoing investigation."

Cirillo stopped at the light on the corner of Flushing and Wilson. "Agreed. So?"

"What was the story with Sergeant Ramos?"

The light turned green, but Cirillo didn't move until several horns behind him blared. "What makes you ask?"

That tore it. "You know what really pisses me off about this investigation? Everybody has something to hide. Nobody has given me a straight answer, yet. Okay, I'll tell you. You reprimanded Ramos over signing out early over half a fucking hour, even though he made up the time, and you switched him to the graveyard shift desk. That reeks."

"He's married and was having an affair with my assistant."

"And you're, what, captain of the morals squad, now? Is that why there's nothing in his HR file about the reprimand?"

Cirillo stopped at the light at Troutman Street. "How the hell do you know that?"

"Not important." No way was he going to tell Cirillo about Vera Koshkin's access to NYPD systems. "What else did you say to Ramos at the time of the change?"

"It got heated, and I said I didn't think someone with his temperament had a future in the department. A week later, he quit. But what difference does any of that make? How would he know the details of our investigation, now?"

"Duh, maybe someone is still friendly with him. He had lots of friends around here." Although Bob realized it might be best not to mention Therese in that context. "I'm curious. Why did you go nuclear on him for canoodling?"

The light changed and Cirillo drove on. "That's none of your concern."

Holy shit. The captain wanted her for himself.

***

Mayor Brandt sat back in his seat at the head of the dining room table in Gracie Mansion. It was just the three of them—Kyle Emory, Fredrick Hammond, and himself—and they'd finished dinner and dessert and were now sipping cognac. The mayor was the only one not smoking a cigar.

His guests had spent the entire dinner fleshing out their idea of privatizing public housing, complete with a subway spur line and police substation, and they now turned to their host to get his decision.

"Am I to understand that you two will be the only major investors?"

"No," Emory replied. "Conrad Vinson, who provided the transportation for your Mr. Cates to fetch your detective back from Bermuda, is also interested. There is one other, but he wishes to remain anonymous for now."

Time to show the whip hand. "No secrets here, gentlemen. There are some things I must know before I can sign on to this project. Who is this anonymous investor, and why does he wish to remain anonymous?"

"Because," Emory said, "he would likely be embarrassed if his participation became public knowledge."

"It's just the three of us here." But their silence spoke volumes. "Ah, so you think I'll leave here and go on television and announce it?"

Hammond spoke up. "You are going on television at 8:00, are you not?"

"I am, and for debunking this rumor about myself and a certain detective, one of several unsavory items that have popped up in the media lately. I wonder, Fred, how you knew about an interview that was only scheduled this afternoon."

Hammond took a sip of cognac. "I have media people."

"Good. Then perhaps you can enlighten me where these unfortunate leaks are coming from, since they are making the department's work more difficult."

Hammond looked stunned. "I don't know. What a strange thing to ask."

"Not so strange," the mayor said. "These leaks have put me in an unfavorable light. If you can provide me with the source, the police can address the problem, as well as the greater one of solving a difficult murder case."

"We're all in a delicate situation here," Emory said. "There will be some strong negative public reaction to this project now that Prinz has launched his first attack. It's vital we make certain we have everything in place. Part of that is making certain we have your complete support."

"Which you will not get unless I know who your other partner is."

Emory turned to Hammond, who was clearly the leader of the consortium.

Hammond considered it for several moments before he replied. "We appreciate your concern and your interest, but our fourth partner has his own reasons for wanting to remain anonymous. He even declined my invitation to join us here tonight. As he will merely be a minority shareholder in our limited liability company, his identity is irrelevant."

"If it were irrelevant, you wouldn't be fighting so hard to keep it from me. But since that is your position, I can only say I will continue to take your proposal under advisement."

CHAPTER THIRTY-SIX

"So," Joanna Dunbar said with a surprised expression, "you're saying that the detective in question has not been taken off the case?"

The mayor stared directly into the camera. "I met with the commissioner earlier today and verified it. I find it disturbing that misinformation continues to flood the news media, and I suspect that those responsible for Sabrina Dunn's murder are behind it."

"Was the report about you and Ivan Koster having worked together true?"

"He was a messenger for the same law firm that hired me out of law school. He and I never had direct contact. I performed some research when the firm defended him on the assault charge, but I still had no contact with him, which is why the name didn't register with me when I was first asked."

"But weren't you fired after the firm lost the case? I'd think that would etch his name indelibly into your memory."

"It might have if I'd been fired because of some interaction with him, but I was fired for missing something in the research, and that was because I was unfamiliar with the research software. At the time I wasn't angry at Koster, I was angry at the firm, but it was the best thing to happen to me because I realized that politics, not criminal law, was my true calling."

"So, where does this leave us with the murder case?"

"The police are working as hard as they can, and they have my complete support. I am getting regular updates, but you'll understand if I don't divulge the details."

***

Kim stared at the screen as the interview ended.

"He lied," Jake said. "You were so taken off the case."

But it made sense. "He's got something up his sleeve. The news media won't be so eager to publicize the next anonymous tip they get on this case, and whoever's behind this may further tip their hand the next time."

The doorbell rang. It was Bob Nolan, with whom she'd already spoken in the afternoon. "What's on Sabrina's phone?"

She gestured to the dining table and sat with him, taking out the cell. "The texts had been deleted."

"So much for Prinz cooperating."

"Right? Fortunately, she had her phone set to back up data to the cloud, so I could use the Restore function. I found lots of political items, but nothing pointing to her funding sources, and no specific mention of the mysterious $125,000. But I saw two from the same number that got my attention. The first was on May 19th."

I think it's time we ended this. Please call me. I'd like to help.

She waited for Bob to read it over several times. "The second was on June 4th."

I thought we had an understanding.

"Did she respond?" Bob asked. "I don't see anything."

"No, but I found four calls between her phone and this one." She handed him a printout showing the owner of the other number. "Two between the first text and the transfer, and two after the second text."

Bob stared at it. "Her father?"

CHAPTER THIRTY-SEVEN

Saturday, July 23rd

The Latino housekeeper glared at Kim as she stood at the entrance to the Dunn house. "Do you have an appointment?"

She flashed her badge. "Official police business. We don't need an appointment. Mr. Dunn can see me now or I can come back with a warrant."

"I assure you that won't be necessary." She showed Kim into the center hall. "Please have a seat and I will inform him you are here."

When Richmond Dunn descended the stairs, she expected him to be huffy, but he was relaxed and pleasant. "Good morning, Detective. Please, let's go into the living room to talk. What can I do for you?"

Kim already had her cell out and opened her Notes app. "When I was here a week ago, you told me you'd had no contact with your daughter since you'd cut her off nine years ago. But that's not true, is it?"

His pleasant manner evaporated. "I don't know what you mean."

They always did it the hard way. She pulled out the printout. "That's your cell number, correct?"

"Yes." It came out in a whisper.

"Her phone log shows four calls within a ten-day period, two from you to her, two from her to you, book-ended by two texts from you she didn't answer. I don't like it when people lie to me, Mr. Dunn."

A pained expression crossed his face. "No father likes to admit that his daughter hates him."

"Uh huh. What were the calls about?"

"I was hoping to reconnect with her after all this time. Her boyfriend was in prison, and I thought she might have been able to rethink her opinions."

"And she called you back for what? To plan for Father's Day?"

"I don't like your tone, Detective."

"That makes us even. Nine years of silence, followed by four phone calls and two texts, followed by more silence, followed by her death."

"I had nothing to do with that." He all but spat the words.

Enough fencing. "Two calls were made before she received a large sum of money, and two calls were made after she'd reversed the transaction. I'm allergic to coincidences. What can you tell me about the payment?"

"I don't know about any payment. Who made it?"

"It was a payment of $125,000 from a foreign corporation controlled by Fredrick Hammond, and it smells to me like an attempt to buy off your daughter. You made the first call before the payment and the first call after it. Now, please be so kind as to cut the shit, Mr. Dunn."

He sprang to his feet. "I'll hold still for a lot, Detective, but I will not tolerate you speaking to me that way in my own house. If you have questions for me, please phone me in advance so I can have my attorney present."

***

Once back at the Castle, Kim briefed Bob and then joined him for an update of Cirillo.

"That's it? After all the maneuvering to get Dunn's phone, you got nothing else?" Cirillo's manner was even more sour than she'd expected. Then again, according to Bob, the mayor had ripped him a new one in the commissioner's presence. She wouldn't be getting any Christmas cards from him.

Keep calm. "I wouldn't say that. Her father's reaction was over-the-top, partly because he never expected me to find out about those phone calls. But they bring into question everything he told me about his relationship with her. He has some connection to that $125,000 payment."

Cirillo pounded the desk with his fist. "You can't prove that."

"No, not yet. But he initiated both the texts and the calls."

"You said the payment originated from a foreign sub of a company owned by Fredrick Hammond," Cirillo said. "How does that implicate Dunn?"

"It doesn't, but the phone calls do. My next step is to ask Rick Conti on Monday to get a subpoena for the records of that sub—with your permission, of course."

To her surprise, Cirillo didn't explode. "Proceed."

CHAPTER THIRTY-EIGHT

Sunday, July 24th

Kim eased her pace while approaching the turn at the halfway point of the loop after two complete circuits despite her elation at pushing her run to six miles, her longest yet. The heat had broken and there was a pleasant breeze coming off the river. For the first half of her run, she'd pushed everything from her mind, focusing only on the exhilaration of the run, but now she was relaxed enough to turn her thoughts to the case.

Rick Conti had been cool to the idea of requesting the subpoena and suggested that she might have better luck seeing what Ken Taylor could get from the IRS. But he agreed to try. Bob had recounted his exchange with Cirillo in the car, saying he intended to talk to Therese Vargas again. Kim would have preferred to do that herself, but since Bob had already broken the ice with her, they agreed to talk to her together.

Vargas had to be the leak, but if Bob's suspicions about Cirillo were true, it would be impossible to plug it without hard proof. She needed a way to prove it.

As she reached Monroe Place, she half expected to see Justin waiting for her. But the only familiar face she saw was the other runner, who sprinted past her as she reached their building.

***

"He's here." The city's First Lady had not lost her disdain for Justin Cates since her husband's election as mayor.

"Thank you, dear."

"Must you have him come here to Gracie Mansion? Couldn't he see you at City Hall?"

The mayor tried a disarming smile. "I have a busy day scheduled and going to City Hall would take me out of my way."

Justin entered and waited for the First Lady to leave. "Ricky is seeing Judge Vickers tomorrow morning about a subpoena of Hammond's foreign company's dealings. Kim Brady will check in with Taylor at the FBI to see what he can get her through the IRS."

"Unless the IRS has already agreed to share what they have with the Justice Department, he won't have anything for her. What's her interest in it, anyway? What does this foreign sub do?"

Cates laughed. "I'm not sure. It's based in the Channel Islands, apparently part of a scheme to move profits from foreign corporations owned by Hammond's main US corporation to the parent company without looking like a dividend, which would be taxable."

The mayor took a moment to absorb that. "I can see why the IRS would be interested in that, but what's Kim Brady's interest?"

"I don't know."

The mayor stared at his trusted assistant for a long time. "Justin, you've withheld nothing from me for as long we've worked together. Why now?"

Cates paused before answering. "Because I don't think you've been completely honest with me about this Brownsville housing thing. And it occurs to me that people passing some secrets along and withholding others is going to get someone hurt. None of us liked Sabrina Dunn, but gunning her down crossed the line, and we all know it."

"And you think I had some involvement with that?"

"Did you?"

"You've been hanging around Kim Brady too much." But when the joke fell flat, the mayor turned serious. "No, I did not. And you should know that, because if I had, bringing her back from exile would have been the last thing I'd want to do. Have I not backed her up every step of the way since she returned? Did I not haul the police commissioner into my office yesterday and order him to put her back on the case?"

"Yes. But then…"

"You think the rumor about her and me is true."

"No, I know you had powerful feelings for her in the past, and I think you still do. And if I've seen it, others probably have, too. I'm not judging you, because we feel what we feel, and no one knows that better than I do. But it occurs to me that your judgment in this case is hampered, and perhaps your feelings for Kim have something to do with that."

"What does any of that have to do with you withholding information?"

"It's not information, it's speculation, and I don't know if it's correct or what effect it could have if it gets out."

Was Cates accusing him? "Why would I tell anyone else?"

"We sometimes blurt things out that we never intended, especially when angry. If my speculation is confirmed as fact, I will tell you."

CHAPTER THIRTY-NINE

Monday, July 25th

Kim and Bob were in the break room drinking coffee before the day started. It was going to be a busy one. Kim had already spoken to Ken Taylor about getting more information on Hammond's Channel Islands company, and he'd agreed to try but hadn't been optimistic. Rick Conti had asked her to join him in Judge Vickers' chambers at 10:00 about the subpoena.

The door to the break room opened and Therese Vargas entered. Kim always marveled at Therese's ability to work a full day wearing three-inch heels. But now she realized Therese had shifted from short skirts to slacks and from snug knit tops to tailored blouses.

"Hi, guys," Therese said.

"Hi," Kim replied, "that's a lovely top. Lavender is a wonderful color for you."

Therese burst into a grin, "Aw, thanks."

"I think the conservative look works," Kim added, "although some of the guys are probably disappointed."

"Hey," Bob said, "don't look at me."

Therese turned serious. "No, Bob, you're always a gentleman. But could you give Kim and me a couple of minutes?"

He didn't hesitate. "Sure, I'll see you outside, Kim."

Therese waited until he'd left, then recapped her conversation with Bob from Friday. "I'm sure Bob told you about our conversation the other day, but I didn't tell him Cirillo had found out about Miguel and me—he saw us together at a restaurant one night—and after that he was constantly on Miguel's case. Then, not long after Miguel quit, the captain started hitting on me. That's when I ditched the skirts for work."

"Have you spoken to anyone else about this? Someone in Human Resources, perhaps?"

"Are you kidding? I'm not even a cop, I'm a civilian employee, and my word against a captain's would count for nothing. No, I just ignored his advances, and dressing differently sent the message on a different level. But I have a favor to ask."

This was a surprise. "Sure, what?"

"I know you have connections elsewhere in the department. Could you tell me if you hear of an open position for a civilian anywhere?"

"It's gotten that bad with the captain?"

"Not yet. But I saw how he made it for Miguel, and I'm afraid it'll get worse for me if I don't get out. Even Miguel says I should get out."

"You told him about Cirillo hitting on you?"

A humorless smile. "Yeah. I thought he'd like to know why the captain was on his case."

"How's Miguel doing now that he's no longer on the job?"

"He works for one of those big banks, Worldwide Investment Opportunities."

Kim made sure her expression didn't change. "How does he like it?"

"He says it's alright, but he misses being a cop." Therese shrugged. "I think it's just a matter of getting used to an unfamiliar environment. He calls me now and then to feel like he's still a part of it."

Kim patted Therese's arm. "I'm sure. And don't worry, I'll ask around about a position for you."

***

"This is getting to be a regular thing, Mr. Conti." Judge Vickers cast a rueful eye at Kim as she took a seat next to Rick in the judge's chambers. "But I appreciate you bringing a warning flag with you—whenever Ms. Brady joins us, I know I'm in for an effort to write new law and a lecture on the difficulties of policing."

Kim replied with a half-smile, saying nothing.

"Oh, dear," the judge said. "No reaction at all? Okay, Mr. Conti, let's get to it. What is this all about? I've read your request and not found even a whiff of probable cause, or a connection to the murder case."

Rick recounted what they knew about the potential Brownsville project, Sabrina Dunn's opposition to it, and the returned $125,000 payment.

Judge Vickers stunned Kim by asking her, "What would you think about such a project?"

"My opinion of a redevelopment project has no bearing on this investigation, your honor."

"Granted. But please humor me."

"Very well, my initial reaction is one of skepticism, although I don't have enough information about it to form a definite opinion."

"Neither do I, nor any of us. So, you're asking me to issue a subpoena based on the majority shareholder of the parent company of a company doing business in the UK, who might be involved in a major project the mayor has not yet approved, making a payment that was ultimately returned which could have been connected to the murder of Sabrina Dunn, but not necessarily. Mr. Conti, not only do I not see any probable cause here, I see nothing other than a prayer heaved from mid-court at the buzzer."

Kim had to smile at the basketball reference and wondered if it was for her benefit.

Judge Vickers softened his tone. "Detective Brady, I appreciate your zeal to solve this case more than you realize, but I can't let that blind me to the requirements of the law. The affidavit mentions you were alerted to the source of this transaction by the FBI, who got it from the IRS. I suggest you follow that path, but do not violate my stipulation on the subpoena I gave you on the will."

"Thank you, your honor. I haven't, and I won't."

They were interrupted by a knock at the door. Vickers' clerk entered. "Your honor, Alec Danson is here and demands to see you at once. It's regarding the matter of Sabrina Dunn's will and the condition under which you granted the subpoena."

"Send him in." Vickers turned to Rick and Kim. "I guess you two better stay."

Danson was fuming as he stormed in and slapped a subpoena down on Vickers' desk. "That's from a federal judge ordering me to turn Sabrina Dunn's will over to the FBI. That can only mean one thing." He turned on Kim. "You broke your pledge and informed the FBI."

"Direct your comments to me, Counselor," Vickers said, "and in a civilized tone, if you please."

Danson took a seat. "Your honor, there is only one way the FBI could have known to ask for a federal subpoena—this detective leaked it."

Vickers turned to Kim. "Did you?"

"I did not violate the condition of the subpoena. I did not divulge the will's provisions to any person outside the NYPD, including the FBI."

"But she told them she had it. There's no other way they would have obtained a subpoena of their own."

"Your honor," Kim replied, "agent Taylor already knew we had the will. He did not hear it from me. And he was angry when I would not share the contents with him. But even if I had informed him we had the will, it would not have violated your condition."

Danson turned red in the face. "That's hair-splitting, your honor. By telling them she had the will, it was a bald-faced invitation for them to obtain a subpoena of their own."

Vickers shrugged. "Which they did, and which a federal judge signed. Detective Brady did not violate my condition, and she wouldn't have even if she suggested the FBI seek a federal warrant. I assume they would have known to do that on their own if they felt there was value in it."

Rick said nothing until they were back on the street. "I assume your next stop is Federal Plaza."

On her way to the subway, she read a text from Jake. *Did you make the appointment with the gynecologist?*

She stopped and texted back. *Yes, I made it this morning online. 6:15 this evening.* Because Jake was right. She needed to know.

His reply was immediate. *Great. I'll pick you up at the Castle at 5:30.*

***

"There were fireworks this afternoon on the floor of the City Council as lawmakers took up a controversial bill governing the construction industry in New York City that would require all construction companies with over two hundred employees to be unionized, except for minority-owned companies. Sponsors have dubbed the bill Sabrina's Law in honor of Sabrina Dunn, who was to make the proposal a centerpiece of her gubernatorial campaign. While the bill has a majority of Council members as co-sponsors, all but guaranteeing passage, Mayor Brandt has said he will veto the bill if passed. The focus of the battle in the Council, now, is to reach a veto-proof majority. Joanna Dunbar, ITN News."

***

"How close is it?" The mayor remained impassive as he awaited the answer from his most trusted advisor.

Cates checked his notes. "The bill has twenty-eight co-sponsors, including the Speaker, plus two more who have voiced support. Sixteen spoke against it today, and five are undecided."

"Meaning they'd like to vote one way, but their districts want them to vote the other way. Where does that leave us, assuming the undecideds go with their districts?"

"Probably 32-18, and the Speaker doesn't get to cast a deciding vote. Worst case is 34-16, and the Speaker doesn't need to vote."

"Let's work on the undecideds. Work up a report on what each of their districts need the most and get it to me as quickly as possible."

Cates hesitated. "You mean you're going to bribe them for their votes?"

"Of course not. I'm simply going to give them good reasons to support this administration's position."

***

It was nearly five when Kim got back to the Castle. She and Bob stopped upstairs to brief Cirillo on Judge Vickers' decision as well as what she'd learned from Ken Taylor.

"Sorry," Therese said, "but he's already gone for the day. He wasn't feeling well. I think his ulcer was bothering him."

"I didn't know he had ulcers," Kim said.

"Oh, yes. He keeps a container of milk in the mini-fridge in his office, and he never drinks coffee, only tea. He says he can't have spicy food, so he likes spicy women."

Kim rolled her eyes. "Suave. Okay, I'll call him tonight." She added to Bob, "He'll be interested in our latest development." She hoped Therese didn't see the look of surprise that flickered across Bob's face, or Kim touching his arm to keep him from walking more than a few steps away. "Thanks, Therese."

But Bob played along. "You still haven't told me."

Therese got ready to leave.

"A woman has come forward and identified the other man in the rear seat of the car with Koster. It's the break we've been looking for." She nodded toward the stairs, and he followed her. Neither said anything until they were behind closed doors in Bostwick's office.

"What the hell are you talking about?"

"Therese is passing information on to Ramos, who works for Worldwide Investment Opportunities, Inc., which is Fredrick Hammond's company."

"Therese is undermining our investigation?"

"Yes, but I don't think she realizes it, yet. She likes to gossip, and it may be innocent. Then again, Cirillo has hit on her several times, so this could be her way of getting back. Either way, if the story I just planted ends up on the news tomorrow, we'll know she's the leak and that Hammond had a motive for Dunn's murder. If nothing else, it will give us probable cause to haul Ramos in."

Kim then laid out what Taylor had provided—that the IRS had turned Hammond's tax fraud case over to the Justice Department, and that he could pass on whatever was relevant to the Dunn case. Hammond's Channel Islands company was the last step in a convoluted process in illegally moving overseas profits back to the US parent company tax-free. The FBI had already demanded documentation of the $125,000 payment.

"It's a good thing Cirillo went home early," Bob said. "We couldn't have told him any of this with Therese there."

Kim laughed. "I wouldn't have tried. I would've waited until she left."

***

Dr. Genevieve Harper sat behind her desk with several printouts arrayed in front of her, peering at them through black-rimmed glasses as if reading them for the first time, her blond hair pulled back in a loosely clipped bun. Kim wondered if Jake, sitting next to her, found Dr. Harper attractive.

Dr. Harper sat back. "Well, Kim, you certainly look a lot better after your Bermuda trip. I'm not sure diving into a major case when you returned was the most therapeutic thing you could have done, but I'm not sure it was such a bad idea, either. In any case, I'm glad you came in."

"Sorry I didn't contact you as soon as I got back."

The doctor's smile radiated warmth and caring. "It's not unusual in cases like yours. Women want to know but don't want to know." She picked up a printout with an image on it. "Your ultrasound showed no indication of uterine fibroids or other abnormalities." She laid the image on her desk and picked up a small sheaf of papers. "We did a lot of lab work, and results were negative for diabetes, thyroid disease, blood clotting disorders, immune system or hormonal disorders. We found no indication of other metabolic disorders that typically cause miscarriages, such as antiphospholipid syndrome or polycystic ovarian syndrome. You didn't drink alcohol, use drugs, or smoke during your pregnancy, and even kept your consumption of caffeine at low levels. And you're certainly not obese."

"So, what's causing the miscarriages?"

Dr. Harper laid the papers back on the desk. "We don't know. You can both go for genetic testing to look for any chromosomal abnormalities."

Jake finally spoke up. "What do we do if that's the cause?"

"You would have the option of in-vitro fertilization, using either donor sperm or egg."

"I wouldn't want to do that," Kim said. It was reflexive.

Dr. Harper leaned forward. "Remember that nearly half of all recurring pregnancy losses remain unexplained. Kim, you're in a small segment of the population, as only 1% of women have three or more miscarriages. But you still have a better-than-even chance of carrying to term."

"But she might have more failed pregnancies before that happens?" Jake asked.

"It's possible. Kim, I'm sorry I don't have a definitive answer for you. But I have a suggestion."

Kim met her gaze. "What?"

"There is no medical reason for you not to try again, so long as that is what you want. On the other hand, multiple miscarriages can wear you down. You need to understand your own heart before deciding. I recall you were in therapy after this last loss. Going back now may help."

Jake didn't say a word, which was one reason she loved him so much.

CHAPTER FORTY

Tuesday, July 26ᵗʰ

A steady drizzle cooled Kim as she ran. Five miles was now her basic run, and she planned to try for eight miles come Sunday. She'd heard nothing from Joanna, but then part of the reason she'd planted the story was to see how long it took to make it into the media. And there was always the chance that Therese might not have passed it on, or that Hammond had not approved using it.

As she made the turn onto Monroe Place, the familiar nameless runner sprinted past her. She had waved to him a few times, but he never returned it, so she had stopped. Strange, because one of the joys of running was how runners greeted each other, even if they were complete strangers. Then again, sometimes when she ran, she was barely conscious of anyone else around her.

As she slowed to a walk, Justin got out of his car. "Nasty morning for a run."

"No, the rain is quite refreshing, although the humid air is heavy."

"Your runs are getting longer. Training for the marathon?"

She laughed at that. "No, just trying to stay fit." But then she considered it. "A 5 kilometer might be fun, though. Anyway, what brings you to my doorstep this rainy morning?"

"The need to see a friendly face."

"Well, you can come on in, but Jake may not be up yet so please keep it down."

He frowned at the mention of Jake. "Any chance for an update on the investigation?"

"I have no secrets from my husband. I'm told my grandfather kept nothing from my gram, but I know my dad kept everything from my mom. So, shortly before we were married, I decided my grandfather's way was better."

Justin smiled as she opened the front door. "Ricky and I are the same way. Maybe we can all go out to dinner sometime."

"I'd like that." She opened the apartment door. Jake was sitting at the desktop in his boxers and a Nets tee shirt. "We're not alone, dear."

Jake bolted for the bedroom. "Sorry, I didn't know we were expecting company."

Justin didn't wait for niceties. "Kim, have you gotten anywhere with the FBI on Hammond?"

Uh oh. "Justin, the answer is yes, but I need to be careful, here, and so do you. I can't risk the mayor passing anything I tell you on to Emory."

"I don't think you need to worry about that. The other night, the mayor demanded to know who the fourth investor was as a condition for supporting the Brownsville project, and the others refused. If one or more of his major supporters are being investigated, he needs to know that."

"This is why you shadow me so often on my runs?"

"No, Kim. It's because you have become a dear friend and my in-stincts tell me you're in grave danger. I always follow my instincts. Also, the mayor will ask me soon about the investigation of Hammond, so I'm multitasking."

"What makes you think I'm in grave danger?"

"Because someone powerful had Sabrina Dunn assassinated, and whoever that was won't hesitate to kill you, too, if you get too close."

Jake entered the room, fully dressed, glaring at Kim.

But she remained cool. "Do you know anything specific, or is this just emotion?"

"If I knew anything specific, I would tell you. But please watch yourself, especially when you run."

***

"Welcome to *City* News, the morning edition. There is a fresh development in the investigation surrounding Sabrina Dunn's assassination. According to one source, police have a witness who can identify another man who was in the getaway car with the gunman, Ivan Koster, and they have launched a manhunt to locate him for questioning."

***

The summons from Captain Cirillo was not unexpected, and Kim closed the door once she and Bob were inside.

"Why the fuck didn't you tell me about this sooner?"

Kim spoke in a soft voice. "I would appreciate you lowering your voice, Captain. They can hear you out on Wilson Avenue."

But Cirillo only grew more agitated. "Don't try to tell me..."

Bob interrupted, "The walls have ears, Captain. Kim thinks it might be partly your fault, so I suggest you listen."

"What the hell is that supposed to mean?"

"Quietly," Kim replied. "The report on *City News* this morning is bogus. Bob and I planted it yesterday to smoke out the leak, and we were right. But before I go further, I must demand that you take no action against the individual involved."

Cirillo snarled but kept his voice down. "Where do you come off..."

"Captain," Bob said, "please."

"Very well. Proceed."

Kim laid out the details of Therese and Ramos. "I made up the story about the witness, so it could not have originated from any other source.

Ramos works for Hammond, whose company tried to pay off Sabrina Dunn."

"So, now you think Hammond was behind the murder?"

"It sure looks that way. I want to bring Ramos in for questioning. But please do not mention to anyone outside this room, including the commissioner, that we planted that story."

CHAPTER FORTY-ONE

Kyle Emory caught the mayor just as he was preparing to leave for City Hall. "We need to talk."

The mayor led him to the living room. "And what troubles us this morning?"

"What's that report about the Dunn case all about? They have a witness?"

The mayor had seen the report and did not know where it came from. "Apparently. Does that bother you?"

"On the contrary, it would be a great relief if this investigation were to reach a satisfactory conclusion. I just wondered if it might be doing so."

"We'll have to wait and see. But I'm glad you stopped by. We have a long, mutually beneficial relationship, and so I'm going to ask you one last time to identify the fourth member of your investment group for the Brownsville project."

"As I explained the other night…"

"Stop it, Kyle. I need it, now."

"And if I don't tell you?"

"Then I'll have to do what I must do."

***

Kim and Cord intercepted Ramos as he left the headquarters of World-wide Investment Opportunities, Inc. on Park Avenue.

"Good afternoon, Sergeant Ramos," Kim said.

"What do you two want?" He did not try to be pleasant.

"Just to take you to lunch," Kim said.

"Yeah," Cord added. "At our place."

"You're arresting me? On what charge?"

"Obstruction of justice," Kim replied, and she recited his rights.

***

The mayor strode to the podium at City Hall as reporters buzzed about the absence of teleprompters. "Thank you all for coming. There have been several rumors lately, and even a protest, about a major redevelopment project involving public housing in Brownsville. I've been asked several times about it and have replied truthfully each time that no such project has been approved by this office. However, I have been approached about such a project and been asked to support it."

He paused for dramatic effect. "Having asked for several pertinent details about the project and not getting answers, I am here to say that I am opposed to it at the present time. The notion of privatizing a large public housing project, though radical, may well have some merit, but only after all the ramifications have been explored and addressed could I consider supporting it."

"Mr. Mayor," a reporter from *City News* called out, "what were the details you wanted and didn't get?"

"That would get into the weeds for no good reason. I will only say that my concerns stem from my desire to protect the city's interests." He pointed to his right. "Ms. Dunbar?"

"Sabrina Dunn was vehemently opposed to privatizing public housing. Is it possible that her death was connected to her opposition?"

He'd had the same nagging thought, himself, but he couldn't say so. "I suppose anything is possible, but I wouldn't assume it. The police are investigating, and I'll leave it with them." He pointed to his left.

"Mr. Mayor, Kyle Emory is one of your biggest backers. Was he involved in this project, and if so, how will your opposition to it affect your relationship with him?"

"There was no firm commitment as to who would ultimately be involved."

***

"The story about the witness was bullshit?" Ramos was stunned.

"Pure fiction," Kim replied. "Therese was the only one I told, and there was no one else around so she had to tell you the same way she's been telling you all the other details that have been leaked to the press. Your experience in law enforcement means you appreciate how leaks can hamstring an investigation, so you understand we have you cold on obstruction."

"Like hell you do. She could have told that story to anyone."

Kim turned to Bob, who had entered the interrogation room. "Let's find out."

Bob opened the door and made a hand gesture to Brogan. A few moments later, Brogan walked in with Therese at his side.

Ramos threw his hands in the air. "Great. A fucking setup."

"Therese," Kim said, "did you overhear me discussing a new witness with Detective Nolan last night?"

"Yes. What's this all about? And what's Miguel doing here?"

"Did you repeat that story to Miguel last night?" Kim asked.

"Yes, but what's…"

"It was bullshit, Therese," Ramos said, spitting the words.

Therese was baffled. "It wasn't true?"

"I'll get to that in a moment," Kim said. "Have you been telling Mr. Ramos other details about the case?"

"I didn't mean any harm." Therese was close to tears. "Miguel told me he missed being here and enjoyed hearing what was going on. He…"

"Will you just shut the fuck up!" Ramos was half out of his seat before Cord grabbed him by the shoulders and forced him back down.

Kim remained calm. "Therese, whether or not you realize it, you have been leaking information about an ongoing investigation, and that's a serious matter."

"But I only…"

Kim cut her off. "I understand the reasons, and that you probably did not realize the seriousness of the action." She turned to Ramos. "But you did, and I suspect you encouraged her to talk."

"You can suspect whatever you like," Ramos said. "She just told you she only passed on what she thought was gossip."

Kim laughed without humor. "That's just not your best option, here, Ramos. Therese, did you tell Miguel about the early developments of the case? I can assure you if you answer my questions truthfully, nothing bad will happen to you."

"Yes." It came out as a whisper.

Kim repeated the facts that had been leaked.

"Yes," Therese said again.

"Did you tell anyone else?"

"No."

"And those details wound up in the media," Kim said, turning back to Ramos. "Sounds like proof to me. But, if you like, I can arrange for a lineup so Joanna Dunbar and her counterpart at *City News* can hear your voice and tell me if they recognize it. And we both know they will."

"No, they won't. I never spoke to her or anyone else in the media."

"Then," Bob said, "you told someone who did."

Ramos stared at the table. "I think I need a lawyer."

"Maybe not. If you agree to cooperate, we won't press charges against you, and if you are fearful for your life, we can place you in protective custody."

"I had no involvement with the assassination."

"Fine. If you didn't tell anyone in the media, you told someone who did. Who?"

"A guy who works for the company."

Kim leaned forward. "Give me a name."

"Brandon Keifer. He works in accounting."

"Cute," Bob said. "How did you get to know him?"

"We take the same express bus. I get on at the first stop, Gerritsen and Lois. He gets it in Midwood, Ocean Avenue and Avenue K. He spotted me as a regular my first week at the company and struck up a conversation. He was really interested in my experiences as a cop."

"What kind of voice does he have?" Kim asked.

"Kind of low, deep."

"Any accent?" She needed to know for when she spoke to Joanna.

"No. Sounds to me like a typical New Yorker." He paused for a moment. "Although he has a funny way of saying New York, more like New Yahk."

Bob chuckled. "Kinda like 'pahk the cahr'. Maybe he's originally from around Boston."

"Let's check that out." Kim focused her attention back on Ramos. "Any other examples?"

"Not that I can think of. What kind of cooperation did you have in mind?"

She made a mental note to check with Joanna on the accent of the caller. "You work for Fredrick Hammond, do you not?"

"Yeah. I'm head of security for his home office."

"Has he spoken to you about this case at all?"

"No, why?"

"Where did you get the information about Brandt and Koster working at the same law firm?" Kim asked.

"I didn't. I knew nothing about that.

Bob spoke up. "You had no contact with Ivan Koster?"

"No, I never even heard his name until they said it on the news. Why did you ask about Mr. Hammond? You think he might be involved in the assassination?"

Kim chose her words with care. "Not at this point. Are you at all involved when Mr. Hammond meets with other top people?"

"Sure. We make certain security is tight and I give my guys the details on when they'll arrive and leave. VIP visitors drive into an underground garage, and we have lots of security there when they do."

"Have you ever been present at these meetings?" Kim asked.

"No, I have guards posted outside Mr. Hammond's conference room, but they're soundproof."

"Do you keep visitor logs?" There had to be an opening here some place.

"Sure, but they're kept in encrypted files. The system records any access to the logs and any printout requests."

Shit, forget that. But… "I would imagine you have reason to access the log frequently."

"Any day there's a meeting, I check to verify that they've been logged in."

"So, you could look over a list of names and then write them down later?"

He nodded.

One other question. "Can you look at logs from past days or weeks?"

"When I log in, I see the log for the current week. If I go back any further, the system records it."

It was a start. "Please keep me informed of who he sees each day."

"Anyone in particular?"

"No, just the names and, if included on the log, their companies."

"They're included. But one thing bothers me. How will I explain no longer getting details on the case?"

He couldn't just stop. "If they ask, say that your friend has been out sick." Sudden thought. "They don't know who Therese is, do they? Good.

See how long that holds them. If they press you, let me know. In the meantime, do not have any contact with Therese."

"Why not?" Therese asked.

"It won't be safe for you," Kim replied.

After Therese and Ramos left, Bob said, "I'll have Cord get started on checking out this Keifer character."

FORTY-TWO

An hour after Ramos left, Brogan and Stransky returned from the field.

"They left shortly before you came back with Ramos," Bob said. "A 911 call from a freaked-out landlady in Bedford-Stuyvesant. What's the deal, guys?"

"Looks like a suicide," Brogan replied.

Bob shook his head. "From the beginning, Tim."

"Sorry, we got a call on a stiff found in a third-floor apartment of a three-story walk-up on Throop Avenue just off Vernon. The landlady got a complaint from a tenant about loud music from the apartment next door having kept her up all night, and when she got no answer to a knock on the door, she let herself in with her own key. The guy, one Willis Hicks, was stone cold."

"And he offed himself?" Bob asked. "How?"

Stransky spoke up. "He had a hypodermic sticking out of his arm, so our first thought was an overdose of some sort, probably smack. But a search of the apartment turned up an insulin kit, so then we figured maybe insulin shock."

"Crime lab guys get the needle?" Kim asked.

"Yeah," Brogan said. "We made sure of that. We interviewed the neighbor and the landlady, and neither knew much about him other than he was quiet, kept to himself, liked classical music, and worked odd hours."

Kim's interest was caught. "What kind of odd hours?"

"Irregular. Sometimes days, sometimes nights, and sometimes he'd be gone for long stretches at a time, like a few weeks. I grabbed his wallet." Brogan held up an evidence bag containing it. "No employer ID, no credit cards, no membership cards, no photos."

Kim's inner warning bell was already ringing. "Driver's license?"

"I got that." Stransky held up another evidence bag.

Kim pulled on a pair of latex gloves and extracted the license. Something about it wasn't quite right. "It's not one of the new Enhanced or Real ID licenses." She popped open her laptop, logged into the DMV database, and entered Hicks' license number. "Describe his face."

Stransky exchanged glances with Brogan before answering. "Light complexion, dark hair, blue eyes, with a…"

Kim stopped him. "The license is either a fake or altered. Did you guys get prints or DNA?"

"CSU took prints from him, and the apartment, and I guess they took anything that might provide DNA. They were still working when we left."

Kim turned to Bob. "I'll touch base with Phil Vitello and with the Medical Examiner's office. Once we get prints and DNA from him, we'll run them through the system, because I suspect we'll get a hit." She turned the laptop so they could all see the screen. "In the meantime, let's try to track down the real Mr. Hicks, if he's still with us."

She pointed to the image on the screen.

Willis Hicks was black.

CHAPTER FORTY-THREE

Wednesday, July 27th

"This is unacceptable." Kyle Emory was shaking as he spoke. "This is a project that could change the face of this city permanently, and you announce your opposition out of personal pique?"

"Not out of pique at all," the mayor replied. "Out of deep concern that you continue to withhold what I consider important information, and that withholding that information may mean there are other facts of which I am unaware."

Emory regarded him with a shrewd gaze. "Are you suggesting that if I tell you, that will change your position?"

"I guarantee nothing, but it would be a required first step before I consider it."

"And what might the other steps be?"

"I'd need to know, and be comfortable with, every aspect of your project."

Emory laughed without humor. "Even we don't know all the aspects of the project, yet."

"Then I'd need to be part of the planning process. And, besides knowing the fourth partner's name, I'd need to know the reason you withheld that name for so long."

Emory considered it, which annoyed the mayor because the group would have discussed how they would respond. A knock at the door interrupted his reverie.

"What?" The mayor had left strict instructions that they were not to be interrupted, so this must be important.

The door opened and Justin Cates entered. "Sorry to disturb you, sir, but I just took this and thought you should see it."

He glanced at the neat, crisp cursive writing: *Eyes only—interesting development yesterday in Bed-Stuy; will fill in JC later. KB.*

He gave the note back to Justin. "Thank you and let me know."

Justin left without another word.

The mayor turned back to Emory. "So?"

"The reason for our reluctance will become obvious once you know the name."

When the mayor heard the name, he agreed it was obvious. "We will have a great deal more to talk about. Dinner tomorrow night at Gracie Mansion."

***

Searching the usual databases, Kim had found a landline in Willis Hicks' name that was no longer in service and a cell number that was answered by someone who'd never heard of Hicks. She and Cord had gone to the address on his driver's license—a modest Dutch Colonial house in Queens Village—but the current occupants also had never heard of Willis Hicks. They'd been renting the house for two years.

The tenant gave Kim the owner's address in Bayside, a middle-aged man with a receding hairline and thickening middle.

She showed him the photo of Hicks. "Do you know this man?"

"Sure, that's Willie Hicks. He was a tenant of mine, an awful nice guy. Died a couple of years ago."

"He was rather young," Kim said. "According to his driver's license, he was born in '85. Do you know how he died?"

"A medical condition of some sort, I imagine. I only found out when he missed a rent payment and I went to see him."

"Did he have a family?" Kim asked.

"None that he ever mentioned to me. He moved here when he was in his late teens, I think, hailed from somewhere in the Carolinas. He was always a loner, except for his girlfriend."

Kim's heart jumped. "What's her name? Do you have any contact information?"

"Sophia Laguerre, nice girl, but a bit flighty. She's the one who told me he'd died."

"They lived together?" Cord asked.

"Sometimes, although she hadn't been staying with him for the last several months. When I got there, she was packing up some personal items. Very upset, she was. Said he'd had a heart attack, but people often say that when they don't know what the cause was."

"Do you know anything else about him?" They needed something, anything. "Where he worked, or where Sophia Laguerre works?"

The landlord shook his head. "Sorry. She was a hospital worker of some sort, but I never knew which hospital." A moment to reflect. "I'm not sure, but they may have worked at the same place."

***

"Fentanyl?" Bob asked. "They're sure?"

Kim handed him the report from the lab, which had been sitting in her e-mail when she and Cord returned to the Castle. "It was in the syringe and a vial marked as insulin in the kit. I'm waiting for a call back from Dr. Shelton over at the Medical Examiner's office, but that must be the cause of death."

Phil Vitello knocked on Bob's door. "Heard back on the fingerprints. We have a match."

Kim leaped from her seat. "Who?"

"His name was Peter Fedorov, did a stretch at Dannemora for assault and a weapons charge."

"Dannemora?" Kim gestured the printout in Vitello's hand and read it. "Seven years, paroled in 2005, meaning he was there the first two years of Ivan Koster's stretch."

"So, they could've known each other," Bob said.

"I'll go further than that. I think they were working together, and Fedorov was the guy waiting in the back of the car for Koster after Sabrina Dunn was killed." She called Cord, Tim, and Martin into the office and briefed them.

"So," Cord said, "you think Fedorov killed Koster and then offed himself."

"Yes to the first, no to the second," she replied. "No way he knowingly injects himself with the same thing he used to kill Koster."

"But," Martin said, "his were the only prints on the syringe. You think he did it at gunpoint?"

Maybe in a film noir, but not in real life. "No, more likely someone switched vials on him without him knowing. We'll have a better idea when we hear from Dr. Shelton. In the meantime, see if you guys can track down this Sophia Laguerre. The landlord saw her packing up Willis Hicks' personal things, so his wallet and driver's license were likely among them. The shortest distance between two points is a straight line, so she was probably the line to Fedorov. Also, she's a hospital worker, so she may be the source for the Fentanyl. Start canvassing the hospitals in Queens, then Brooklyn and Manhattan if Queens doesn't check out. Also check the usual databases. And have the crime lab check the vials in the insulin kit for prints."

"In the meantime, Kim," Bob said, "let's go upstairs and give Cirillo the latest."

***

It was a few minutes before five when Kim and Bob reached Cirillo's floor. Therese Vargas wasn't at her desk, so they approached Cirillo's office.

Therese rushed out, obviously upset.

"Are you okay?" Kim asked. But Therese turned down the hall, toward the ladies' room.

Bob knocked on the open door.

"Come," Cirillo said.

Kim took a seat in front of his desk. "We have some new information."

Bob took the other seat. "Cord Washington is looking into this Brandon Keifer character, the guy Ramos was feeding information on the investigation. He's not just a staff accountant, he's a senior consultant whose specialty is forensic accounting. He's got a B.S. in computers and an MBA in accounting. His work history includes some time with the IRS."

"I also checked with Joanna Dunbar," Kim said, "who confirmed her informant did not speak with Ramos' heavy Spanish accent, but more like a New Englander, much as Ramos described Keifer's." She laid out what they'd learned about Hicks and Fedorov.

Cirillo did not try to hide his irritation. "And what the hell does any of that prove?"

"None of it proves anything, conclusively," Kim said. "We're taking steps, here, trying to piece together a conspiracy to assassinate a political figure."

Cirillo glared at her. "So, now it's a conspiracy?"

Kim adopted a tone of exaggerated calm. "Yes. You see, when a person or persons plan for someone else to commit a criminal act, that's called a conspiracy. And unless you believe Koster shot Sabrina Dunn on his own, hailed a cab that wasn't really a cab, reached around halfway to his back and stabbed himself with a syringe full of Fentanyl and then dumped himself in Newtown Creek, this is a conspiracy."

Cirillo rose halfway out of his seat. "Don't you patronize me, bi—" He froze.

Kim stood. "Bitch? You were about to call me a bitch? Watch yourself, Captain, because you've come as close to the line as I'm willing to allow."

She walked out. Therese still wasn't at her desk, so Kim followed the path she'd taken and found her in the ladies' room, staring at herself in the mirror. "You okay?"

Therese nodded. "Just a bad day."

"I saw you rush out of Cirillo's office, and when Bob and I talked to him, he definitely had a thorn in his paw. Did something happen?"

"No."

"Your face is telling me something else. What's more, he blew up at me and called me a bitch. Well, he caught himself mid-word, but it couldn't have been anything else. If he hit on you, that's sexual harassment and a direct violation of department policy."

"He didn't."

"Then why have you been crying?"

"I can't afford to lose this job."

"Did he threaten you?"

"No. He said he knew about me telling Miguel about the case, and he trusted I would never do something so foolish again. He said it was all forgotten."

"And…?"

"Then he said how much prettier I look in skirts and heels, and how I should go back to wearing them to work."

CHAPTER FORTY-FOUR

Thursday, July 28th

Kim walked down to Millie's Cuban Kitchen, following the text she'd gotten from Justin Cates. She wasn't surprised to see a black Chevy Suburban parked a hundred feet beyond Millie's, only that Justin was alone in the back.

"Sorry," Justin said as she closed the door behind her, "but this is the first chance I've had to see you since I got your note, and the mayor wouldn't go for my idea about burner phones."

She filled him in on Peter Fedorov, as Dr. Shelton had confirmed the cause of death as a Fentanyl overdose. "We still don't know what he'd been doing since he got out of Dannemora, which suggests he'd been working for someone. Elsewhere, we've discovered the source of the leak." She explained Ramos' connection to Hammond. "He didn't contact the media, and I've confirmed that with Joanna Dunbar, who said her informant did not speak with an accent. But he told someone named Keifer, which explains how information was leaked that Ramos didn't know."

Justin's usual poker face evaporated.

Kim's inner alarm went off. "What?"

"Emory was in yesterday for a chat, and it wasn't pleasant. He's still pushing for that privatization thing in Brownsville, and he's plenty pissed that the mayor came out against it. Hammond is one of the four partners, along with Emory and a guy named Conrad Vinson. They're all having dinner with the mayor at Gracie Mansion tonight to try to change his mind about the project."

"You mentioned three names. Who's the fourth?"

"Richmond Dunn."

***

Kim was still sorting out the ramifications of Richmond Dunn being a part of the circle that stood to gain the most from his daughter's death when she briefed Bob back at PBBN.

"You think he could have had his own daughter killed?" Bob asked.

"It doubles down on the personal gain motive. But if we question him about his involvement, it risks outing Cates as my source."

Bob sat back. "And if we question Keifer about what he did with Ramos' information, we out Ramos as our source and risk blowing his story about Therese being out sick. So, how do you want to proceed?"

"Justin overheard the mayor and Emory talking, which he's certain the mayor doesn't know. Dunn might be at the dinner. I suggest we wait to see if Justin gleans any details from it. In the meantime, how are the guys coming along on Sophia Laguerre?"

Bob broke into a grin and handed her a printout. "Cord tracked her down."

"She's a nurse's aide at Cypress Hills Hospital. Lives on Van Buren Street just off Patchen Avenue." Kim pondered that. "That's only a few blocks from Fedorov's place. I wonder if…"

Cord knocked once and entered. "I see you're getting the latest. I just got off the phone with the head of human resources at Cypress Hills Hospital, who confirmed that Willis Hicks was working there at the time of his demise."

Bob grinned at Kim. "You were saying?"

"Indeed, I was. Let's investigate Mr. Hicks' cause of death."

"You think she offed him?" Cord asked.

"The landlord said she gathered up his personal items," Kim replied. "Peter Fedorov, who lives nearby, ends up using Hicks' driver's license to assume his identity. She may have killed Hicks, or she may have just taken advantage of the opportunity when he died. Let's see if we can find out, and, while we're at it, check with the hospital to see if they've had any problems with thefts of anesthetics, lately."

Cord shot her a grin. "Anything else?"

"Yes," Kim replied. "Dig into Hicks' financial records, and Fedorov's. See what turns up."

Another knock, and Therese Vargas walked in and handed Bob a sheaf of papers. "Captain Cirillo says these reports need to be completed by five o'clock today."

She turned quickly, causing her short skirt to flare a bit, and walked out, her spike heels clip-clopping on the linoleum floor, without making eye contact with Kim.

"Well," Cord said when she'd gone, "that'll earn her some extra attention around here."

Not now. "Cord, you mentioned that this Keifer character had worked for the IRS. Any idea what he did there?"

"Audits, I assume."

"Yes, but in what area of tax law?"

Cord was stumped. "They have specialties?"

"Never mind." She retrieved her cell and pulled up the number of her cousin, Jim Brady, whom she hadn't seen since his fiftieth birthday party back in April and gestured for Bob and Cord to leave.

When she'd told him she was pregnant.

After some hesitation, she touched the screen to place the call.

"Hey, Cuz!" His booming greeting forced her to jerk the phone away for a moment. "You must be getting very big in your field."

Oh, shit. "No, Jim, I lost the baby."

"I'm so sorry, Kim. Are you okay?" He sounded crushed.

"Just focusing on the job at the moment." Not wanting to prolong the condolences, she added in a brighter tone, "I actually called you about something work related."

His voice brightened as well. "Cool. Your work or mine?"

Which was why she loved this cousin she hadn't known until Dad's funeral. "Both. Do you ever get involved in tax cases in your law practice?"

"Only as part of my trust and estate work. Why?"

"But you understand how the IRS functions?"

He turned serious. "Have you received a notice from them?"

"No, it's not personal, it's business. I'm working on a tough case…"

"Situation normal, as I recall."

"More than usual. I need to ask you some things about the way the IRS works without you knowing what it's about."

"If I can help, I will."

"Thank you. If someone is an auditor for a multinational corporation and has a reputation for being strong in forensic accounting, what area of the IRS might he have worked for?"

At first, he said nothing. "Kim, it could be anything. Auditing is forensic accounting. It's what the IRS does. Going from the IRS to a multinational indicates he likely worked on the international side, which the IRS keeps separate from other areas of corporate auditing. If he has a high-level position at this multinational, he was most likely an International Issue Specialist at the IRS. But I'm only guessing."

"I understand, Jim. And thanks for the help."

"Keep in touch, Kim. We'd love to have you and Jake over for dinner one of these days."

"I'd like that. I'll call you when we finish this case."

One more call, this time to Ken Taylor.

CHAPTER FORTY-FIVE

"So," the mayor said as he sat back and sipped his cognac, "I presume you will all try to convince me to support this grandiose plan of yours." He turned to Dunn. "Your involvement in this came as a great surprise to me. I'm sure it would come as an even greater surprise to our fellow New Yorkers."

"Which is why I've worked so hard to keep my involvement out of the public eye," Dunn replied. "It's no secret that my daughter and I were estranged, and I hesitated to join in this project because I knew it would put us at loggerheads." He paused.

The mayor filled the void. "But in the end, you decided in favor."

"Yes. I tried to reconcile with Sabrina, but an ill-considered attempt to influence her by other parties…" He glared at Hammond. "… rendered that impossible."

Hammond stirred in his seat. "I misread your intentions, Rich. It was an unfortunate error."

"Any other unfortunate errors I should know about before we proceed?" the mayor asked. When no one replied, he turned back to Dunn. "You look as if you expect someone to say something more."

Dunn glared at each of his partners but no one said anything.

Finally, Emory spoke up. "I think we're all eager for the murder investigation to reach a successful conclusion. Have you had any news on that?"

"No," the mayor said. "I believe the leaks to the press have hampered the police investigation."

"Just as those leaks have stirred up premature opposition to our proposal," Hammond replied.

The mayor set his snifter on the table. "Are you suggesting a connection between the two?"

But Hammond didn't back down. "Only that it seems like a coincidence."

"Gentlemen, the last thing I would have done is leak this thing to the press. Any idiot could see that it would energize Sabrina Dunn's campaign…"

"And we couldn't have that," Dunn said.

The mayor fought to keep his temper. "Let me make one thing clear, Richmond. I think the biggest thing working against your proposal is your daughter's death. It's also the biggest thing working against me in what, until now, had been a widely successful mayoralty. Whoever engineered her assassination did not have the city's best interests at heart, or mine, and I am determined to do everything possible to bring those responsible to justice."

"Are you suggesting we might have been involved with it?" Hammond asked.

He thought of Kim. "Should I?" When he got only stunned expressions in response, he continued, "No, of course not. So, here's where we are. Your plan might very well be a breakthrough in the realm of affordable housing, but it would also place considerable strain on the city's resources, even without the spur line and police substation, both of which I agree would be necessary. So, if I agree to this—and I'm still not convinced I should—it would have to be with the understanding that your group would purchase the property at least a year before beginning the first demolition phase…"

Emory spoke up. "What do you mean, the first phase?"

"I mean it would not be practical to empty the entire housing project at once, it would have to be in stages. We simply could not find relocation facilities on that large a scale. Moreover, I would expect that from the time of purchase through the entire demolition and construction phases, the old buildings would be managed by the city, but with all staffing, maintenance, and repair expenses borne by the new owners."

"That's one hell of a condition," Emory said.

"Finally," the mayor continued, "the plan would need to be vetted and approved by the City Council."

"You mean the same City Council that's expected to pass that construction industry bill?" Hammond struggled to control himself.

"The same. If I sign on to this, I will do my best to see it gets approved, but I won't go against them if it doesn't. Also, I will need detailed answers to detailed questions before we go public. I also want to see how this murder investigation goes before we move forward."

"What the hell does that have to do with it?" Emory asked.

The mayor shrugged. "That's what I need to find out."

CHAPTER FORTY-SIX

Friday, July 29th

Kim had just taken a seat on the B38 bus when Justin boarded and sat next to her. "You didn't run this morning."

"Setting aside, for the moment, that I shouldn't need to clear my running schedule with you in advance, I'm trying to adhere to a 5-day running week, taking Mondays and Fridays off. This case makes that a challenge."

Justin chuckled. "Too bad, because it's a delightful morning, with a cool breeze coming off the river."

She turned serious. "You waited in the park, and when I didn't show, you camped out at the bus stop? What's going on?"

He glanced around the bus, even though no one else had boarded, and only continued when the bus pulled away from the curb. "My boss had his dinner last night. Everyone was there but Vinson, who apparently had a prior engagement. I wasn't present for any of it, but the mayor recapped it for me. He and Hammond fenced over leaking stuff to the press, but no one admitted anything. There was also tension between Hammond and Dunn, which suggests that Dunn did not appreciate Hammond's clumsy attempt to bribe Sabrina." He then explained the mayor's conditions before he would support the project.

"Does he really plan on supporting it if his conditions are met?" she asked.

"I asked him the same question, and all he did was give me the blank stare."

She nodded. "So, either he's stringing them along hoping to keep them at bay while we complete our investigation, or he's hoping he gets enough cover from the City Council to support the plan."

He pressed the button to signal a stop. "See, that's why you're the best."

***

Marshal Dhillon greeted Kim with a covered plastic container at the main desk. "Good morning, Detective Kim. We are having a family gathering tomorrow and my wife prepared too much food. I thought you might like to try this. It's *baingan bharta*, mashed grilled eggplant mixed with chopped tomato, onions, herbs and spices, including chili peppers. You've mentioned liking eggplant, so I thought you might want to try it."

"Thank you, Marshal. I'll have it for lunch." She placed a post-it with her name on the cover and found a place in the break room refrigerator for it.

"You really going to eat that?" Bob asked.

"Jake always says that eating is an adventure." She lowered her voice. "So, if I don't like it, I'll take it home for him."

She nuked the coffee she'd bought at the Firehouse Deli, made herself comfortable, and popped open her laptop. A search revealed no arrest record for Sophia Laguerre, so she turned her attention to Dunn Holdings, Inc.

After a couple of hours, all Kim could discover was that they invested mostly in other investment funds and did not offer their services to the public, although Richmond Dunn held a broker's license.

Cord broke her concentration. "Anything new?"

"Nothing that helps. What did you find at the hospital?"

"I talked to the head nurse, who had nothing bad to say at all about Sophia Laguerre or Willis Hicks, and she confirmed they were involved. Hicks' death came as a shock to everyone at the hospital, as he'd never taken a sick day in the entire six years he'd worked there."

Interesting for someone who supposedly died from a serious illness. "How about disappearing anesthetics?"

"I spoke to the Director of Pharmacy, didn't mention any names, and just asked if it was a problem. She said, no, absolutely not."

"She was that emphatic?"

"Yeah, and my reading of her manner was a loud and clear warning not to go there, so I backed off."

She'd have to follow up, herself, taking a different approach. "Okay, you and Tim keep digging into this guy Fedorov and see what you come up with. I'll ask Martin to head up to Dannemora to see if anyone remembers Fedorov and Koster. And I'll get a hold of Hicks' death certificate and check out his cause of death."

***

"*City News* has received reports of a pending federal investigation into the financial transactions of Mayor Raymond Brandt. According to informed sources, the mayor is suspected of violations of the Bank Secrecy Act of 1970, which requires any U. S. person to report any interest in a foreign bank or financial institution exceeding $10,000 in a year. Failure to report any such holdings can result in civil or criminal penalties, including up to five years in prison. *City News* will continue to monitor developments in this story."

***

The mayor snapped off the set, jaw clenched, neck flaming. It was only after a minute or two that he noticed Justin Cates studying him. "Oh, for God's sake, of course it's not true. I have no investments in foreign institutions. Someone's trying to get at me."

Justin hesitated before he spoke. "They're doing a good job. This is the kind of thing in which a person is guilty until proven innocent. If I may suggest, sir, you need to have your accountant go over your tax returns to be sure he has missed nothing that could be construed as a violation of the law."

"I just told you, I don't have any investments in foreign institutions, period."

"But your backers do, and I'd make sure you can't be connected to any of their dealings. Hammond is already under the microscope, and after last night, don't be surprised if he tries to serve you up to take the heat off himself."

The mayor leaned forward. "Go on."

"Last night, you slapped them down pretty hard, and I think it was long overdue. But it will have repercussions. Out of that group of four, your only real friend is Kyle Emory, and he's in the weakest position. Dunn could be a decent friend and ally, but then he's also in a weak position."

"Why?" But then, the mayor already knew. Dunn Holdings had suffered badly in the roiling markets of recent months, and Richmond Dunn was desperate to regain his financial footing, even if it meant throwing in with people like Hammond. He wondered if that extended so far as to having his own daughter killed.

CHAPTER FORTY-SEVEN

It had taken Kim thirty minutes to track down the head of Anesthesiology at Cypress Hills Hospital, and then he'd kept her cooling her heals for another twenty. She flashed her badge as she entered his office despite having presented her credentials to his receptionist.

The inference was not lost on the doctor.

"I'm investigating two homicides in which the victim died following an injection of a large dose of Fentanyl. Does this hospital keep supplies of Fentanyl?"

"Why? Do you suspect us of being involved?"

"Questions like that always suggest to me someone has something to hide. Please answer mine."

He was appropriately flustered. "Sorry, no, nothing of the sort. Yes, there are some surgeries that require the use of Fentanyl. We maintain strict inventory controls."

"Have you had any recent instances of discrepancies in your inventory of the drug?"

"I'd have to check our…"

She stood and leaned forward on his desk. "No, you don't. Fentanyl is in the news a lot these days, and not in a good way. If you've had a problem with theft—and you have, otherwise you wouldn't be stalling—

you'd know damned well. So, either answer my question now, straight, or I go to the DA, get a subpoena, drag your ass before the grand jury, and you can answer under oath."

He held up both hands. "Okay, okay. Sorry. A few months ago, our new Director of Pharmacy noticed that certain drugs, including Fentanyl, were running lower than the documented dosages indicated they should. She reviewed our protocols and found that some nurses were leaving medication carts unsecured."

"Unsecured how?"

"They're equipped with drawers with electronic locks, but the locks don't work if the drawers are left open. When that happens, anyone could come along and take vials of drugs if they know what they're looking for."

Kim sat and made entries into her Notes App. "So, what did you do?"

"We terminated the two worst offenders and pulled all the other nurses into retraining for security protocols, and the supervising nurse on each floor was tasked with making spot checks to ensure compliance. Since then, our inventories have stabilized."

"Do you suspect anyone in particular of the thefts?"

"No, but I'm guessing you do."

She finished her notes. "Thank you, doctor. Before I go, I'd like a listing of all your nurses, aides, and support staff and the shifts they work, from just before your Director of Pharmacy began her investigation to the present."

***

The mayor studied his guest, Leroy Barnett, Councilman from Washington Heights and the Speaker of the City Council, who had just made a thinly veiled accusation. "I realize we disagree on several issues, and that in today's politics, scorched earth is the order of the day with one's political opponents. But, as we are both in positions of significant responsibility to the city and members of the same party, let's try to tamp down the drama for a moment."

Barnett shifted in his seat but said nothing.

"For the record, the *City News* report this morning was complete and utter fiction. I have no foreign holdings, period."

"But you oppose protecting workers rights and have entertained the notion of privatizing public housing."

"Let's take those one at a time. I entertain many ideas that never reach fruition. The Brownsville proposal is likely one of them. But let's be honest. This city's management of public housing has hardly been a matter of pride, and fee-based management by private companies has been little better. But if private buildings included public housing, then the standards of maintenance would need to be the same for public and private residents, wouldn't they?"

"What about the servants' entrances?"

The mayor allowed himself a chuckle. "What about them? So far, the residents of the public units in existing private buildings appear to be coping quite well. And if we considered this project, I'm sure the Council would have some ideas on improvements. As for your other concern, I support protecting workers' rights, including the right to unionize. But I oppose saying one race of owners must have a union shop while another need not do so."

"Easy to say when one race already enjoys a major advantage over the other."

"This city already has in place preferences for minority-owned and female-owned businesses. Tell you what: I'll call a news conference today and announce that I have no intention of terminating any of our existing programs intended to foster investment in those businesses if you announce at that same conference that you've concluded the so-called Sabrina's Law is a bad idea and you will do your best to see it is not passed."

Barnett stared at him, dumbfounded. "I'd be thrown out as Speaker."

"Wanna bet? You already know you don't have enough votes to override a veto, so everything else is just posturing. And if they dump you, who replaces you? Most of your committee chairs are first-termers, and the handful of second-termers are disgruntled at being passed over for the speakership. Such is the reality of term limits. By the way, how is the crime situation in your district these days?"

Barnett had been a vocal opponent of the mayor's policing reforms and had argued strenuously against the additional funds in the departmental budget. "Better. The new precinct commander has been a welcome addition. He understands community policing."

"The latest data shows violent crimes significantly lower, and the anti-weapons program has taken 900 guns off the street just in your precinct." The mayor decided not to mention that the ruling by a federal appeals court reversing a lower court decision banning stop-and-frisk as inherently racist had helped.

"So," Barnett said, "what's your point?"

"Simply that the city is better off when we work together than when we are at cross-purposes. Shall I schedule that news conference?"

"I'll get back to you on that."

***

"Did you hear the latest on Brandt?" Bob asked the minute Kim walked into the Castle.

"Yeah, heard it on the radio. I called Ken Taylor and asked him if there's anything to it. He's checking it out." She walked to the break room and put Dhillon's *baingan bharta* in the microwave.

"What exactly is that, anyway?" Bob asked.

"Marshal Dhillon thought I'd enjoy it. A Punjabi eggplant dish." The microwave beeped, and she took it out, the fragrant aroma filling the room.

"Doesn't smell too terrible." Bob poured a cup of coffee.

She took a bite. "It's quite good. I…" She stopped as the chili peppers took effect, and her eyes began to tear. She raced to the water cooler and gulped down one cup and then another. And a third.

Dhillon walked in and burst out laughing. "No, no, no, Kim. Water makes it worse. Take a bite of the *naan*."

"What's… that?" she asked.

He pointed at the container. "The flat bread. It will absorb some of the spice."

She took a large bite, then washed it down with another cup of water. "Wow. That's really hot."

"You must have eaten a chuck of chili pepper. *Baingan bharta* is not usually so hot. I hope it didn't ruin it for you."

Bob laughed. "No, I'm sure she loves setting her tongue on fire."

She took another bite and followed it with a bite of the *naan*. "It's excellent, now that I know what to look out for." She held the dish out to Bob. "Want to try some?"

"Er, no, thank you. I've had lunch."

Dhillon left and Kim told Bob what she'd learned at the hospital. "I still have the shift records to look over. That may take a while."

Bob gestured toward the door and the TV set beyond. "I assume the Brandt thing is just another attempt to slow him down."

She didn't answer. There was something about it that bothered her. "Except the other leaks proved to be at least partly true. He and Koster had worked at the firm concurrently, and not only had Brandt worked on Koster's case, but it had cost him his job."

"So, where are we going with this?"

She took the last bite of eggplant and followed it with the last of the *naan*. "No idea, but I'm sure we won't like it when we get there."

CHAPTER FORTY-EIGHT

"In a hastily called press conference at City Hall this afternoon, Council Speaker Barnett charged the mayor with 'double dealing' and revealed that the mayor had admitted he still might support the controversial proposal to privatize public housing in Brownsville. Speaker Barnett vowed to oppose any such effort, saying he had a veto-proof majority of the City Council behind him. He also promised that Sabrina's Law would be passed by a similar majority. This is Joanna Dunbar reporting for the Independent Television Network."

***

"Well," Justin said with a wry smile, "that went well."

The mayor snickered. "I note he said that 'a similar majority' would pass Sabrina's Law, suggesting that he may not, in fact, have two-thirds of the Council."

"As of now, it looks like 32-18, so he doesn't, but he's close."

"Who are the two undecideds leaning our way?" The mayor picked up a sheet listing all fifty-one members.

"DiNapoli of Glendale and Pagan of East Williamsburg."

The mayor nodded with satisfaction. "Both first-termers who won by narrow margins."

"Yes, sir. But I understand Pagan has been promised a plum committee appointment if she supports the Speaker."

"Doesn't she have a beef with the Parks Department?"

Justin nodded. "Cooper Park, which had a major upgrade about five years ago, is fraying around the edges. Benches have broken slats, some bleachers at the basketball courts have been damaged, and there's increasing activity in there at night."

"Tell Parks to get appropriate repairs under way, immediately. I'll contact the local precinct and have them step up night patrols in that area. Then, you can tell Ms. Pagan that the safety and well-being of her community is very much on our minds. What about DiNapoli?"

"Had an easy time in the primary, but only won by a nose in the general election. I think he's worried they'll put up a stronger candidate next time around, even with the drop in crime."

The mayor thought for a moment. "Their precinct has a strong community council, don't they?"

"Yes, they do. Good crowds at every monthly meeting."

"Excellent. Please tell Mr. DiNapoli that I'll speak at their next meeting, and I'd be honored if he'd join me. When he accepts, I'll arrange it with the commissioner. Now, who among the three leaning to yes because of their district would be the easiest to turn?"

"I'd say Elliot Anastos of Throggs Neck, up in the Bronx. He's got some fire-breathing progressives up there, but he's already bucked them on a couple of issues."

***

It was after nine in the evening. Checking the shift lists was proving more time-consuming and tedious than Kim had expected, so when her cell buzzed, she was grateful for the interruption. She recognized the number on the screen as Miguel Ramos'.

"Never play the game if you don't know the rules." It wasn't Miguel's voice.

The shift lists would have to wait.

CHAPTER FORTY-NINE

Saturday, July 30th

By the time Cirillo called Kim and Bob in for an update, Kim's head was swimming from all the loose ends. Nothing to do but lay it all out. Martin was still up at Dannemora, and Tim and Cord had yet to find anything about Peter Fedorov. Ramos' wireless carrier had identified the tower pinged by the call Kim had received as being in Greenpoint, right by the East River. There had been no pings since, and the pings prior to the call were from two hours earlier in midtown Manhattan.

"All of which adds up to what?" Cirillo asked.

"The facts at this point don't support a specific conclusion," Kim replied.

"Then give me your best guess."

"Sherlock Holmes said guessing is destructive to the logical faculty."

Cirillo broke into a slight grin. "He also said that any truth is better than infinite doubt."

Bob stifled a laugh. "Maybe you should call it a best probability based on known facts, Captain."

"Fine. Detective? About Sergeant Ramos?"

"Very well. The comment about playing the game likely refers to our investigation, specifically using Ramos as a source of information. He never had a chance to provide information on who was meeting with Hammond, so..."

"You mean he hasn't yet had a chance, don't you?" Cirillo asked.

"I strongly suspect Ramos is dead. The tower ping in midtown was just after one yesterday afternoon. I got the call from Greenpoint at 9:22 last night. His wife reported him missing this morning."

Cirillo gestured with his right hand. "And...?"

"According to the tide tables, low tide at Greenpoint was at 7:51 last night, high tide at 1:29 this morning. Sunset last night was at 8:13, so it was already dark when I got the call."

"Meaning?" Cirillo asked.

"Ramos was likely dumped in the river shortly before I got the call at 9:22. As the tide was rising, the current was flowing north at slightly faster than two miles per hour, which suggests that the body may well be lying on the rocks somewhere along the river." She glanced at Bob. "You may recall I had a case a few years ago with a similar fact pattern."

Bob rolled his eyes. "The Cove shooting."

Nice that he remembered. "Related to it, yes. In that case, the body washed up on the rocks at Gantry Plaza State Park in Hunters Point, but it had only been in for a couple of hours. If Ramos was dumped in the river, say, between 9:00 and 9:30, that means the killer had up to four-and-a-half hours before high tide."

Cirillo's interest was caught. "Meaning what?"

"North of Newtown Creek, the speed of the current picks up, so anything drifting on it moves faster."

"So, we aren't likely to find him in Hunters Point," Bob said.

Kim asked Cirillo for a map of the East River, and she studied it for a couple of minutes, taking rude measurements with her thumb and forefinger. "Theoretically, he could have traveled to Hell Gate or beyond."

Cirillo peered over her shoulder. "But there are turns in the river."

"And the water flows with the turns," she said. "It's possible he could've gotten snagged at Hallet's Cove."

"Or," Bob added, "he could've been pushed into the Harlem River."

Kim shook her head. "Not likely. The tidal flow is north and east. If he made it around Hallet's Point, he could have made it to North Brother or South Brother, conceivably even to Rikers."

"But that's a rising tide, Kim," Bob said. "If he didn't get caught on anything, when it started going out at 1:30…"

"Then, back downriver he'd go." And there was no way to predict where, or even if, he'd wash up. "Captain, I think the best course of action is to alert the Harbor Unit to search upriver to Rikers Island and downriver to Upper New York Bay."

Cirillo glared at her. "For someone we don't even know is dead."

She met his glare with her own. "You're the one who wanted guesswork."

"The clock is ticking, Captain," Bob said.

"One other thing," Kim said. "I got a copy of Willis Hicks' death certificate. He didn't die from a heart attack; it was a Fentanyl overdose."

***

"I realize this is a prickly situation for you," the mayor said to Elliot Anastos as they sat in the same room in which he had asked Kim Brady to come back to work the Dunn assassination case.

"Worse than that," the council member replied. "Right now, the mail, e-mail, and phone calls to my office are running about two-to-one in favor of the construction bill."

A much wider margin than Justin had estimated. "I didn't think your district was so heavily progressive."

"It's a mix, Mr. Mayor, and it's not just progressives who are driving this. A lot of folks who normally would balk at racial preferences are apparently willing to accept it for the union requirement because a lot of contractors rely on undocumented immigrants for labor. The thinking is the racial preference will keep Sabrina's Law from reducing the number of opportunities for them."

"And you agree with that assessment?"

"No, Mr. Mayor, I don't. But if I vote against the bill, I lose my next election, and, more than that, I become toxic for any other position I could seek. It's not just about this bill."

The mayor braced himself because he'd already guessed what else it was about. "Go on."

"With all due respect, sir, these rumors about you being investigated make it dangerous for me to be seen as allied with you."

"The rumor is nonsense. I have heard nothing from the IRS, or the Justice Department, and I have no foreign holdings, period."

The council member considered that. "That's good news. Let's see how this thing plays out."

CHAPTER FIFTY

It was just after five when Kim figured she had all the pieces nailed down. Two additional nurses had been discharged at the time of the retraining. The Head of Anesthesiology hadn't mentioned that. A phone call and a threat of a full investigation, with full disclosure to the public, had elicited the truth from him and from the Director of Pharmacy.

Both nurses had been found to have left their medicine carts open and unsecured regularly, with far greater frequency than the rest. Both had been offered the chance to keep their jobs if they disclosed the identity of the person for whom the carts had been left open, but they'd refused and had resigned rather than be fired.

Sophia Laguerre had consistently worked the same shifts as the two nurses.

One nurse had dropped out of sight, and Kim figured she'd likely relocated. But the other, Elaine Shields, was working at a local clinic and living in Canarsie. Kim waited for Cord to return, and they both headed out to interview her.

On the way, Cord briefed her on what they'd found. "Not a lot. Fedorov's parole officer told me the dump on Throop Avenue had been his residence since getting out, that he'd worked a series of minimum wage jobs for the rest of his parole term, and confirmed he was diabetic. Checked in regularly, obeyed the rules, an ideal parolee."

"Sounds a little too perfect."

Cord chuckled. "That's what I said, and the parole officer laughed. Said he'd always had the sense something was going on beneath the surface, but he could never figure out what. We also talked to the detective who'd busted Fedorov, and he told us Fedorov had worked for Vladimir Gorkov before his stretch in Dannamora."

"Think he could be Russian mob?"

"Possibly. Gorkov dropped off our radar not long after Fedorov got sent up. Neither we nor the FBI have heard a whisper about him since. The prevailing theory is that he went back to Mother Russia."

"What does the detective think?"

"He's not sure. But Tim's been digging into Fedorov's finances. Garden variety checking and savings accounts with modest balances. But every so often he'd get a wire transfer from a bank in the Caymans, with amounts ranging between five and twenty grand."

Whoa. "Same bank as the attempted bribe to Sabrina Dunn?"

"Same bank, different account. Either way…"

She got it. "A hired hand for somebody. Anything else?"

"Yeah. Willis Hicks had a credit card in that wallet. His last purchase with it was at a local electronics store for four grand."

"Sounds like he was expecting to come into money, himself."

Cord shook his head. "Don't think so. The charge was dated a week after Hicks died. Martin went to the store and checked it out. Got this photo of the guy who used the card."

It was Peter Fedorov.

Cord chuckled. "I thought it was weird, seeing a 77-inch UHD TV in his apartment."

***

They pulled up to Elaine Shields' residence, a semi-attached two-family just off Flatlands Avenue. She answered the door wearing a low-cut, vibrant red sheath dress that came to mid-thigh, and black stilettos. Kim and Cord displayed their badges and identified themselves.

Shields crossed her arms across her breasts. "Can't this wait? I'm on my way out."

"We won't be long," Kim replied. "You once worked at Cypress Hills Hospital?"

"Yeah. So, what?"

"You didn't leave on good terms," Cord said.

"Says who?"

"Save the outrage, Ms. Shields," Kim replied. "We wouldn't be here if we hadn't already checked. You resigned rather than be fired because you wouldn't reveal the name of the person you allowed to steal from your medication cart."

"But we now know who that was," Cord said.

Kim picked it up without a break. "And we need to know what Sophia Laguerre had on you."

"I never heard of her."

Kim took a step closer. "Bullshit. You worked the same shift as her for more than a year, so either answer our questions here, or we arrest you as an accomplice."

"You can't do that."

Cord closed in from the side. "Watch us."

Defiance turned to panic as she glanced from one to the other. "Okay, okay. But you can't tell nobody I told you, 'cause that bitch'll kill me if she finds out. One night, I went to check on a patient on my floor and found he was dead. Before I reported it, I went through his wallet and took some of the money."

"They teach you that in nursing school?" Cord asked.

She grew defensive. "I know, but I was in a major jam, money-wise, and he had two hundred bucks on him. I took half of it."

"And Sophia Laguerre caught you?" Kim asked.

"No, her piece-of-shit boyfriend, Willie Hicks. When I looked up, he was just grinning at me. I panicked and offered him forty to keep quiet, but he just said, no, we'd work somethin' else out. At the end of my shift, he and Sophia grabbed me as I left the hospital, told me from now on, I was to leave the drawers on my cart open when it was unattended. Willie would keep an eye on it and distract anyone who came by who might report it. At first, Sophia only took a couple of things at a time, but then she started snatching multiple vials and bottles, and I got called in for questioning, but before I went, Sophia cornered me and said if I squealed, she had friends who would hunt me down and kill me."

"And you believed her?" Kim made it clear that she didn't.

"Shit, yeah. I'd already seen her screwin' some white guy in a car in the parking lot while Willie, who was supposed to be her man, was on duty. He saw it, too, and didn't say a word. Just shook his head and went back to work."

"So, you said nothing about her involvement," Kim said.

"I said I didn't know nothin' about it. They let it go, but they called me in two days later and said that my cart had more thefts than any other in the hospital, and if I didn't tell them who the thief was, they'd fire me. So, I quit instead, and while I was packing my stuff in the locker room, Sophia came up to me and whispered, 'Smart choice.' I got outta there and ain't never looked back."

"What drugs did she take the most?" They needed to nail this down.

"I never checked."

"Was she a user?" Cord asked.

"Not as far as I could tell."

"Any idea who the white lover was?" Kim asked. "Could you describe him?"

Shields shook her head. "Ain't never seen him before or since."

Kim nodded. "Thanks. Do not discuss this interview with anyone else. We'll be in touch."

***

As soon as Kim saw Bob Nolan waiting for them at the Castle, she knew.

"They found Ramos in Hallet's Cove," he said. "Harbor Unit reported it just a short while ago. One in the back of the head. The body is with the

Queens Medical Examiner's Office, and they'll handle getting the slug to ballistics. I suppose we should be glad it wasn't Fentanyl."

"Only because it helps clarify things." Kim recapped their interview with Elaine Shields. "The guy in the car must have been Fedorov, whom Laguerre may have supplied with Fentanyl to kill Koster and most recently swapped for a vial of Fedorov's insulin. The hospital's investigation occurred after the parking lot incident, and she offed Willis Hicks, in case he decided to expose her. Afterward. she provided Fedorov with the means to assume Hicks' identity."

Bob glanced at the clock. It was now getting on toward nine. "I know it's late, and it's been a long day, but..."

Kim turned to Cord. "She's on the four-to-twelve. Let's go pick her up."

As she slid into the passenger seat, her phone buzzed, signaling a text from Ken Taylor. *Eyes only. I heard from a friend of mine at Justice. Brandt holds an interest in that UK entity of Hammond's and has apparently failed to report it. Working on your request for info about Keifer.*

CHAPTER FIFTY-ONE

Sunday, July 31st

Sophia Laguerre had lawyered up before they'd even gotten her into the car, and the sun was up before a legal aid attorney arrived at the Castle. Kim had slept in Bob's office, and she awoke in a foul mood, having missed her morning run.

Rick Conti walked in.

"I thought you were now executive ADA," Kim said with a grin.

"I am, but I didn't want to leave this with anyone on my staff. Mitchell wants to make sure there are no screw-ups on this one."

Bob and Cord joined them in the interrogation room when the attorney arrived, where Laguerre sat with her legs and arms crossed.

"She looks like Kiersey Clemons," Cord said in a whisper just before they entered the room. He'd mentioned Laguerre's likeness to the young actress the night before, too.

Kim had to admit he was right.

"What, exactly, are you charging my client with?" Legal Aid asked.

Kim took charge. "That's what this interview will decide. Ms. Laguerre, you have been identified by an eyewitness as the individual responsible for a string of thefts from medication carts at the hospital at which you are currently employed."

Laguerre tossed her head back. "You mean formerly employed. They gonna fire my ass after you took me outta there last night."

"They would've fired you long ago if you hadn't intimidated two nurses into silence," Kim said. "It seems Fentanyl was your drug of choice. Your former lover, Willis Hicks, died of an overdose of the same drug. His landlord identified you as the person he found cleaning out Hicks' personal things, including his wallet and driver's license, which were never found. You gave his license to Peter Fedorov, allowing him to steal Hicks' identity. A diabetic, he also died of an overdose of Fentanyl after someone switched out a vial of insulin from his kit. But before that, a third victim, Ivan Koster, also died after being injected with a lethal dose of the same drug."

Legal Aid pounced. "Koster? The guy who gunned down Sabrina Dunn?"

"The same," Kim replied.

"I don't know any Koster," Laguerre said, pouting.

Kim smiled without humor. "I believe you. But you supplied Fedorov, who was also your lover, and he injected Koster shortly after the shooting."

"Hold on," Legal Aid said. "My client has already said she didn't know Koster. You've already admitted that Fedorov injected himself. And, for all we know, Hicks may have simply injected himself with Fentanyl that he had the same opportunity to steal from the cart. So what do you believe you can charge her with?"

"A neighbor places her in Fedorov's apartment the night he died," Kim said. "Since he'd already injected Koster, he wouldn't have been stupid enough to inject himself intentionally with Fentanyl. Also, he injected himself with a syringe from his insulin kit, which he filled from a vial in the same kit, a vial with two sets of fingerprints on it. One set was Fedorov's. We took your client's prints last night when we arrested her."

"On what charge did you have probable cause to arrest her?" Legal Aid asked.

"Robbery, for the theft of the drugs, and the murder of Fedorov," Kim said.

Conti spoke up. "The case against her for the Fedorov murder is circumstantial at the moment, but once her prints come back as a match on that vial, I'll have everything I need."

Thanks, Rick, I owe you one. "However, none of the three murders occurred in a vacuum. Koster's was a classic case of assassinating the assassin. Fedorov's was the same. Hicks was killed to test Fentanyl as a killing agent and to give Fedorov a new identity."

Laguerre slapped the table. "Hold it. Willis injected hisself. He was the one first told me the carts were often left unlocked, and he asked me to cop a vial for him so he could try it. We worked together after that, with me coppin' whatever I could grab off the carts for him to use or sell. The night he OD'd, it was a accident. He was pissed at me 'cause he'd seen me with Fedorov, so he took more than he was used to. I called 911, didn't give my name, and got outta there. When I went back the next day, a neighbor told me he'd died. When I told Pete, he asked me to snag his wallet, that he had a job coming up and it would be helpful."

"Including his credit card." Kim didn't make it a question.

"Everything."

Kim turned to Legal Aid. "All of that suggests a higher order of organization."

Legal Aid looked baffled. "Meaning?"

"Meaning she was working for someone else, someone who had a great deal to gain from Sabrina Dunn's death. Hicks was clearly a poor sap in the wrong place at the wrong time, but Koster and Fedorov were working for someone with powerful connections, and I want to know who."

"You think they were working for the mayor?" Legal Aid asked.

"No, of course not." Kim had to tamp down the doubts that Ken Taylor's text had raised. "But Fedorov had stayed off police radar since getting out of prison, and his employment record grew sketchy after his parole ended. So, someone was keeping him in the game. I need to know who. And since she was intimate with Fedorov, I think she can tell me."

Legal Aid frowned. "May I have a moment with my client?"

They stepped out of the interrogation room.

"Do you think she knows?" Conti asked Kim.

"The guy's name? Perhaps not. But she knows more than she's told us."

Legal Aid opened the door and waved them back in. "My client doesn't know the extent of the operation in which Fedorov was involved, but she can provide some details. In return, we ask you to drop the homicide charge, as she was told to switch the vials."

Kim exchanged glances with Conti before she spoke. "As a health professional, she knew Fentanyl's lethal capabilities. There was no way she could not foresee the consequence of that act."

"I have to agree," Conti said. "I'll consider a lesser charge, but only if she provides significant useful information on the larger crime."

Legal Aid turned to Laguerre and nodded.

"Hey," she said, "can I have a cigarette? I'm dyin' for a smoke."

"Sorry," Kim replied, "no smoking. It's the law. Whose idea was the scheme to steal drugs from the carts?"

"I told you, that was Willie. He used some, sold the rest. Weren't nothing more to it than that."

It pulled Kim up short. "So, the vial you placed in Fedorov's insulin kit didn't come from the hospital?"

"Uh uh. One night, I went over to Pete's. We were supposed to see each other. Only Pete wasn't there, this other guy was. Said his name was Ramos, that he was the pharmacist and that he'd given Pete the wrong prescription for insulin, and that I should switch the one in his kit for this new one. I didn't believe that shit, but he looked tough, and he said if I let Pete or anyone else know about it, it would be bad for me."

Kim leaned forward. "Was Fedorov working for him?"

Laguerre shifted in her seat. "Don't know. Pete never mentioned the name of his boss, but they'd known each other a long time, going back to when they lived in Russia. Pete did jobs for him."

"Did the man who gave you the vial speak with an accent?" Kim asked.

"Kind of. Couldn't say what. He was just your basic tall, skinny white guy."

Okay, Laguerre was scared, but she wasn't being much of a help. "What kind of jobs did Fedorov do?"

"Collecting debts, settling disputes, stuff like that."

"So, he worked for a gangster?"

"No, he always referred to him as a businessman, in high finance."

"Sorry," Kim said, "but legitimate businessmen do not employ hit-men to collect debts and settle disputes."

"Apparently, this one does," Legal Aid said.

"Are you sure he never mentioned a name?" Rick asked. "Because so far, you've given me very little I didn't know, and nothing I can use."

Laguerre's cool finally slipped. "He never told me anything else. I'd tell you if he had."

Yeah, she was scared shitless. "Nothing about where they knew each other from in Russia?" Kim needed something, anything.

Laguerre thought for a moment. "He once told me he grew up in a place called… Lobya?"

Conti glanced up from his notes. "Lobnya?"

"Yeah, that's it. Lobnya."

Conti turned to Kim. "It's a town north of Kimkhi, which is north of Moscow."

Laguerre's eyes lit up. "Kimkhi. He mentioned that, too. Said they'd done business there in the old days, but he never said what."

"Excuse us for a moment." Conti stood. "Kim, guys, a word, please?" Outside the interrogation room, he said, "Kim, didn't you say Fedorov had worked with Vladimir Gorkov before he got sent up?"

"Yes, why?"

"Gorkov was from Lobnya, and his connections in Russia were in Kimkhi."

Kim turned to Cord. "While we finish up here, call Ken Taylor, verify that what Rick just said aligns with his records on Gorkov, and brief him on what we have. Find out if the FBI has anything more recent on him, and especially any aliases they might have for him."

Conti nodded agreement, and when they entered the interrogation room, he took the lead. "Ms. Laguerre, as meager as the information is that you've provided, we're going to see where it leads. If it pans out, and if you will testify to it in court, I'd be willing to reduce the murder charge."

"To what?" Legal Aid asked.

"That depends on how this all pans out."

"What happens to my client in the meantime? She should be placed in witness protection."

Kim spoke up. "And if what she's just told us is a lie, she could then run away."

"I ain't lying," Laguerre said.

"If she's cooperating, she doesn't belong in jail," Legal Aid said.

Kim swallowed her shock and turned to Conti. "Protective custody should work. She'd be guarded and safe, but in comfortable conditions."

Back outside, Bob finally spoke. "Now, we need to track down this Gorkov character, or whatever he calls himself these days."

CHAPTER FIFTY-TWO

Ever since Kim had learned that Richmond Dunn was part of the group pushing the Brownsville project, she'd been itching to question him, hesitating only for fear of revealing she had a source in the mayor's camp. But she needed to know more about this investment group, and now that Ramos, who worked for Hammond, had been identified as more than just a leaker…

Ramos had played her. He'd probably known the entire setup and was feeding tidbits to the press to throw them off. No doubt he would have given her more misinformation. How ironic that he'd been caught at it and eliminated.

Although, if he was just feeding her misinformation, there would have been no need to do anything at which he could be caught. She shoved the thought aside.

She couldn't go as she was, grubby in yesterday's clothes, wrinkled from a night on the couch in Bob's office, and needing a shower. So, it was home to freshen up.

"You look like hell," Jake said as she walked into the apartment.

"I got a few hours of sleep at the Castle."

"So, you can chill the rest of today?"

"Afraid not."

The shower helped, and she changed into fresh clothes, slacks, a light blouse, and a linen blazer.

"That jacket's going to be awfully warm today," Jake said.

"It's okay, I got a car from the unit, and I'll have the air conditioning on high."

***

"I thought I told you I would only talk to you in the presence of my attorney," Dunn said as he gestured for Kim to sit.

"If you'd like to call him, I'll be glad to wait," she replied. "We can even schedule a meeting tomorrow at the District Attorney's office if you'd prefer that. But I thought a quiet chat would be best for now."

He considered it. "All right. Have you learned anything further about my daughter's death?"

"Nothing conclusive. I'm here about another matter, which could be pertinent to the murder case. I have it on good authority that you are a partner in this controversial Brownsville Project which your daughter opposed."

He fought to control his temper. "And exactly who is this authority?"

"I can't say, and it isn't relevant. Are you denying it?"

"I see where you're going with this, Detective. You're looking for a motive so you can hang Sabrina's murder on me."

"I already have an excellent motive," she replied, "in the trust fund that reverted to you upon her death. This would simply amplify an existing motive. I'll lay down my cards, Mr. Dunn: if you didn't have Sabrina killed, you may very well be in business with whoever did. So, I'll ask you once more: are you a potential investor in the Brownsville Project?"

"Get out of my house."

***

It was mid-afternoon when Kyle Emory, the last man the mayor wanted to see on this scorching July afternoon, was shown into his Gracie Mansion office. But there was nothing to do but put a pleasant face on it.

"Something cool to drink?" the mayor asked.

"No, thank you. I've come about two matters. First, what is this about you being investigated?"

"It's nonsense. I've done nothing that would warrant an investigation of any kind. You of all people should know that."

Emory glared at him. "Lately, I'm not so sure what I know and don't know about you."

"I've kept every promise I ever made to you..."

"Until now."

The mayor studied him. "If you're referring to my concerns about the Brownsville Project, that goes way beyond any redevelopment project you've proposed in the past."

"Speaking of which, earlier today, your hand-picked detective paid a call on Richmond Dunn. She knew about his membership in our little group, a fact that was only recently disclosed to you on the condition of absolute secrecy for obvious reasons."

"I haven't spoken with Detective Brady since before you informed me of Dunn's participation, and I haven't revealed his participation in the Project to anyone."

"Perhaps someone in your inner circle eavesdropped on our discussion that night, a colorless little man who seems to turn up in the oddest places with the most interesting information. Someone who sleeps with an assistant district attorney."

"Justin Cates is the most loyal member of my staff, and I trust him implicitly." He tamped down the thought that lately, that trust had not been returned in full. "I can't imagine he would have revealed this to anyone if he did learn of it on his own, and I certainly didn't tell him. But while we're on the subject, what other members of your consortium might there be whose names have not yet been revealed to me?"

Emory spread his hands. "None."

"What about hidden sources of funding to the members you have disclosed?"

Emory turned in his seat and gazed around the spacious office. "Is this place bugged? Am I being recorded, with the tape to be turned over to the FBI or the police?"

"I think you've been watching too many crime shows."

"And what about that construction bill?"

The mayor relaxed a little. "As of now, it looks like it will pass the City Council, but not by a veto-proof majority."

Emory nodded with apparent satisfaction. "Not ideal, but at least a positive outcome. I'm profoundly grateful."

The mayor sat at his desk deep in thought for a long while after Emory left. Not once in all the time they'd known each other had Emory ever expressed his appreciation for the mayor's actions on his behalf in such a florid manner, and it made him nervous that he'd done so now.

CHAPTER FIFTY-THREE

Monday, August 1st

"Good morning from ITN, it's a lovely 71 degrees this morning, going up to a high of 82 as the heat wave that has gripped the city for more than a week has finally broken. In the headline story this morning, the Justice Department will announce today that Mayor Raymond Brandt is being investigated for failure to report foreign financial investments under the Foreign Account Tax Compliance Act. If true, the mayor could face penalties of up to $60,000, and if he is found guilty of tax fraud, he could face a prison term of five years…"

***

Kim turned off the television. Having missed her Sunday run, she was determined to get a run in this morning, especially with the weather finally cooperating. As she began her first loop in the park, she tried to work through the implications for the Dunn case of Brandt being investigated.

She couldn't believe he'd lied to her. And if he'd lied about the investigation, then he might very well have been lying all along about his innocence in Sabrina Dunn's assassination. He also hadn't told her about Richmond Dunn's membership in the Brownsville Project. Justin had done that. And Dunn throwing her out had cemented in her mind that he was, indeed, involved.

And Ramos had played her. Or had he? After all, he'd been killed, too. She'd gotten a text from Phil Vitello that ballistics had identified the slug removed from Ramos' skull as a nine-millimeter from a Glock 19, one of several weapons issued by the NYPD.

She picked up her pace as she reached her turnaround point for the first loop, trying to will away both the growing sense that the case was spinning out of her control and the now-familiar black cloud of depression brought on by the latest consultation with her gynecologist.

***

The mayor invited his tax accountant to sit and join him for a cup of coffee.

"Let me understand this," the accountant began, "you've never received a failure-to-file notice from the IRS?"

"Never. And correct me if I'm wrong, but you've collected all my tax information and assembled and filed all my tax returns since I was first elected to the State Senate, and you know I've received no statements of any kind from any foreign investment."

"Yes."

"Then I'm at a loss about this," the mayor said.

"I can only surmise that there has been a mistake, most likely a whistleblower has provided erroneous information to the IRS. What troubles me more is that this has been leaked before you've received any official notification. That's damned irregular and could violate federal law. I suggest you sit tight and wait for any official notice."

"What about dealing with the leak?" the mayor asked.

"I'll file a complaint with the Treasury Inspector General for Tax Administration—TIGTA for short. They investigate breaches of IRS confidentiality. Folks who work at the IRS are scared to death of TIGTA."

"In the meantime, I'll issue a public statement denying any wrongdoing."

His accountant frowned. "I don't think I'd do that. It might be awkward if the IRS notifies you."

"You don't understand. I can't afford to let speculation fester."

***

Kim was at the top of her second full loop when she was passed by the now-familiar runner in his usual red tee shirt. "Good morning."

But he didn't look back, turning right toward Furman Street while she turned left on her normal loop and headed south at her brisk pace.

She needed to talk out these recent developments with Justin. He hadn't been around on her last few runs, but she hoped she'd see him this morning. Maybe he'd be waiting on her front steps for her.

***

"Where's Justin?" the mayor asked his chief of staff.

"I don't know, sir. He's not in yet."

"This business of him going off on his own and no one knowing where he is must stop. When you see him, you're to tell him that regardless of where he's going or what he's doing, he is to inform either you or me, directly, beforehand. I know he thinks he's helping, but he isn't."

"Yes, Mr. Mayor. Anything else?"

"Schedule a press conference down at City Hall for 9:00 this morning. Then, invite Speaker Barnett and tell him I expect him to be there. The same for the Public Advocate." This shit was ending today.

***

Kim was nearing the end of the shaded path at the south end of Pier One when she saw Justin walking toward her, a worried expression on his face. Just as she arrived at the merge with another shaded path several yards before the main greenway, he glanced to his right and the look of worry flashed to horror.

Out of the corner of her eye, she glimpsed the red tee shirt of the familiar runner.

Justin rushed toward her waving his arms.

A blur of the runner's arm.

Justin yelled.

Two shots.

Screams from bystanders.

Kim dove for the grass, with Justin landing on top of her.

Dead weight.

She shrugged him off and pulled her Chief's Special from the back of her shorts, but by the time she got to her feet, the runner was out of sight. "Oh, God, Justin, no."

She fished her cell from the pocket in her running shorts and called 911.

CHAPTER FIFTY-FOUR

The mayor's staff had set up his podium in the massive vestibule of City Hall, which was now packed with members from every segment of New York's media.

Council Speaker Barnett approached the mayor before he walked out. "You mind telling me what this is all about?"

"You know damned well what it's all about. I want you to listen, and, if you like, ask me whatever questions you like about any topic I discuss, but only about what I discuss."

The Speaker studied him through squinting eyes. "Meaning what?"

"Meaning that this is going to be an exercise in clarification, not obfuscation." He walked out to the podium with the Speaker trailing behind. Several members of the Council arrayed themselves behind him and the Speaker, an excellent touch that the mayor wished he'd thought of himself.

Arc lights game on and the babble of chatter died down.

"Thank you all for coming on such short notice," the mayor began. "I want to address a report that began as whispered rumor and that is now circulating as assumed fact, to the effect that I am being investigated by the Justice Department for alleged violations of the federal law requiring disclosure of foreign bank accounts, known as FATCA. I want to make four things clear."

He paused to let that sink in. "First, I have never invested any amount in any foreign banks, investment companies or other corporations, and my accountant assures me that my records reflect this. Second, I have not yet received any notification from the IRS of any failure to comply with FATCA. If they had evidence of such failure, their procedures would have required them to notify me of such and to give me 90 days to comply. I have never received any such notice."

He gestured to quell the undercurrent of murmurings. "Third, if there is any kind of examination into my financial accounts, it is illegal to disclose it to anyone without a need to know, and if someone not working for the IRS has accessed their records, that is also illegal. Therefore, I have formally requested an investigation into this matter by the Treasury Inspector General for Tax Administration, and I expect the leakers to face the full weight of the law."

When he paused, a reporter in front called out, "That's three points. What's the fourth?"

"Simply this: in criminal matters, it's generally true that anyone resorting to a 'leak' probably has an ulterior motive, one that's not aligned with the cause of justice. And when you report those leaks without verifying, you are likely hurting investigations rather than helping, and the investigation of Sabrina Dunn's assassination is a case in point. Now, before I open the floor for questions, I have invited Speaker Barnett to ask whatever questions he may have for me."

The collective gasp from the gathered reporters was audible.

The Speaker stepped up to the podium. "Mr. Mayor, you have made clear your opposition to the construction bill currently under consideration in the Council. Isn't it true that Sabrina's Dunn death made it easier for you to oppose a law she held dear?"

"No, it isn't true at all. If anything, it made it more difficult because so many Council members now feel they owe it to her to vote for it, perhaps as a memorial to her. Had she lived, we would have been debating the merits of the bill itself."

"What makes you believe members want to pass it as a memorial to her?"

The mayor shrugged. "You said so yourself during last Friday's session."

The mayor's chief of staff rushed up to him and said in a hoarse whisper, "Mr. Mayor, Justin Cates is at NYU Langone in Cobble Hill. He's been shot."

**

Kim paced around the waiting area, still wearing her running clothes, turning everything over in her mind. She should have suspected the other runner when he never greeted her the way runners usually did, especially when they saw each other regularly. Justin had said he had his reasons for tailing her, and he was right there when the runner attacked. How had he known that?

Rick Conti rushed in, blinking back tears. "Where is he?"

"Still in surgery." She repeated what the doctor had told her. "He was hit once in the chest and once in the side. He lost a lot of blood." Her throat tightened. Focus on the facts. "I rode in the ambulance with him. The EMTs got a transfusion going right away. They have a good chance of saving him. He was trying to…" This time, she couldn't go on.

Jake came in carrying a bag with a change of clothes. "Came here at best possible speed. You okay?"

She swallowed it all, despite her desire to fall apart and let Jake put the pieces back, as he had following her last miscarriage. Deep breath. Force it all back in the box. "Yeah, fine." She took the bag and started for the ladies' room.

Conti stopped her. "Kim, what was he trying to do?"

Another deep breath. "Protect me. I told him not to, but he wouldn't listen. Why?"

"He told me he was concerned about you," Conti said, "that you were in danger. He said he wished you wouldn't run so much, but he never said more than that."

Bob and Cord joined them. Kim gave them the update on Justin, still holding the bag with her change of clothes.

"I know this is hard, Kim," Bob said, "but can you tell me what happened?"

"I was running in Brooklyn Bridge Park when I saw Justin running toward me, yelling." She closed her eyes, forcing the movie in her head to slow down. It helped keep the black cloud at bay. "He was frantic." Frame by frame. "Then, shots were fired from my left. I pulled my piece and turned to fire, but the shooter was already running toward Furman Street, where there were a lot more..." She stopped.

"What is it, Kim?" Cord asked.

Stop the film. Rewind, then frame by frame. "When Justin went down, and I was pulling my piece, the runner had a wide-open shot at me."

"What's your point?" Bob asked.

CHAPTER FIFTY-FIVE

A commotion at the entrance to the waiting area interrupted their conversation.

Bob groaned. "I believe hizzoner has just arrived."

The mayor strode in and made a beeline for Conti. "What happened?"

"Go get changed," Bob said to Kim, "because the press will be here any minute."

"My people are setting up for the press up in the lobby," the mayor said. He pulled Kim aside. "What the hell happened?"

She repeated what she had told Bob, but she was still rewinding and repeating the sequence in her mind. "Justin must have thought the guy was stalking me."

"So, you'd seen him before?" Bob asked. "You can describe him?"

"Yes, he's not quite six feet, very thin—a runner's build—dark brown hair, long on top, very short on the sides, dark complexion, maybe Slavic, large nose, square jaw, lots of dark hair on his arms and legs." She turned to Conti. "Did the hospital give you Justin's personal items?"

"Just his wallet, keys and cell phone."

"Give me the phone." He hesitated, so she added, "Now, Rick. We're losing precious time."

Conti fished it out of his pocket and whispered Justin's passcode. "But why?"

"Hold it," the mayor said. "No one does anything until I know what this is all about."

Kim kissed Conti on the cheek. "Please give me the word immediately when you get news about Justin." She turned to the mayor. "Sorry, gotta run. Come on, guys."

Bob and Cord followed her out.

***

The mayor wheeled on Rick Conti. "What the hell is going on?"

"I don't know, sir. I was in the process of finding out when you barged in."

Well, all right, the fellow had reason to be upset. "My apologies. We're all upset. Do you at least know why Justin felt Kim was in danger?" He realized his mistake the moment he saw Conti's stunned expression, but it was impossible to unsay it.

"I didn't even know he thought she was. I only know he was deeply troubled about the shooting and the investigation."

"But he never said why?"

"No, sir."

The mayor was losing his grip on events, and that had to stop. "Mr. Conti, when you contact Detective Brady, you are to tell her to report to me. Am I clear?"

***

"Back to the Castle." Kim struggled to change in the back while Bob drove. "Fast."

"I can understand you not wanting to spoon-feed the mayor," Bob said, "but maybe you could give us a clue what's going on."

Instead, she was on her cell repeating her description of the runner.

"Who was that?" Cord asked.

She pulled on a pair of slacks over her running shorts. "The captain. I asked him to distribute that description department-wide with orders to concentrate on points of exit." She glanced at the time on her cell. "The bastard already has a ninety-minute lead on us."

"Kim," Bob said, "please slow down and explain."

"Can't." She entered the passcode into Justin's phone. It worked. She selected Photos. Nothing among the most recent. She scrolled back. "Come on, Justin, I know you got at least one."

"Kim..." Bob was growing frantic.

There. Taken on Monroe Place as she was ending a run. She had probably just slowed to a walk, but it was hard to tell because the focus wasn't on her, it was on the unknown runner, looking her way, his face slightly blurred.

Shit.

But it was the third in a sequence, the previous shot had been taken seconds earlier, before he turned to look. Perfect shot of his face. And the first in the sequence showed Kim more clearly, still running, and the unknown runner several yards behind.

"I knew he wouldn't let me down," she said in little more than a whisper.

"Kim!"

She reviewed in her mind the moment of the shooting once more. "I wasn't his target, Justin was. The shooter's weapon was already out before he even knew I was there. What's more, after he shot Justin, he had a clear shot at me, but he turned and ran, instead."

She forwarded the second photo in a text to both Captain Cirillo and Ken Taylor. *This is the man who shot Justin Cates. Imperative we cover potential exit points from the city.*

Next, she texted the same photo to their contact in the Face Recognition Unit. *I need an ID ASAP!*

"But why would he want to kill Justin?" Cord asked.

"He told me stuff Brandt was holding back, about Dunn's involvement with that Brownsville thing, and I confronted Dunn about it, hoping to get him to cooperate. But he threw me out, instead. The runner and Dunn are somehow connected."

CHAPTER FIFTY-SIX

The mayor had returned to his office at City Hall after making a brief statement to the press. The concern his wife had expressed frequently—that Justin's relationship with Rick Conti might become public knowledge—was now a fact. Hanging around the hospital wouldn't have accomplished anything except generate more gossip, so an orderly retreat had been his best bet.

Back in his office, he turned on the television. Joanna Dunbar was on the screen. "The victim in this morning's shooting in Brooklyn Bridge Park has been identified as Justin Cates, a member of Raymond Brandt's mayoral staff…"

He changed channels to see how *City News* was handling it. "Police have no leads yet on this morning's shooting in Brooklyn and ask anyone with information to please call the Crimestoppers hotline. The victim, Justin Cates, is an aide to Mayor Brandt and reportedly the lover of Richard Conti, an ADA for Bryce Mitchell, the Brooklyn DA…"

Well, that didn't take long.

His cell trilled. Kyle Emory. He decided to take the call.

"The media now knows about your fag staffer. You've got a major problem."

"That doesn't sound like concern for a crime victim."

Emory snorted. "Save it for the media. They're about to make a meal out of this. And that puts me in a tough position. Continuing to subsidise a pol who tolerates such slack morals…"

Time to push back. "And you can save that for the media."

But Emory wouldn't be deterred. "It will make working with my fellow investors impossible. As it is, they have little stomach for supporting anyone from your party."

"But they do because they understand the only alternatives would be considerably worse. So, let's stop with the bullshit. We both know what this is about."

Emory chuckled. "Fine. Unless we get your buy-in on the Brownsville Project, I will be forced to withdraw my support."

"Fine. Withdraw your support and I'll sign the construction bill when it passes."

"You wouldn't."

"Wouldn't I? You want to go nuclear, I can go nuclear."

***

Kim had gone to the restroom and washed up the moment they entered the Castle. Jake had been kind enough to pack a deodorant stick with her clothes.

Feeling refreshed, she went back over the latest details, including her last interview with Sophia Laguerre. Ramos had provided the fentanyl to put in Fedorov's insulin kit, which meant Ramos had been double dealing.

Wait.

Laguerre referred to Ramos as tall, skinny, and white. Ramos was Latino, rather short and stocky.

As she returned from the restroom, Sergeant Dhillon approached with a printout. "This just came in for you."

"Thanks, Marshal." One glance and her spirits rose. She took it into Bob's office. "The Face Recognition Unit got a hit on runner's image. Art Cowens, with aliases John Jackson, Henry Smith, and Gerald Lang."

"Kind of surprising he didn't get a Jones in there," Bob said. "All nice, clean, American names."

"Which he likely isn't. Check out his mug shot."

Bob studied it. "He looks a bit like Vlad Tepes."

Dracula. That made her laugh, but it didn't last. "Where has he gone?"

A text from Conti. *Justin's out of surgery. Critical but stable condition. Doctor estimates he has a 90% chance of making it. Next 48 hours will tell.*

She repeated the news to Bob and texted him back. *We have a line on his shooter. Let me know when Justin can see visitors.*

Bob responded by answering her question. "Maybe Vlad's hiding out somewhere in the city."

"Perhaps. But if he's connected to Sabrina's assassination, he knows he's not long for this world, and his best chance is to clear out."

"That's a big if."

Only one way to find out. She called Conti. "And I'll bet good money it was Cowens, not Ramos, who provided the vial for Fedorov."

***

The mayor was still calming down from his war of words with Emory when his administrative assistant walked in. "Sir, Mr. Jefferson is here. He says it's urgent."

Lucas Jefferson was the mayor's Legislative Liaison, although lately Justin Cates had been doing some of that work. "What could be so urgent? Okay, show him in."

The mayor waited until she withdrew before shaking Jefferson's hand. "What's up, Luke?"

"Sorry about Cates, sir. Hope he's okay."

On an urgent matter, but pausing for small talk? Either it wasn't that urgent, or it was extremely urgent and he just didn't know how to begin. "Thank you, he's out of surgery, stable but critical if that makes any sense. What's up?"

"The Council just opened debate on Sabrina's Law. I know, they weren't scheduled to report it out of committee until the fifteenth of the month, but Barnett pushed for a vote in the committee an hour ago, and then he kicked it to the head of the pack."

"He's violating his own procedures." But the mayor felt foolish as soon as he'd said it. "Can you check with DiNapoli and Pagan? They were leaning our way. And Anastos, who wants to vote our way but fears backlash in the district."

"I'll do that, but you can forget Anastos. The progressives in his district are heating up the oil."

After a moment, the mayor decided. "Tell him if he wants to vote yes, do it, and perhaps express some misgivings. But we may need him to at least abstain on the vote to override my veto. And let me know about the other two."

CHAPTER FIFTY-SEVEN

It wasn't easy getting through the security at Dunn Holdings, but Kim and Cord managed.

Richmond Dunn was already standing when they reached his office. "I already told you I wouldn't talk to you without my attorney being present."

Kim walked past him and took one of his guest chairs. "Fine. Call him. We'll wait. Or, if you like, he can meet us at PBBN."

"I'm not going anywhere, but you are. Get out of my office, or I'll have you removed by my security men."

Cord sat in the other guest chair. "Now, see, that's clearly the wrong move, unless you want them to be charged with assault and face an obstruction charge, yourself."

Before Dunn could react, Kim added, "You might want to at least wait until we tell you why we're here." She glanced at her watch. The timing on this would need to be perfect.

Dunn remained standing. "I would assume you want to coerce me into confessing to my daughter's murder, which I will not do because I knew nothing about it until it happened."

Cord laughed. "Wrong."

Kim remained serious. "I'm ready to believe you, Mr. Dunn, but that is not why we are here." Another glance at her watch. Where the hell was Brogan?

"Then why are you here?" Dunn asked.

There was a commotion in the outer office. "Let us in, now."

Relief. "That will be Detective Brogan of my unit. And if you refuse him entry, I'll have grounds to arrest you." Before Dunn could reply, Brogan and Stransky entered the inner office. Brogan gave Kim a sheet of paper.

She scanned it before thanking him. Then, she stood and showed it to Dunn. "This is a material witness warrant."

"I see. You're going to detain me until I confess to knowing something more about Sabrina's murder."

"Hey, man," Cord said, "you mind telling me how anyone so dumb could get to be so rich?"

Although Dunn's anger flared, he restrained himself from taking a step toward Cord.

Cord snickered. "Smart move, Bro."

"As it happens," Kim said, "we have no intention of detaining you to obtain a confession, nor do we expect you to have pertinent information about Sabrina's murder. If you read the warrant, this relates to information that I passed on to you in our last discussion that resulted in Mr. Justin Cates being shot this morning. I need the names of anyone you told about it. And I'm willing to wait until your attorney arrives to get your response."

Dunn called to his secretary. "Call Wilfred Renwyck and ask him to come over right away."

Kim returned to her seat. "Tim, Martin, thank you. Please get back to the Castle and alert me the moment hear from the feds."

"Oh," Martin said, "one more thing." He handed her a printout.

***

"This just in. The City Council has just passed the construction bill known as Sabrina's Law by a vote of thirty-four to sixteen. Mayor Brandt has already said he would veto the bill, but today's vote suggests the majority is enough to override his veto."

***

"What the hell happened?" the mayor asked Luke Jefferson.

"Not sure. I never had the chance to talk to either DiNapoli or Pagan."

"So, we have 30 days to move two votes to our side of the ledger." He reached for his phone to call Cates, then remembered that Cates wasn't available. And he wouldn't be for quite some time.

CHAPTER FIFTY-EIGHT

Wilfred Renwyck's expression of distaste upon entering his client's office might have amused Kim under other circumstances, but in her mind the clock was ticking and there just wasn't time.

"Now," the attorney said as he closed the door behind him, "please tell me what this is all about."

"Yesterday, I revealed my knowledge of certain facts to your client, facts I could only have reasonably gotten from one of two sources. This morning, one of those two sources was gunned down a few feet away from me."

"And you suspect my client?" Renwyck asked in a dismissive tone.

"No. But if he told anyone about what I'd discovered, he may have unwittingly set into motion a series of events that resulted in this morning's shooting."

"If you're looking to pin an accomplice charge on him…" Renwyck began.

Kim stopped him. "I'm not, at least not yet. I'm willing to accept that any revelation was likely made in an agitated state and that he could not have anticipated the result. But that could change if he's not completely forthcoming now."

"And you believe this is somehow connected to the murder of his daughter?"

"Yes." She addressed Dunn. "And if I'm correct in my suspicions about how Justin Cates came to be lying in a Brooklyn hospital fighting for his life, I would think you would be as anxious as I am to get to the bottom of it."

Dunn blanched but remained silent.

"Before we proceed," Renwyck said, "how can I be certain that Bryce Mitchell will go along with this?"

"Call him."

Renwyck called and got through to the Brooklyn DA. After a brief discussion, he ended the call. "Detective, Mr. Mitchell confirms your claim." He turned to Dunn. "Rich, I suggest you answer the detective's questions."

Dunn nodded but said nothing.

"Very well," Kim said. "Did you speak to anyone after our brief meeting yesterday afternoon?"

"Yes."

"And did you reveal to any of them the substance of our conversation, or that I had learned about your participation in the proposed Brownsville Project?"

Dunn glanced at his attorney before answering. "Yes, I spoke to Fred Hammond. He had invited me to invest in the project, and I'd agreed provided that my participation be kept secret. I was furious that our confidence had been breached."

"Why were you so anxious to keep your participation secret?" Kim asked.

"My wife had become adamant that I reconcile with our daughter, and I agreed to try. I knew that if my participation became public, any chance of that would be lost."

Time for a little misdirection. "Does the name Peter Fedorov mean anything to you?"

"Why?" Renwyck asked.

Kim ignored him. "Does it?"

Dunn remained calm. "No."

"What about Vladimir Gorkov?"

"Are you going to quiz him on the entire Moscow phone directory?" Renwyck asked.

Kim's eyes never left Dunn. "So, you admit you know they're from Moscow."

"Hey," Dunn replied, "he said it, not me. I've never heard of either of them."

"I assure you, Detective," Renwyck put in, "I only mentioned Moscow because the names sounded Russian. What is their significance?"

"I'll come back to that. Mr. Dunn, Sabrina's cell phone records suggest you knew of Hammond's attempt to bribe her with a payment of $125,000. I expect that disrupted your attempted reconciliation."

Dunn was shaken by the revelation. "When I first approached Sabrina, she was skeptical but willing to listen. When she learned of the wire transfer, she didn't know who was behind it, so she called me. When she told me the source entity, I blurted out it was Hammond's company, and we got no further."

"And yet you remained as part of the consortium. Sounds like you weren't all that torn up about the failed reconciliation."

Dunn shrugged. "I wasn't."

Time for another change of direction. "So, how did Hammond react when you told him of the leak?"

"He was furious. He said the only people who knew I was involved were the partners and the mayor, and he'd have Kyle Emory deal with him since the mayor is Emory's boy."

"Whoa." Cord laughed. "He used those words?"

"Yes. Hammond doesn't hold Mr. Brandt in very high regard."

"Did Hammond ever get back to you on how Emory dealt with it?" Kim asked.

"No."

"Has he ever mentioned the names Art Cowens, John Jackson, Henry Smith, or Gerald Lang?"

Renwyck had had enough. "No more name games, Detective. What's this all about?"

"Your client complained to Hammond about his involvement having been leaked to me, which it was. Hammond confirmed that the only person who knew of his involvement outside of the investors themselves was the mayor. My source was Justin Cates, the mayor's top aide who was shot this morning only ten feet in front of me by a man named Art Cowens, who uses the aliases I mentioned." Back to Dunn. "Please answer the question."

The color drained from Dunn's face. "You think Hammond had some involvement with this?"

"I think Cowens' attack was ordered by a member of your consortium." She showed him the printout Martin had given her. "This is a ballistics report on the slug recovered from Justin Cates during this morning's surgery. It matches the one recovered from the body of Miguel Ramos, a former police sergeant who was working for Hammond when he was killed, and in that capacity had obtained information about our investigation of Sabrina's murder and then facilitated a leak to the media. He was murdered after agreeing to provide information to us on the other members of the Brownsville consortium."

Renwyck stood. "That's enough, Detective. You've now gone far afield of the terms of the warrant."

"You don't get it, dude," Cord said. "She ain't after him."

Kim kept her focus on Dunn. "It's all related to Sabrina's murder. Koster killed her, then Fedorov killed Koster, then was killed. Ramos tried to assist our investigation, and Cowens killed him. Justin Cates told me you were involved in the project, and Cowens tried to kill him after stalking me from the moment I was assigned to this case. The mayor refused to support the project, so the consortium doesn't need you and will probably look to kill you the first chance they get. So, I'm exercising the authority under the warrant and taking you into custody as a material witness."

Renwyck stood. "We'll just see about that."

CHAPTER FIFTY-NINE

Tuesday, August 2nd

For the first time since she'd taken on the Dunn case, Kim did not see the previously unknown runner, whom she now knew as Cowens, as she ran. Not a surprise. The photo Justin had taken was now being flashed regularly on television news shows, and the FBI had launched a national dragnet.

She nursed no fantasies that he'd be apprehended.

As she ran, she caught herself looking for Justin. But he was still in ICU, fighting for his life.

He was trying to protect me, and all the time I should have been protecting him.

She forced the thought and the blackness away. Focus on the case.

Three hit men, two dead, one vanished. Hammond was looking like the epicenter of the conspiracy, but, as much as she disliked Hammond, he wasn't likely to have a stable of hit men. But he had to know something, if not everything.

As she ended her run, Conti emerged from a parked car wearing yesterday's suit and sporting a shadow of a beard. She had to laugh. "Keeping up the tradition, I see. How's Justin?"

"Still critical, but stable. I stayed with him all night."

"You look like you could use a cup of coffee. Come on in."

Jake was already up, and the coffee was already perked. "I'll grab a shower."

"How did your chat with Mr. Dunn go?" Rick asked.

Kim took a sip of coffee. "He's challenging the warrant, saying I abused the terms of it. I hope you have a good person to send to argue today."

His cell pinged with a text, and he read it. "My office received notice late yesterday. We're due in Judge Vickers' chambers at two this afternoon."

"We?"

"I don't trust anyone else with this, Kim, and I'll need you there to connect the dots."

Which didn't give her much time.

***

"We have a problem," Luke Jefferson said. "DiNapoli and Pagan both plan to vote to override your expected veto, and DiNapoli says he'd prefer that you not appear at the precinct's community meeting tomorrow night."

The mayor struggled to control his anger. "Fuck DiNapoli, I'm going, and if he doesn't come, I can talk about how unhelpful he's being. Tell Pagan that we've hit a snag on the Cooper Park project and I'm unsure when we'll be able to start. If she asks if that's a threat, tell her she's goddamned right it is. Finally, find out what Anastos will need to support a veto. If it's a promise of support for a future office, tell him he's got it. We'll even find him a good district to run in."

When Jefferson left, the mayor picked up his cell and sent a text to his attorney. *Any word on the investigation yet?*

A few moments later, he received a response. *TIGTA doesn't move that fast. You need to be patient. However, the IRS is preparing to issue a 90-day letter, meaning you have 90 days to report your foreign holdings, regarding a UK investment. Will advise when you receive it.*

It was time to ask Kim Brady for a favor.

***

Shit. Time was running out, and she had none to spare for side issues. Except that this wasn't really a side issue. "I'm due downtown in a couple of hours."

"So, you have the time," the mayor replied. "It's a phone call."

"It's more than that, and you know it. You are asking me to obtain, through unofficial means, information to which I am not entitled and have no need to know, to pass on to you before official notice can be given." She couldn't tell him she'd known for more than a week and hadn't told him because she still hadn't been sure of his innocence in Sabrina Dunn's death. "That could not only get me severely disciplined by the department, but possibly prosecuted."

"I'm being got at, goddamn it!"

She'd never heard him so angry. "I understand. But you've never been completely truthful with me, so how can I trust you now?"

"I put you on the fucking case to start with, and I put you back when your captain tried to pull you off."

"Oh, thank you so much." No, can't get bitchy with him. Besides, someone was trying to get at him, and if they succeeded, the person responsible for Sabrina Dunn's death, as well as all the others, could go free. To uphold the law, she might have to break the law. "You're still not telling me the whole truth. I'll give you one shot, and only one, right now."

"Anything."

"There are four partners in the Brownsville Project—Emory, Hammond, Dunn, and some guy named Vinson, who was not at your little dinner at Gracie Mansion last week. Tell me about him right now and how he fits in with this group."

A long pause. "He's a financier. I know nothing about him or how he came to belong to the group."

"Didn't you ask? Or were you afraid to find out?"

No response. That said everything.

"I'll take that as a no to the first and yes to the second. May I also assume that the reason was that you were afraid he might have a less-than-savory past?"

"I didn't know what to think. Emory had never been secretive with me before, and I didn't like it. But his manner has turned hard assed over this project, and I'm worried where it could all lead. Justin being shot brought that home to me."

A long silence.

"If I don't get out in front of this federal investigation, I could be forced to resign. I need your help, Kim."

"Detective Brady, please. Are you certain you can't think of any investment?"

"I may be rattled now, but I have a firm handle on all my investments, and my accountant has all my financial records. My lawyer tells me it may be something in the UK, but I have nothing there… unless… oh shit!"

"Exactly what I was thinking, Mr. Mayor. I'll see what I can find out."

***

Judge Vickers listened as Wilfred Renwyck ranted about his client being railroaded and Kim being a scheming liar trying to bring down a grieving father. Kim struggled mightily to keep her best poker face.

When Renwyck finished, Judge Vickers turned to Conti. "Counselor?"

"To the extent defense counsel has elucidated the facts, as opposed to histrionics, they are correct. Detective Brady's purpose was to establish a connection from her confronting Mr. Dunn with a piece of information to Mr. Dunn complaining to a fellow partner about it. Thus, the conditions of the warrant have been met."

"But to what end?" Renwyck said. "She has proven no wrongdoing by my client, either in the matter of the attempted murder of Mr. Cates or the murder of Ms. Dunn."

Conti turned to her and nodded.

"And that wasn't my goal," she said.

"Then why are the police so eager to place my client in custody?" Renwyck was not quite yelling.

Judge Vickers frowned. "Please keep your voice at a civil level, Counselor. Detective?"

"Protective custody, your honor." She recapped the string of murders. "This record suggests a level of organized criminal activity much more advanced than just a single assassination. If Miguel Ramos was killed for trying to get information for the investigation, it's reasonable to assume that Mr. Dunn could be in similar danger if the remaining dominoes fall."

"What dominoes?" the judge asked.

Kim handed him the new affidavit completed by Rick that morning. "Based on my interview with Mr. Dunn, we are requesting a material witness warrant for Fredrick Hammond..."

Renwyck appeared ready to explode. "Barefaced bootstrapping, your honor."

"You have no standing to object, Counselor," Vickers replied.

"They have no right to present that request here, your honor. We are discussing my client."

"Your honor," Conti said, "this is the perfect time to present it, as it shows the police were correct in questioning Mr. Dunn and that they have sufficient reason to want to question Mr. Hammond."

"With all due respect, your honor," Renwyck replied, "my client could be more than adequately protected in his own home."

"Really?" Kim asked. "Does he have a standing army we don't know about?"

"That's enough, Detective." But the judge was struggling to suppress a smirk.

"Sorry, your honor," she said, "I just can't understand why a defense lawyer would be so eager to place his client's life at risk."

Renwyck trembled as the needle sank home, but the judge forestalled an outburst. "My thoughts, exactly, Detective. Counselor, I reaffirm my approval of the material witness warrant, and your client will cooperate forthwith. You and he are excused. Mr. Conti, Detective Brady, please re-main."

"Thank you, your honor," Kim said. "Detectives Stransky and Washington are right outside, and Detective Brogan is in a car downstairs waiting for them."

After they left, Vickers turned to Kim. "Before I grant your request, I'd like to know just what you think you're going to find, and how finding it will help in the case of the attempt on the life of Mr. Cates."

"Dunn complained to Hammond about being 'outed', and Hammond knew that either the mayor or Mr. Cates had been responsible. Either Mr. Hammond ordered Mr. Cates killed or he knows who did."

"And you want to explore that," the judge said.

"Yes."

He stared at her with eyebrows arched. "Anything else?"

She made brief eye contact with Conti, who'd warned against mentioning it for fear Vickers might consider it all speculation, which it was. She'd already stepped over the line once, which Vickers didn't know, yet, but might find out.

"Detective?"

Deep breath. "Mr. Cates revealed a fourth potential investor in this Brownsville project, a man named Conrad Vinson. My team spent the entire morning dredging the internet for records of this man and could only find material dating back about fifteen years. And Ken Taylor at the FBI could find no birth record for him in any jurisdiction."

"And you think this Vinson is the person Hammond turned to with Dunn's complaint. All right, granting that you are right, where does that get us? Can you establish a connection between Vinson and Mr. Cowens?"

He had her there. "I don't know, yet. We have to follow the trail one step at a time."

Conti frowned as the judge sat back.

All in. "Your honor, you may have seen the leaked report about the mayor and some foreign holdings he didn't report."

"I have. He claims he has no foreign investments. But in my experience, the IRS makes certain they have all their facts straight before proceeding with an investigation."

"They also make sure nothing gets leaked, as leaks violate due process," she replied. She reminded him of the battle over Sabrina Dunn's cell phone. Another deep breath. "This is all linked, your honor: Sabrina Dunn's murder, the Brownsville Project, the other murders, the leaks, and the investigation of Mayor Brandt. I'm satisfied Mr. Dunn was not complicit in his daughter's death, and I've also eliminated the mayor as a suspect. But that consortium smells like week-old fish."

Vickers leaned forward. "As does your request, given this new information. You're looking for far more than you've suggested in your affidavit, and based on what you're telling me now, you don't have anywhere near probable cause for any of it."

"But I have probable cause for what's in the warrant, and if I discover more than that in the process, it would be admissible, such as finding a gun while executing a search for drugs. Besides, in the final analysis, probable cause is subjective, isn't it?"

"Is that how you're justifying this to yourself?" he asked.

"Perhaps."

He picked up a pen and signed and dated the warrant. "Mr. Conti, I've been remiss in not congratulating you on your recent promotion. We often disagree, but I have a great deal of respect for you. Good luck in your new position. Good luck to you, too, Detective."

CHAPTER SIXTY

This time Kim didn't ask questions in Hammond's office or grant his request to wait for an attorney. "You can have your attorney meet us at Patrol Borough Brooklyn North." She and Cord escorted him out of the building with Brogan and Stransky right behind.

Hammond kept muttering about the outrage all the way to the Castle. Once there, she placed him in an interrogation room until his attorney arrived, which wasn't until just after six.

"Mr. Hammond, did Richmond Dunn complain to you about his participation in your Brownsville Project consortium being leaked to police?"

"You will not railroad me like you did with my son."

Kim turned to his attorney. "Please advise your client that we are not railroading anyone, and that answering falsely is perjury, and when he's prosecuted for it, that won't be railroading, either."

The attorney leaned over and whispered to Hammond, who snarled but said nothing. "My client will answer your questions to the best of his knowledge."

She faced Hammond. "Peachy. Did Dunn complain to you?"

"You must understand," Hammond replied, "he was very anxious to keep out of the public eye."

"So, he did complain."

"Yes."

"And you agreed he was right to be angry?"

"Yes."

"And you passed your complaint on to Kyle Emory?"

"Yes. He had a relationship with Mayor Brandt, and he was certain that the mayor had been your source, or someone on his staff."

"Did Emory tell you whom he thought that someone might be?"

"No."

Too fast. "Mr. Hammond, are you sure? Under penalty of perjury?" She turned to the attorney. "You must know I will confirm his answer with Mr. Emory."

The attorney whispered to Hammond, who now looked worried.

"Let me think," he said, his manner more reserved. "I believe he mentioned a name, but I can't recall what…"

"Justin Cates." She made certain it didn't come out as a question.

"Uh, yes, that was the name." Hammond was now openly fearful.

She smiled at him. "Relax, Mr. Hammond, you're doing fine." But then, she was sure he knew what lay ahead. "And did Mr. Emory have a suggestion about a solution?"

"He said he would talk to the mayor, and I believe he did."

"And did that satisfy you?"

Hammond spread his arms. "Not really, but I didn't see what else he could have done?"

Kim made a show of checking her Notes App. "What did you do, next?"

A blank stare. "I'm sorry?"

"Did you turn to anyone else after Mr. Emory told you he would contact the mayor? Did you seek any other resolution of the leak problem?"

"No."

Again, too fast. This time, she let it pass. "Do you know a man named Miguel Ramos?"

"He worked for me."

The attorney started. "That's beyond…"

"Your client has already answered." Back to questioning Hammond. "I note your use of the past tense. You know that Mr. Ramos is dead?"

"Yes."

"And that he was murdered?"

"Yes."

"By someone using the same weapon that shot Justin Cates."

The attorney stood. "That's all. Detective, you are now way beyond the scope of the warrant. A material witness is one who can provide evidence of probative value to a matter at dispute when a subpoena is unlikely to guarantee the witness' presence at trial. There is no trial and you have no defendant, although it appears you are trying to turn my client into one. I'm going to Judge Vickers in the morning and demand that he revoke the warrant. If he refuses, I'll file an appeal." He turned to Hammond. "Until then, say absolutely nothing to them about anything."

***

While questioning Hammond, Kim had gotten a text from Rick that Justin was out of ICU. With her hands now tied on Hammond, she stopped at the hospital to visit.

"Only twenty minutes left," Rick said as she entered Justin's room. "But thanks for coming."

"Hi," Justin said, his voice weak. "Get anything out of Hammond?"

She laughed, but with little humor. "I see Rick's kept you up to date. No, not much. His lawyer is going to Vickers in the morning to revoke the warrant."

"You pushed the envelope, didn't you?" Rick asked.

"That was the whole idea, wasn't it?"

"Yeah, and Vickers knew that. He'll have no choice but to revoke it."

"And that means Hammond can jump on his private jet any time he wants and bug out. We need to figure out a way to prevent that."

"By tomorrow morning," Justin said from his bed.

Only one card left to play. "Gotta make a call."

***

"A little late to be calling at Gracie Mansion, isn't it?" the mayor asked.

But Emory was fuming. "Fred Hammond and Rich Dunn are both in custody. What in blue blazes are the police doing?"

"They're trying to solve what has become a string of murders. Dunn complained to Hammond who complained to you, and my aide was shot and nearly killed. I don't blame you for being upset, Kyle, since you were the last one in the chain."

"You think I was responsible for the little fag getting shot?"

"That depends on what you did with the information." The mayor sat back, waiting. When Emory said nothing, he added, "The chain goes a link or two further, doesn't it?"

Still no response.

"Who brought Conrad Vinson into the partnership? And, for that matter, who is Conrad Vinson? My information is that Dunn doesn't know him, so that leaves you and Hammond."

"I don't know him very well. To me, he's just another investor."

"So, it was Hammond. And presumably you reported back to Hammond it was Justin who revealed Dunn's participation in the project to the police. So, either Hammond arranged for Justin to be shot or he had someone else do it."

Emory could only sit silent and fume.

The mayor pulled out a single sheet of paper from his desk drawer. "You've been pressing me to veto Sabrina's Law. But a veto is useless unless it can survive an override vote, and this one will take a great deal of effort, which will engender significant ill will in the Council."

Emory leaped to his feet. "You wouldn't sign it."

The mayor shrugged. "Why not? It certainly would make my life easier. Besides, it might not survive a judicial challenge."

"That could take years. You promised…"

"I said I would give you free rein on any new development projects. I did not say I would stand by while you took over public housing, nor did I promise to do everything you asked." He picked up the sheet of paper. "But here's what I will do: I'll announce tomorrow night that I'm vetoing Sabrina's Law, and I'll do my level best to defeat the override vote. In return, you will write and sign a declaration, here and now, that you informed Fred Hammond that Justin Cates leaked Dunn's membership to the police."

"What about the project?"

"The project is dead. Dunn will back out and Hammond will have way too much on his mind." The mayor drew another paper from his desk. "I received this today. It's a letter from the IRS requiring me to complete information filings on my financial investment in a company in the United Kingdom. My accountant assures me I have no such investment. I'll have no trouble beating this, but it's going to create some problems for Hammond. You've used terrible judgment in choosing your friends."

Emory sank back into his seat.

The mayor held out the blank sheet. "Do we have a deal?"

"You're an ungrateful bastard, aren't you?"

The mayor shrugged. "You've abused your privileges. This will square it with us. You can continue to support me or not. As they say, it's a free country."

Emory snatched the blank sheet and wrote and signed his statement.

CHAPTER SIXTY-ONE

Wednesday, August 3rd

"Mr. Conti," Judge Vickers said without even glancing at Kim, "your Detective Brady seems to have gone rather far afield."

Best to let Rick do the talking.

"This case is a tangled web, your honor," Rick said.

"That's no excuse for abusing a material witness warrant," Hammond's attorney said. "And, from where we sit, there is no case. Just a tangled mess that the police are desperate to solve, so they're trying to frame my client. I ask that you revoke the material witness warrant."

The judge turned back to Rick. "Unless you have something else for me, Counselor, I'm afraid I have no choice."

Kim pulled out the sheet of paper she'd received earlier by messenger. "This might be of interest, your honor—a signed statement from Kyle Emory stating he revealed to Mr. Hammond that Justin Cates informed me of Richmond Dunn's participation the Brownsville Project, which led to the shooting of Mr. Cates. Mr. Hammond knows what he did with Emory's information, and whomever he told set up the shooting."

"Pure conjecture, your honor." The attorney didn't hide his smug expression.

Kim looked directly at Hammond. "Do you know a Vladimir Gorkov?"

Hammond blanched, but then recovered. "No, never heard of him."

"Wait," Vickers said. "Who is this Gorkov?"

"A member of the Russian underworld. Peter Fedorov, the man who killed Ivan Koster, worked for him." She turned her attention back to Hammond. "Did you tell someone about Cates, or did you arrange for the shooting yourself?"

The attorney placed a hand on Hammond's arm. "Don't answer that."

"Is he pleading the Fifth Amendment?" Kim asked.

The attorney glared at her. "Is he a suspect?"

"He is, now," she said.

"You will both direct your questions and comments to me," Judge Vickers said. "Mr. Conti, the material witness warrant is revoked. Mr. Hammond, I recall that you once assisted an accused criminal in fleeing this jurisdiction. You haven't been accused of anything, yet, but it sounds as if you have become the focus of the police investigation in the assassination attempt on Mr. Cates, and I suspect you may consider flight yourself. I promise you, that would have very serious consequences."

"Your honor," the attorney replied, "until and unless the police have enough evidence to sustain an arrest warrant, my client will go and do as he will."

"Just a moment, your honor," Rick said. "Before you let Mr. Hammond go, and to save time, the people have a request." He handed over a sheaf of papers. "Earlier today, Mayor Brandt supplied this copy of a notice from the IRS regarding allegedly past due FATCA filings for an investment in Mr. Hammond's overseas entity. He also supplied that affidavit from his accountant attesting that Mayor Brandt holds no such investment."

Vickers scanned the documents. "Seems to me this is a federal matter, Mr. Conti."

"The FATCA issue is, your honor, but the mayor has sworn out a complaint of fraud against Mr. Hammond. The people are requesting a warrant for his arrest."

"That's absurd," the attorney replied. "Mr. Hammond is a shareholder and is therefore protected by the corporate veil."

Kim spoke up. "Your honor, Mr. Hammond is not just the majority shareholder, he is the Chief Executive Officer of the corporation which holds a controlling interest in the UK entity."

"Thus," Rick added, "he is criminally liable."

"I agree," Vickers said. "The arrest warrant is granted." He turned to the attorney. "If your client can offer proof that Mr. Brandt does, in fact, own an interest in this company, I will rescind the warrant."

"We'd like to go further than that, your honor." Rick handed the judge another affidavit. "People request a subpoena for the accounting records for all transactions involving Raymond Brandt's investment in this company."

"Granted, Mr. Conti."

Cord and Tim were waiting outside the judge's chambers.

"He signed the arrest warrant," Kim said. "Take Mr. Hammond directly to Central Booking."

Hammond's attorney turned to Rick. "You have forty-eight hours to arraign him. One second longer, and your ass is mine." In a more soothing tone, he said to his client, "We'll post bail as soon as you're arraigned."

***

Therese Vargas was waiting for Kim when she returned to the Castle. "Captain Cirillo said to call you and Detective Nolan in the moment you return." She had once again ditched the short skirts and high heels. Cirillo stared after her as she left, and there was no mistaking the look of irritation in his eye.

"You wanted to see us, Captain?" Kim asked.

"Yes. What the flying fuck were you doing in Vickers' chambers this morning?"

Kim recapped the meeting, ending with the fact that they now had Hammond in custody.

"And what, exactly, does a fraud count do for our murder investigation?"

"Well, for one thing, it makes certain the guy who either ordered Cates' shooting or asked someone else to order it doesn't jet off to an island someplace to avoid prosecution," Kim replied. "In case you haven't noticed, these guys have been playing us like a mark in a Three-Card Monte game."

"I can't believe Judge Vickers, the ACLU Man of the Year, went along with this."

"Why not?" Bob asked. "The arrest was a legitimate request, as was the subpoena. Hell, he could even claim the subpoena assisted the defense in establishing his client's innocence."

"What I can't believe," Kim said, "is how you have resisted virtually every step we've made in this investigation. When you've bothered to pay attention, that is."

Cirillo didn't back down. "You're running around cooking up half-baked material witness warrants, keeping someone in protective custody who hasn't given us anything, letting her walk on a possible murder charge, and now trying to help Brandt get out from under an IRS problem. Oh, I've been paying attention, all right." He turned to Bob. "You have anything that can get us out of this mess?"

Bob didn't even glance at Kim. "The hidden character in all of this has been this guy Vinson. We haven't been able to find much on him at all, which is odd considering how much money he has. We should get some eyes on him. It's possible he's the guy Hammond turned to after finding out about Cates."

"What do you have on him? Besides mere suspicion, I mean."

"We've eliminated Emory and Dunn, and we're not sure about Hammond. That leaves Vinson."

"What about this Gorkov guy?" Cirillo asked.

Kim started to answer but Bob beat her to it. "We've got the FBI looking into him, but they haven't gotten back to us, yet. Fedorov worked for him back in the old country and probably continued here. It's possible that either Hammond or Vinson had contact with him. Sabrina Dunn, Ivan Koster, and Peter Fedorov—all murders that form a trail of breadcrumbs to Gorkov."

"Unless he's dead." Cirillo shook his head. "This is all conjecture."

Kim couldn't sit still any longer. "Then what would you suggest, Captain?" When he didn't answer, she said, "So, can we put a stakeout team on Vinson?"

"Yes, all right."

On their way out, Kim told Bob she'd meet him back downstairs, then waved Therese out into the hallway. "I'm glad to see the more professionally dressed you."

"I felt like a vulture was circling overhead and might strike at any moment." She shook her head. "Now, his eyes shoot daggers at me whenever he sees me. Is there anything you can do?"

"I'll see, but watch the job postings, and if you see a chance to get out, take it."

***

Back downstairs, Bob said, "Sorry about that, but I was afraid he was going to explode."

"No, it's okay. At least we got the stakeout."

"What were you and Therese talking about?"

"Nothing much."

"I see she's ditched the sexy look. Cirillo looks displeased."

So, he'd figured it out. She said nothing.

"Have any ideas?"

"Not really." But she did. She just wasn't sure how to go about it without burning another bridge. But she knew someone who might help.

***

The applause the mayor received upon being introduced at the meeting of the 104th Precinct Community Council meeting was encouraging. He spoke glowingly about the work the 104th was doing and about the significant drop in crime over the past two years. "I have every confidence that trend will continue."

The crowd cheered.

"Now," he said when they'd quieted down, "there is another matter that has dominated the headlines in the past few days, concerning a bill recently passed by the City Council that purports to support unionization in the construction industry, but gives a free pass to any contractor whose skin is the right color."

A rumbling of boos.

"I am fully committed to protecting the rights of all our citizens. But that means all citizens, equally. I recognize the rights of workers to unionize if they so choose, as well as not unionizing if that is their preference. Therefore, tomorrow morning I will veto the so-called Sabrina's Law. There will be a subsequent vote in the City Council to override that veto, a vote that must receive a two-thirds majority to pass. And I'm counting on fair-minded members like your good Mr. DiNapoli to defeat the override."

As the crowd cheered, Councilman DiNapoli gave a weak smile and nodded.

CHAPTER SIXTY-TWO

Thursday, August 4th

Kim finished her morning run, reaching six miles, her high for a weekday. She hoped to hit ten miles on Sunday. The combination of an aggressive running program and the complicated case allowed her to ward off the black cloud of depression.

Jake had the television on when she arrived back at the apartment.

"Council Speaker Leroy Barnett reacted to the mayor's announcement that he would veto Sabrina's Law this morning with anger, saying he had the votes to override the veto. He also charged Mayor Brandt with ushering in a new era of racial discrimination and toadying to wealthy financial interests."

Kim was still toweling off when she heard the ping signaling a text from Tim Brogan. *Got the response to the subpoena last night by messenger. Shows a transfer in June from a Caymans account they say is Brandt's. He ain't gonna be happy.*

The Caymans? That would mean Brandt had two foreign accounts he hadn't reported. He wasn't that stupid.

June. That caught her attention, and she texted back. *Don't do anything, yet. Let me see it when I get there. I'll be there in a couple of hours. I have an errand to run, first.*

***

As soon as Brandt arrived at his City Hall office, he vetoed Sabrina's Law and sent the notice over to the Council chamber. Nothing to do now but wait.

***

It had been over four years since Kim had left Internal Affairs, so it felt a little like returning to her old high school. Her old unit had turned over twice since her departure, but her old supervising officer, Lt. Steve Colangelo, was still there. "Uh oh. An in-person visit with no preceding phone call. This must be unofficial."

She took a seat opposite his desk. "Very. Do you have a position for a non-Member of Service support staffer?"

Colangelo's brows arched downward. "Why?"

She answered with a slight smile. "Do you?"

"Not in my unit, but my captain's admin just went out on maternity leave. Officially, we must assume she's coming back and guarantee her a position, but she and her husband just bought a place in Tom's River, New Jersey. Now, please answer my question."

She explained about Therese Vargas.

His furrowed brow grew deeper. "I see your luck with supervising officers continues."

"Lt. Bostwick is fine. We had some turbulence at first, but we worked that out long ago."

"But Cirillo already tried to pull you off the Dunn case."

She wasn't surprised word had gotten around. "He thought it was damage control. Mostly, he's been okay, or at least no worse than the rest. Present company excepted."

His smile was genuine. "Thanks. But if he finds out you're trying to pry his admin away from him, he'll likely go nuclear."

"That's why I need you, or your captain, to post the position. Encourage Therese to apply. And if you can put in a good word for her, I'm sure that will go a long way."

"Says she who's always hated departmental politics."

She didn't laugh. "Yes, and I still do. But, in the old days, she'd have been trapped with a lecherous boss and no one would've lifted a finger to get her out. She's an excellent assistant, professional and organized."

Colangelo thought about it. "Captain Cirillo will smell a rat the moment he finds she's applied for a position in Internal Affairs. That won't be good for you."

"I'll live, and if it's listed with all the other job postings, he won't know for certain it was me."

"I see. Plausible deniability. Okay, let me talk to the captain about it." He hesitated. "You understand I'll have to give him the full story."

She stood and shook his hand. "Understood. Please text me after you speak to him so I can tell Therese to be alert and ready to apply the moment the listing is posted."

***

Council Speaker Barnett entered the mayor's office, a mixture of angry and wary. The wariness deepened when the mayor stood and gestured for him to sit. "I'm not sure what you think we can talk about at this late date. I'm determined to override your veto and you're determined to defeat that attempt. There is no middle ground."

The mayor shrugged. "If you say so." He sat back and waited.

The Speaker gave in. "Okay, what?"

"It seems to me that neither of us wants a vote on this. I think I've got the votes to defeat an override. DiNapoli and Pagan voted with you the first time to satisfy their consciences, but their districts are up in arms about it. DiNapoli has already pledged in public to vote against the override, and Pagan has agreed privately to do so."

"After some not-so-subtle arm-twisting on your part."

The mayor shrugged. "We do what we must. Anastos voted yes to satisfy the progressives in his district, but he detests the bill and will abstain on the override."

"He'll look like a coward."

"I agree, which will probably inflame people on both sides of the issue. Then again, it's his career. In this matter, an abstention is as good as a no vote, and if you lose it, you will be significantly damaged, as will your wing of the party. You will appear to be elitists, out of touch with the city that voted for me by an overwhelming majority."

"At least according to your friends at the Independent Television Network."

The mayor grinned. "Whose market share has been steadily increasing every month, in part because they draw a sharp line between reportage and opinion. On the other hand, if I'm wrong and you win the override vote…"

A small grin crept across the Speaker's face. "Then you're the one who looks like the out-of-touch elitist."

"And very well you put it. Politics is often a zero-sum game. But there are exceptions."

"If I don't bring this to a vote, it's as bad for me as if I lose the vote."

"Agreed," the mayor said. "But if you bring an amended bill to the floor for a vote, one on which we can agree in advance, I will sign it. I'll even ask DiNapoli to sponsor it."

The Speaker's eyes narrowed. "I'm sure you've already asked him. All right, what changes do you have in mind?"

"I'll agree to a requirement for all construction companies with a minimum of two hundred full-time employees to offer unionization to their employees, but with the right for those employees not to do so, with no race-based exemption."

"A right not to unionize? That makes the provision toothless."

"It's consistent with federal labor law. Anything more restrictive likely would not survive judicial review. And I'd be fine with stiff penalties for companies who unduly interfered with a fair vote."

Barnett thought about it. "Full-time employees? That's a loophole that you could drive a truck through."

"Part-timers would still be covered by the benefits of working in a union shop."

The Speaker didn't hesitate. "But with such a large base needed to make a union shop, most firms wouldn't qualify. Make it one hundred."

"One-fifty." Although he'd probably said it too quickly.

"No, Mr. Mayor. I'd consider one-fifty if we dropped the full-time requirement. Your choice."

The mayor considered it. "Very well, one hundred full-timers it is." He extended his hand, and the Speaker took it, if with some wariness.

***

"Good morning, Detective Kim," Sergeant Dhillon said upon her arrival at the Castle. "Your group is waiting for you in the conference room."

"Thanks, Marshal. If anything comes in for me from the DA's office, please let me know immediately." She walked straight to the conference room where Bob, Cord, Tim, and Martin were all waiting. "First, what's the news from the stakeout team?"

"In place. Vinson's gone to his office down on Rector Street. Residence is on Central Park West. Not sure what you expect to find."

"Neither am I. Let me see the stuff about Brandt's account with Hammond."

Tim spread out the printouts, including a transaction list from June that included the $125,000 transfer. Kim stared at it, then pulled up an image on her cell. "Tim, please pack this back up, along with a copy of the subpoena. I need to make some calls."

As she returned to her desk, her attention was caught by the image of the mayor and Council Speaker Barnett on the large screen TV.

"... met with Speaker Barnett this morning to discuss the fate of the construction bill which I vetoed yesterday. After considering the matter with care, we have arrived at a compromise that we both believe will best serve the people of this city and not cause further divisions..."

Bob sidled up next to Kim. "He caved?"

But after listening, she replied, "No, he just got rid of the racial preference. Emory and his pals will be pissed. But then..." She explained what she'd found on her cell. She made three phone calls, starting with Ken Taylor.

"You go," Bob said. "I'll brief the captain." She started to protest, but he added, "He needs to inform the chain of command, and if you wait until after your meeting, he'll blow you out of the water."

Marshal Dhillon approached, a worried look on his face. "I just heard from the officers guarding Sophia Laguerre. She has slipped away."

It took all of Kim's strength not to explode. "How long ago?"

"They discovered she was gone approximately thirty minutes ago, but they last checked on her last night. I am so sorry."

"Not your fault, Marshal. Text me with any updates."

"I'll have the captain alert the precincts," Bob said. "Although Christ only knows where she could have gone." He caught Kim's furrowed brow. "What?"

"Fentanyl has popped up three times: Koster, Hicks, and Fedorov. But Laguerre said only Hicks was using from the vials snatched from meds carts. So, the fentanyl used to off Koster and Fedorov came from someplace else. Someone in this thing has a major supply source."

Bob considered it. "And?"

"Why would Laguerre run, now? We already told her she'd skate on the thefts, and we left her involvement in Fedorov's death unaddressed."

"You're thinking she had more to do with his death than she's letting on?"

"Exactly. Possibly with Hicks' death, too." She checked her watch and turned to the group. "Martin, I need you with me at Federal Plaza. Cord and Tim, hang tight in case we pick up any intel on Sophia Laguerre. If you find her, bring her back here under arrest for the murder of Peter Fedorov."

"Based on what?" Cord asked.

"Her fingerprints having been found on the vial of insulin in Fedorov's apartment."

"But," Bob said, "her story is that she was told by someone claiming to be a pharmacist that the vial contained insulin. We have no proof that she knew better."

But Kim was adamant. "And she's offered no proof that she had reason to believe it was true. It's enough to arrest her."

CHAPTER SIXTY-THREE

As they climbed the subway stairs to Centre Street, the sound of an angry crowd grew louder. When they reached the covered plaza at street level, City Hall Park was jammed with protesters, many of them waving signs.

"Don't sell us out!"

"Sabrina's Memory Disgraced!"

"Barnett = PINO!"

Stransky turned to Kim. "What the fuck is a PINO?"

"Progressive in name only. Let's walk down Centre to Reade and turn there."

When they reached Federal Plaza, Rick Conti, one of the three people she'd called from the Castle, was waiting for them. "I assume you saw the latest from CHE."

Kim nodded. "Seems pretty tame so far."

"No doubt Mr. Prinz learned a thing or two from his stretch in the pen." Martin nodded toward the group of police from the Manhattan South Strategic Resource Group. "Or maybe they're providing a re-minder."

Ken Taylor was waiting as they came through the security check-point. "Not a word until we're upstairs." Once on his floor, he led them to his office. "Sorry if it's cramped, but I don't want to be overheard."

Kim gave him the printout of the list of wire transfers. "Check that account number. Look familiar?"

Taylor stared a moment. "Shit."

"Am I crazy?" Kim asked, "or is that a very sloppy attempt to make the return of the attempted bribe of Sabrina Dunn look like a buy-in to the corporation by Raymond Brandt?"

"You're definitely not crazy," Ken replied, "because that's what it looks like. Now, the next thing you're going to do is suggest that I shoot this over to the IRS to clear Brandt's name. I can't do that, because I got the information unofficially, and the IRS already has TIGTA giving them an unanesthetized colonoscopy over this case. But you got this pursuant to a subpoena on Brandt's fraud case, so you can inform him, and he can respond to the IRS."

"Won't that be simply giving them what they already have?" Martin asked. "The key is that we know that account belonged to Sabrina Dunn. You already provided that."

"Unofficially."

"Wait," Kim said. "We got it legally when we checked Sabrina Dunn's other bank records and saw the activity. And Felipe Prinz confirmed it in a conversation we had. My concern isn't Brandt's tax problem, although I'm glad we've been able to deal with it..."

"And we can prosecute Hammond on the fraud case," Rick added.

Kim pointed a finger at him. "Therein lies a problem. Once we prove the fraud charge, he'll book at his first opportunity, because it looks like he's neck deep in the Dunn murder and possibly the string of killings that have occurred since then." She recounted Sophia Laguerre's disappearance and her new thinking on the supply of the Fentanyl.

Taylor considered it. "You're right. Most of the Fentanyl sold on the streets comes into the country from the cartels in Mexico, and the amount is massive and, according to the latest from the DEA, growing every week here in New York. But do we have anything linking Laguerre to that kind of operation?"

"The fact that she slipped away from us tells me we're getting close," Kim said. "Maybe she panicked, but she must know that, eventually, we're going to track down whomever she's working for. And, since she first mentioned Gorkov, I've had the sense that he is still somehow in the picture. Hammond's behavior has also had my nose twitching."

"I agree," Rick said. "When we were all in Vickers' chambers, you could almost smell the panic on him. Do you think Gorkov is involved with the Brownsville Project?"

A humorless laugh. "I'd stake my life on it, only my dad once told me never to stake my life on anything. Ken, have you been able to dig up anything on him?"

"We hadn't, but this new twist on Fentanyl bothers me. Let me do some digging."

"What do we do about Hammond?" She asked Rick. "How can we keep him here?"

"However much he might want to help on this," Rick replied, "Vickers can't revoke Hammond's bail unless he tries to flee, or you find probable cause to arrest him on a more major charge."

"We could let him see what we have and where we're going," Martin said. "He might give us what we need on Gorkov, or whoever is behind these killings."

"Gorkov was, and probably still is, Russian mob," Taylor replied.

"Which means Hammond will be way more scared of him than us." Kim thought back on their last session in Vickers' office. "The judge was rather emphatic about flight. What do you think he'd do if Hammond tried to get away and failed? Wouldn't that be a bail violation?"

"Yes, but that would require one hell of a specific fact pattern. I see where you're going. At the arraignment, we'll make sure the judge orders Hammond to turn over his passport and the keys to his plane."

It might not be enough. "Okay, it was just a thought. Ken, please keep me posted on anything you turn up, and I'll do the same."

"Sure thing, Kim. Oh, and one other thing. We've been going over Sabrina Dunn's will. We found nothing suggesting additional funding sources. Her campaign spending was well within the means of what her Campaign Finance filings reported as contributions."

"What about the Norfolk Street condo?" Kim asked.

"Looks like it was purchased with the proceeds from her trust."

"Martin," Kim said, "let's give the mayor the latest. Rick, perhaps you'd like to join us."

Back at the courthouse entrance, Kim stopped. "Rick, is Justin taking phone calls or texts?"

He laughed. "Are you kidding? He's living for them. Texts are better, since he's up and around a little more these days."

"Okay, please give me a moment." *Hi, Justin. Quick question: when you flew down to Bermuda to fetch me, whose plane were you on?*

CHAPTER SIXTY-FOUR

The crowd of protesters now made it impossible for them to get into City Hall.

Rick sized up the situation. "We wouldn't want to try, anyway. The last thing we want is to have videos of us entering City Hall plastered all over the evening news. Give me a minute."

As he turned away and pulled up a number on his cell, Kim studied the antics on the far side of Chambers Street, where Felipe Prinz was working the crowd. An ITN truck stood nearby, and Joanna was probably there, too. Which meant that she wouldn't be able to get started on the favor Kim had asked of her for several hours. More time lost.

Rick ended his call. "Just as I thought. The mayor left right after his presser with Barnett this morning. He's back at Gracie Mansion. Let's grab the Number Four train. He'll have a car meet us on the northeast corner of 86th and Lexington."

Kim's cell pinged with Justin's response to her text. *Conrad Vinson's.* She texted back. *Where did you take off?*

***

Kyle Emory had turned up an hour after the mayor returned from City Hall. His opening comment set the tone. "Please turn off whatever listening devices you have here."

The mayor gestured for his guest to take a seat and chuckled with a humor he didn't feel. "I don't have any. Richard Nixon proved nearly half a century ago that any usefulness of such a system is outweighed by the likelihood that someone, someday, will discover something one would prefer to keep secret." He gestured for his guest to get on with it.

"It appears you didn't have the votes you thought you had to prevent a veto override."

"No, I had the votes."

"Then why did you give in to Barnett's compromise? You could have broken him and his ridiculous progressive movement."

"It wasn't his compromise, it was mine. And defeating his override wouldn't have broken his wing of the party, it would have made them more determined the next time, when they would have pushed harder for something even more ludicrous. And it would have put the mayor and the council in diametrically opposed positions instead of the give-and-take that good governing requires."

"Do you realize what this does to the construction industry, and what it means to enterprises like mine? You've made it impossible for us to continue the process that has made this city livable again."

"Nonsense."

"Is it?" Emory pointed to the muted television that the mayor hadn't thought to turn off. On it were images of the protests down at City Hall. "You've energized the unwashed mob."

The mayor guffawed. "Kyle, I believe you have lost all ability to judge matters objectively. Why do you think Prinz and his ilk are upset? Because he's lost his issue. Look at the signs. You don't see my name on any of them, only Barnett's."

"I'm not following you."

"That's apparent. By engaging in compromise with me, Barnett has moved out of lock-step with people like Prinz, and that means Prinz has lost his grip on the system."

"You think he'll just disappear?"

"No. He'll withdraw and try to figure a new angle. People like him always need to be agitating about something. But then, he's not who you're most worried about, is he?"

Emory studied him. "Don't get too big for your britches. I'm sensing a lack of loyalty lately, a lack of gratitude. Frankly, you've pushed my patience to its limit."

"You mind translating that?"

"This legislation, your rhetoric notwithstanding, is a slap in the face to every developer in this city. You're forcing every major contractor to unionize. You may have killed gentrification for good."

"Unless?" Might as well get it out in the open.

"The Brownsville Project. Either I get a commitment from you here and now to support it, or my support and the support of my associates for your political career ends here and now. You've given something to the little people, so it's only fair to give something to us."

The mayor leaned forward, looking his guest in the eye. "Let's both step lightly, here, and be careful we don't let emotions carry us to places we'd both rather not go. I've already stated the conditions under which I would reconsider my stance on the Brownsville Project."

Emory stood. "Then we have nothing left to talk about."

***

Kim was taken aback by the warmth of the mayor's welcome as they were shown into the same room in which he'd first asked her to take on the Sabrina Dunn murder case.

He shook Rick's hand and placed his other hand on Rick's shoulder. "Hello, Mr. Conti. Please tell me, how is Justin doing?"

"Better. He needed surgery to repair where a bullet nicked his aorta, but he's been out of ICU for a couple of days and has been out of bed several times. He should be home soon." A weak smile. "It may be some time before he's ready to return to work, though."

"Please give him my best and tell him to take his time." He turned to Kim. "Your presence suggests you have something for me."

She handed him the printout. "We received this from Hammond in response to our subpoena on the fraud case." She handed him the statement from Sabrina Dunn's Cayman Islands bank account. "This is the account from which the payment to Hammond's company was made." She explained about the bribe attempt.

"That unvarnished bastard." He turned to Rick. "May I use these in my IRS problem?"

"That's why we're giving them to you, Mr. Mayor. Detective Brady uncovered the Caymans bank account in her investigation of the Dunn murder. We'll begin presenting to the grand jury on the fraud charge this afternoon, but I must ask you not to disclose that or your knowledge of these documents to anyone other than your accountant for the time being."

Kim spoke up. "You know Hammond will run as soon as he hears of them."

"I understand. What else do you have on the murder case?"

"Cases." She recapped where they were. "I must ask you, is there anything else about this Brownsville group you can tell us? Anything about this guy, Vinson, for example?"

The mayor remained deep in thought for several moments. Not a good sign.

"Mr. Mayor," she said at last, "I've had the sense from the beginning of this investigation that you've been holding some things back. It's why I had such a difficult time eliminating you as a suspect."

"What changed your mind?"

"The fact that someone was working so hard to make you look guilty. Sergeant Ramos got a raw deal in the department and then got used and finally killed. He worked for Hammond, but Hammond didn't order him killed."

The mayor snorted. "Hammond wouldn't have the guts."

"Exactly. But Ramos swore he never leaked the details he learned of the investigation to the media, he only told someone who worked for

Hammond, someone who speaks with a Boston accent. He also had no way of knowing the details about your past that were leaked. Moreover, someone knew when Ramos had ceased to be useful. If not Hammond, someone who worked for him and could deal with the problem."

"You think it could be Vinson?"

She met his glare. "You tell me. Who is Vinson? Where did he come from? Why does he have no history prior to fifteen years ago?" When the mayor had no answer, she added, "Have you ever spoken to him?"

"I only met him once."

"Did he speak with an accent of any kind?"

The mayor thought about it. "Yes, but nothing I could identify and nothing consistent."

"What did you notice that was different?" Martin asked. "What did he struggle with?"

"It's hard to say." After a moment, he added, "Occasionally, he had trouble with words beginning with t-h. For example, 'this' came out 'zees' at times."

"So, he also had a problem with the short 'eye' sounds. Anything else?"

"I recall at one point, 'what' came out as 'vhat', which I thought was odd."

Martin turned to Kim. "Russian might have been his first language."

"You think Vinson might be this character Gorkov?" the mayor asked.

"Let's not get ahead of ourselves," Kim said. "Anything else you can tell us?"

"He listened a lot more than he spoke, and he triggered my distrust alarm, but I couldn't tell you why."

"Can you explain why you didn't check into his background, or at least grill Emory on it?"

After a moment, he replied, "Poor judgment on my part."

One more question. "If you didn't know him well, and had only met him once, how was it you sent for me on his private jet?"

"I asked Emory to ask Hammond to send his, because I knew if I'd asked him, it would be awkward. But Hammond was having problems with his Learjet and was selling it, so he asked Vinson to send his."

"Emory or Hammond?"

"Hammond. How did you like it? It's a Bombardier 7500, quite an aircraft."

"You sound as if you'd like one, yourself," she said.

"I would, but way too rich for my blood. Besides which, it wouldn't look good for an elected official to go jetting around in something like that."

Perhaps Ken Taylor would come up with something.

CHAPTER SIXTY-FIVE

Friday, August 5th

The first thing Kim did after arriving at the Castle was to check her texts. There was one from Rick. *Arraigned Hammond this morning. The judge ordered him to surrender the keys to his airplane and his passport. Think that will be enough?*

He knew damned well it wouldn't. *Working on a plan B.*

***

As Joanna Dunbar sped eastward on the Long Island Expressway in her red Toyota Solara convertible, she had to admit that Kim Brady didn't ask many favors, but when she did, they were epic. Then again, Kim had helped Joanna save her career by somehow getting Raymond Brandt to agree to do an interview with her after she'd been sabotaged at her old job at *City News*, and Brandt had gotten her in the door at ITN.

As she crossed the border into Suffolk County, it started to rain, affirming her decision to keep the top up. She wondered how she would even broach the subject with Matt, the mechanic at MacArthur Airport whom she'd first met years earlier while chasing the story of Fred Hammond's son fleeing to Jamaica and then returning at his father's insistence. She'd coaxed information from the mechanic without a hint of shame and no small sense of satisfaction, and then realized that the attraction he showed was mutual.

After the story broke, she'd gone back to the airport to thank him for his help. He'd asked her to dinner, which had led to a nightcap at his place in Babylon, which had lasted until breakfast. The relationship had continued for over two years until the storm of passion had finally blown out.

It was now fourteen months since they'd agreed to call it quits, without so much as a text or an e-mail exchanged. The rain intensified as she parked the Solara in the hangar area, and she wondered how he'd react to her just turning up unannounced, not to mention what she was planning to ask of him.

She saw no one outside, so she stepped inside the hangar and asked the first person she saw if Matt was around.

"Right here," Matt said from behind her, making her jump. The person she'd asked walked away.

"Hi."

Matt shook his head. "Now, that's funny. After all this time, you show up and just say hi, like we just saw each other last week. Tell me you're not looking for a story."

Shit. "Can we talk someplace a little more private?"

He nodded toward the spot where the other worker had been standing. "He left. It's just us. Now, what's the story?"

"I'm not looking for one, because I've already got one."

He sneered. "Go on."

"No. I'm sorry, Matt. We had something special and…"

"And then you pulled the plug. You said I was interfering with your work."

"I did not say that; I said my work was increasingly demanding, and you needed to understand there would be times when I was unavailable. You got upset, and I suggested we step back for a time and reflect."

"And that was the last time I heard from you until today."

She had to blink back tears. "And if I hadn't come, were you ever going to call me?"

It pulled him up short. "Okay, fair point. Sorry. So, what brought you out today?"

No, Kim was going to have to figure out another way. "It doesn't matter. I shouldn't have come. I'm sorry." She walked back to her car.

***

Kim was bringing Bob up to date when a text came in from Cord. *Stakeout team spotted Sophia Laguerre near Vinson's apartment building and grabbed her.*

"Holy shit." She immediately texted back, *Bring her here ASAP.*

"We need to brief Cirillo," Bob said.

But as they left his office, Therese Vargas pulled Kim aside. "There's a posting for an admin for a captain in Internal Affairs. Did you do that?"

Kim shushed her. "Don't sabotage it. Yes, I spoke to someone over there. Apply for it but keep it quiet until you go for the interview."

A cloud crossed Therese's expression. "But he'll know, won't he?"

"I believe you can request that your supervisor not be notified."

"Thanks, Kim. You're the best."

***

Matt caught up to Joanna as she reached her car. "Wait. I'm sorry, but when I first saw you, I thought maybe you came out to get back together, but then it was more like the first time you came here, working on a story. I felt like I was being used again."

She turned away. "I never used you. I was attracted to you the first time I saw you. Okay, full disclosure, here. I came here today because someone asked me for a favor that probably only you can provide, and I saw it as one last chance to see if we could get back together. I should have known you'd take it the wrong way. You don't know how many times I picked up the phone to call you but didn't because I was afraid."

"Same here."

She searched his eyes. "Honestly?"

"Honestly. Ask your favor; let's deal with that, first." It was raining harder, and he led her back into the hangar.

She explained the situation with Fredrick Hammond.

Matt snorted. "Him again? Well, you have little to worry about, there. His jet is grounded now. He's trying to sell it but not having any luck."

"So, until then, he's given up flying?"

"Not a chance. He has a friend who lends him his plane whenever he needs it."

She turned serious. "Conrad Vinson?"

Matt turned serious, too, and scanned the hangar for anyone who might be listening. No one was around. "Let's get a coffee. Your car."

***

Cirillo sat and listened, stone-faced, until Kim finished. "You both should have kept me in the loop, especially since you were dealing with the mayor."

"With all respects, Captain," Bob said, "this thing has been moving quickly, and you haven't been very accessible. I assumed you wanted me to handle direct supervision."

The captain glanced first at Kim, then at Bob. "Very well. Have you decided how you're going to keep Hammond from jetting to Jamaica or wherever else he might go?"

"We have some ideas on that," Kim replied, "but we need to deal with Laguerre first. Cord and Tim are on their way in with her."

"I assume you want to return her to protective custody."

"No, Captain. Nor do I see her as having much value as a witness. I've already talked with Rick Conti. Her prints on the vial of Fentanyl are enough to charge her with his murder."

"At the very least," Bob said before Cirillo could react, "she's an accomplice."

"You don't have enough to convict," Cirillo said.

"No," Kim replied, "but the murder charge should motivate her sufficiently to tell us who else is involved."

"You might have pursued that when you first interrogated her. I'm trying to understand why you didn't." Cirillo sat back and waited.

The black cloud she'd been holding back bore down on her. "Poor judgment on my part."

"My thoughts, exactly. Perhaps you came back too soon."

No, not taking the bait. She repeated what Ken Taylor had said about illegal Fentanyl supplies from Mexico. "I'm betting Laguerre will tell us about that, too."

***

Joanna finished explaining Kim's Plan B, having pulled into a parking lot next to the Ronkonkoma railroad station.

For a moment, Matt could only stare at her. "What, exactly, does she think I can do?"

"She didn't say. Maybe make something look like a breakdown?"

"Any mechanical problems would be reported by the pilot, and we'd be expected to make immediate repairs. How much of a delay would she want?"

"As much as you can manage."

He pondered the problem for several minutes. Finally, he said, "There is one thing I might be able to manage, but it'll only delay him a half hour at the most."

Joanna pulled out her cell. "I'm sending you her contact information. If Hammond shows up, please text her an alert and let her know how much time she has."

"What will that accomplish?"

"Damned if I know. But it's probably better than nothing."

He laughed. "Fair enough. Now, when can I see you again?"

CHAPTER SIXTY-SIX

Sophie Laguerre glared as Kim, Bob, and Captain Cirillo walked into the interrogation room.

Kim took her favorite seat, directly across from the suspect. "You broke our agreement, Ms. Laguerre. We agreed to hold back on any prosecution on the condition that you remain in protective custody." She picked up a sheet of paper. "This is a fingerprint analysis report that states your prints were on a vial of Fentanyl in Peter Fedorov's insulin kit."

"So? I told you some guy who said he was a pharmacist gave it to me."

Kim picked up another sheet. "This is a credit report showing your employment history, which has been rather spotty."

"She means you've gone long stretches without a legitimate job," Bob said.

Laguerre shrugged. "It be tough out there, sometimes."

"But you always rolled with it," Kim replied. "Who's been keeping you afloat between jobs? Because I know as well as you do that person is the one who sent the mysterious pharmacist."

"I told you the pharmacist said his name was Ramos."

"But you know he wasn't a real pharmacist. After all, how many pharmacists do you know who make house calls?" Kim didn't give her a chance to answer. "You already explained that the only fentanyl taken from the carts in the hospital were for Hicks to use or sell. Also, the vial with your fingerprints on it had no lot number on it, which means it wasn't from a legitimate source. One glance at the label would tell you all you needed to know."

Laguerre stared at her, mouth agape.

"I'll spell it out for you," Kim said. "Even if the label said 'insulin', the lack of a lot number should have alerted a health-care professional like you to the likelihood of it being bogus. The legal term is willful ignorance. As a health-care professional, you are no doubt also aware that most abused fentanyl is smuggled into this country by organized cartels. We have good reason to believe your benefactor, whoever he is, is connected to such a source."

"I don't know, and I want me a lawyer."

"That is your right, and we'll make the call right now." Kim put her papers back in order. "But…"

Cirillo interrupted. "Detective, I believe we need to stop questioning her here and now."

"Absolutely," Kim said. "But I would like to give Ms. Laguerre an idea of what information we will seek when counsel arrives, so that she may consider just what's at stake."

"Understood, but procedure is procedure, and we don't want any risk of this prosecution being disrupted by a failure on our part."

Kim stood. "Then I guess we'll leave it at that until her lawyer arrives." Out in the corridor with Bob and the captain, she closed the door and said, "Thanks, Captain. That'll leave her stewing for a while."

He shrugged. "Least I could do."

Cord rushed up to them. "Yesterday, Cowens used a credit card under the name of Gerald Lang, one of his aliases, at a hotel in Elmhurst, Queens. So, we checked video surveillance at the Elmhurst Avenue station on the M and R line." He pulled out a printout from the video.

"That's him," Kim said.

"The Venus Lodge is a block from that station, on 83rd Street and 45th Avenue."

Cirillo laughed. "The Venus Lodge? Good Christ, why not call it the No-tell Motel and get it over with?"

But Bob was serious. "Okay, Kim, get over there, all four of you. That's the One-fifteen, correct?" Department shorthand for the 115th Precinct.

"No," Kim replied, "the One-ten."

"I'll alert them in the event you need to call for backup," Bob said. "I want this motherfucker."

She thought of Justin. "Not as much as I do. And let's alert them now. Cowens is almost certainly hiding out, not venturing out." She turned to Cirillo. "Captain, I have one hunch to play. I need to ask Laguerre a simple question that cannot incriminate her of anything."

He shrugged. "Your call."

Laguerre jumped when Kim and Cirillo returned to the interrogation room. "One simple question that will help us if you can answer it, and it won't incriminate you of anything." She laid the photo of Cowens on the table. "Do you recognize this man?"

At first, Laguerre refused to even glance at the photo.

Cirillo spoke up. "Ms. Laguerre, you can only help yourself with this. That's why I gave Detective Brady permission to ask you."

Laguerre eyed them both with suspicion, then turned to the photo and gasped. "Holy shit. That's the pharmacist."

"Thank you." Kim gathered the team in the conference room, where Cord already had a map of the area on the wall. The Venus Lodge was outlined in red marker, with an "X" at the entrance on 83rd Street. "The Elmhurst Avenue subway station has five entrances, two at the north end of the park with the playground, and three at the southeastern point of the park."

"So," Bob said, "his natural inclination if he slips out will be to turn left, toward 45th Avenue, and head for the subway."

"Unless he's thought about it and knows to turn right, heading toward Whitney Avenue and then back onto Broadway." Cord considered it. "Of course, he'd then have to run six or seven blocks to the next stop."

"Or lose us in the side streets," Kim said. "But you've highlighted our task. Bob, we need the One-ten to cover both ends of 83rd Street so he doesn't get away. Then all four of us can cover the hotel."

"Five," Bob said. "I'm coming with you."

Kim was ready to argue, but Cirillo stopped her. "He's right. You need to cover every exit. I'll stay here and make sure you have the backup. Also, if Laguerre's lawyer shows up, I can question her."

"Please don't Captain," Kim replied. "I'll let Rick Conti know we're holding off until we can bag Cowens. Because he may not be hiding just from us, and if I'm right, he might prove more useful than Laguerre."

***

The One-ten already had four units in place when they arrived, two at the 45th Avenue corner and two at the Whitney Avenue corner. The Venus Lodge had been converted from a large three-floor house and had fire escapes on either side. She had Cord at the bottom of the north side fire escape and Tim at the south side. Bob took up a post at the main entrance, and Martin accompanied Kim inside.

The furniture in the cramped lobby was bargain-basement cheap, the front desk quite small. A sign hung behind the desk: "All the comforts of the country, all the conveniences of the city." The powerful odor of air freshener didn't completely screen that of weed.

Kim flashed her badge. "Police."

The desk clerk, an Asian boy about twenty years old, held up both hands. "We don't do nothing illegal here."

"Relax." Kim pulled out the photo they'd gotten of Cowens. "This man is currently staying here." She made sure it didn't sound like a question.

The boy responded in a vigorous nod. "What's he done?"

"That's not important. He should be registered as Gerald Lang. What room is he in?"

He checked the register. "Room 103."

"Which fire escape do the windows from that room face?"

The clerk pointed to his left.

She texted Cord. *First floor, your side. Be ready.* "Give me the passkey."

She and Martin walked around to 103. No sounds from inside. She gestured for Martin to stand to one side of the door while she stood at the other, the passkey card at the ready.

"Think we should knock?" Martin asked in a whisper.

Good question. If they knocked, he'd most likely try to slip out the window, right into Cord's waiting arms. But if she just used the passkey, she and Martin would have the numerical advantage. She shook her head and pulled her Chief's Special, the .38 that had once belonged to her grandfather, while Martin pulled his piece and stood to one side.

She waved the passkey card over the lock, stepped back to the edge of the doorway, and turned the handle.

Two shots blasted through the center of the door.

Just where she'd have been standing if she hadn't taken the precaution.

Five more shots splintered the door.

She kicked the door open before ducking back. Three more shots hit the opposite wall.

That was ten. The Glock 19, which he'd used on Ramos and Justin, had a magazine which held 15 rounds, plus one in the chamber. "Drop it, Cowens. Police. We have this place surrounded."

A window shattered.

A shot, but not at her.

Kim swiveled into the doorway. Cowens stood, panicked, not knowing where to find cover. Cord was still outside the shattered window behind cover. She took a two-handed stance. "Drop it, Cowens. It's over."

CHAPTER SIXTY-SEVEN

Saturday, August 6th

"Police last night announced the arrest of a suspect, Arthur Cowens, also known as Gerald Lang, in the attempted murder of Mayoral Aide Justin Cates. Cowens is also the prime suspect in the murder of former police sergeant Miguel Ramos. Police believe the two shootings are connected to the assassination of Sabrina Dunn five weeks ago. Joanna Dunbar, ITN."

***

Bob called Kim into his office as soon as she arrived at the Castle. "Laguerre's attorney arrived late yesterday and demanded that we either arrest her or let her go, so Cirillo arrested her. She was booked last night."

"Which means both she and Cowens must be arraigned today." Kim thought a moment. "And after that, they go to either the Brooklyn Detention Complex or Rikers. Shit, Rikers is the last place I want them, especially Cowens. I'll call Conti and ask they be held here in Brooklyn."

"The captain already made that request last night."

"That was unusually helpful of him."

Bob shrugged. "He's getting used to us."

But Kim wasn't prepared for the captain to be waiting when she came out. Judging by his expression, this might not be pleasant, so she led with gratitude. "Thanks for arranging for Cowens and Laguerre to be held at the BDC."

"No problem. Would you mind?" He gestured toward the conference room. "I found out this morning that Ms. Vargas has applied for another position in the department. Over at Internal Affairs, your old stomping grounds. I wondered if you could shed any light on it."

This would lead nowhere good, and it was the last thing she needed right now. But he also wasn't about to let it go. "I was only at IAB for thirteen months, Captain."

"From what I've seen, you build loyalties quickly and easily. I suspect that thirteen months would be sufficient. Just please answer my question."

"If you're asking if I knew about her desire to find another position, the answer is yes. Therese came to me and asked me if I knew of anything. I suggested she follow the job postings, and I guess she did."

"Why did she want to leave?"

Nope. Not playing this game. "People change jobs all the time and for a variety of reasons. My advice would be to wish her well and let her move on. I'm sure you'll find another competent admin. Now, if you'll excuse me, I've got a couple of lowlifes to interrogate."

***

Fredrick Hammond couldn't believe what he was hearing. "You know that's not possible. They've taken my passport and the keys to my plane."

The voice on the other end remained cool and dispassionate, as always. "Zhat makes eet more difficult, but not impossible." The lapse into a Russian accent suggested he was not as cool as he would have Hammond believe. "My associate does not believe Cowens will hold up well under police questioning. If he doesn't, we are all in jeopardy."

"Meaning what?"

"You know what zhat means. Do not pretend otherwise. I will pick you up in my car in two hours. Please be ready."

***

Kim was surprised when Rick Conti showed up at the BDC with Lauren Davis, a young, attractive ADA who spoke with a light patois of her native Jamaica which she sometimes intensified for effect. Kim had worked with her a few times before the last miscarriage. "What's the matter, Rick? Don't you think Lauren can handle this on her own?"

But it was Lauren who spoke up. "He just can't stand to sit back on a big one like this. I said he can come along if he don't get in my way."

Rick's laugh suggested Lauren was probably telling the truth.

"I'm glad to have you both here." Kim introduced Bob to Lauren.

"Kim made me promise not to get in the way, either," Bob said. When the laughter died down, he turned serious. "I've been making inquiries among my former associates in Narcotics about the recent influx of Fentanyl from Mexico. The DEA recently discovered a tunnel at the border big enough for a two-track subway line."

"Any idea who might be using it?" Rick asked.

"A cartel, I'm sure," Bob replied. "Narcotics will keep me posted."

"I smell Gorkov," Kim said.

Rick shook his head. "Let's not jump to conclusions."

"I suggest we question Cowens first," Lauren said.

CHAPTER SIXTY-EIGHT

For a hardened criminal, Art Cowens looked terrified, like life in prison might not be the worst thing in the world. Kim led with the obvious. "We have you cold on one murder and one attempt, and Sophie Laguerre fingered you as the one who provided the vial of fentanyl that killed Fedorov. The slugs recovered in both shootings match the weapon you fired at me yesterday—so that's two more counts of attempted murder, one on me and one on Detective Stransky—and we have this." She slid the printout of the photo Justin had taken shortly before he was shot.

"We gonna lock you up and t'row away da key." Lauren said. Then, to Rick, "You t'ink of anything might change dat?"

"That depends on what else he has to say." He gestured to Kim to take over.

"Right after I began the investigation of Sabrina Dunn's murder, you started tailing me on my morning runs. Why?"

"I live in the same neighborhood."

"No, you don't. You've lived in East Williamsburg for several years until you tried to hide out in a cheap hotel in Queens. But I'll rephrase: who ordered you to tail me, and who ordered you to shoot Miguel Ramos and Justin Cates?" She pointed at him before he could respond. "You get one chance to cooperate."

Lauren spoke up. "I don't need no confession to put you away for the murder and the three attempts."

Cowens froze.

"Going once," Kim said. "Going twice…"

"Okay, okay. I'll tell you whatever you want to know, but you gotta protect me. He's got guys all over, and he'll come get me. I know it." He stared at Kim. "I didn't know you all were cops yesterday. I thought it was his guys comin' to take me down."

"Who's guys?" Kim asked, unmoved.

"Promise to protect me, first. 'Cause if I sell him out, he'll come after me wherever I am."

Lauren turned to Rick. "You buyin' this shit?"

"I don't know," Rick replied. "He hasn't told us anything, yet. But if he gives us anything about Vladimir Gorkov, I'd say we could arrange for him to serve his time someplace Gorkov would never find him."

Cowens' eyes grew as big as quarters at the mention of the name. "Yeah? Where?"

"A maximum security setting with a special housing unit to keep you apart from the general population. The term, and whatever comes after, depends on what you can tell us." Rick gestured for Kim to continue.

"So, you were working for Gorkov?"

Cowens nodded.

This was like pulling teeth. "Speak, Mr. Cowens, in complete sentences if that's possible."

"Or." Lauren added, "there be no deal."

"Okay, I've been working for Gorkov for about ten years, mostly collecting debts. He has a lot of private security around him since he took a lower profile."

"And why did he do that?" Kim asked.

"Cops were getting too close, I got busted, and so he disappeared for a while. When things cooled down, he changed his approach."

"What's his connection to Conrad Vinson? How did they hook up?" It was a shot.

"Who?"

Kim jumped up. "Don't fuck with me, you little piece of shit. You killed a good cop, you tried to kill a good friend of mine, and you tried to kill my partner and me." She pointed to Rick. "He might want to give you a deal, but I'm fine letting you rot… in the general prison population… with no protection. Now how the fuck does Gorkov know Vinson? And what's Sophie Laguerre's connection to either of them? Tell me now, or your ass is fried."

Lauren held up a match. "And I be lightin' da fire."

For a moment, Cowens buried his face in his hands.

Lauren leaned forward and glared at him. "I would advise you to think very carefully before you speak, because this is your only chance."

The sudden disappearance of her Jamaican manner left Cowens speechless for a moment. "I don't know when or how Gorkov first hooked up with Vinson. I think they were old pals from the old country. Vinson emigrated after Gorkov and they were doing a lot of shit together. Vinson got into drug dealing early, and Gorkov provided protection. Guess who made more money? After Gorkov had gone underground…"

"Which is when you started working menial jobs," Kim said.

"When I got paroled, one condition was that I have a regular job. I'd been out for two years before Gorkov contacted me. Vinson had gone legit. He used the proceeds from his drug business to make legitimate investments, and then he started providing money laundering services to other illegal enterprises. Sorry, but I have no idea how that worked. He used Gorkov to provide his own private security, and so Gorkov hired me back and a bunch of other people…"

"Including Ivan Koster, Sophie Laguerre and Peter Fedorov?" Kim asked.

"Yeah."

"And has Vinson been smuggling Fentanyl in from Mexico?"

"Yeah, for a few years, now. It kicked his drug business into high gear. He sees himself as a wholesaler. Lots of lower-level dealers buy from him, so he doesn't have his own network."

"But he provided Fedorov with enough to kill Koster," Bob said.

"Indirectly, yeah. By then, he'd started fucking Sophie, and she'd told him what a splendid weapon it would be. So, he provided Sophie with enough for Fedorov to kill Koster."

"And how, exactly, do you know all this?" Kim asked.

"Because he told me when he ordered me to give Sophie a vial to switch with Fedorov's insulin."

Lauren jumped in. "Why use you? You just said he was dippin' his pen in her ink pot."

"He didn't want to give her anything to use against him. Sophie didn't know who I was, and even if she didn't believe I was a pharmacist, she wouldn't be able to link Vinson to killing Fedorov."

Nice and neat. "Who ordered Sabrina Dunn's assassination?"

"Vinson didn't tell me that, but I'd guess it was Gorkov, since he ordered me to tail you and to kill Cates."

"Did Gorkov tell you why he wanted you to tail me? After all, I'd only just come back to the city."

"Gorkov never told me 'why' about anything. Just told me to monitor you, where you went, who you met. When I told him about seeing you running that first morning, he told me not to tail you anywhere else, but to keep an eye out for a good place for a hit if it was needed."

"But when the time came, you shot Justin Cates, instead." How odd to be discussing a possible attempt on her life in such detached terms.

Cowens shrugged. "Orders."

Kim made notes. "How does Brandon Keifer fit into all this?"

"Keifer was on an audit of one of Vinson's legit businesses a few years ago and uncovered some shit. Vinson bribed him to sabotage the audit, then offered him a job with Hammond's company as a way out."

"How did Hammond feel about that?" Bob asked.

Cowens shrugged. "Vinson probably didn't give him a choice. As soon as Vinson learned Hammond had hired Miguel Ramos, he had Keifer contact him."

Kim exchanged glances with Rick. "That would have been back in May. You mean he knew then that something big was going to go down with Sabrina Dunn?"

"Yeah, the timing is right," Cowens replied. "As for the why, sorry, that's above my pay grade."

Kim added to her notes. "Where is Gorkov now?"

"I don't know. He's gone underground again."

***

Sophie Laguerre was already angry when she walked in with her legal aid attorney. "You ain't got shit on me."

Kim's cell, sitting in her hip pocket, buzzed. Whatever it was would have to wait. "You know what I hate? When people are both stupid and arrogant. You had a sweetheart deal, being in protective custody with no charges filed against you, and you thought you could slip away. Well, sweetie, now charges have been filed, for the murder and accessory to murder."

The legal aid attorney stopped her. "If you think her alleged thefts from a cart at the hospital proves your charge of..."

So, he hadn't done his homework. "Wrong, Counselor. That's not our theory. Your client had a much more reliable source for a much larger supply of Fentanyl." Kim turned back to Sophie. "Didn't you?" Her cell buzzed again.

"Don't answer that," the lawyer said to Sophie.

Kim's sense of shit about to fall on her suddenly kicked in, a sense that rarely proved wrong. She pulled out the cell.

A text from Cord. *Just got word from the stakeout team, who followed Vinson in his limo. He just picked up Hammond and his wife, with suitcases.*

Kim jumped up and turned to Rick. "We have a situation. She's small potatoes."

She waited until they were outside before telling Rick and Lauren what was going on.

"And just what can we do about it from here?" Lauren asked.

"That's what I need to learn. I'll keep you posted. Right now, we need to get our asses out to MacArthur Airport as quickly as possible. In the meantime, run everything Cowens told us about Laguerre's involvement by her and see if she'll verify it."

"I'll drive," Bob said, "while you coordinate."

Once in the car, she called the number Joanna had provided, then called Cord and finally Ken Taylor.

CHAPTER SIXTY-NINE

"Why are we heading downtown?" Hammond was alternatively trying to understand the plan and tend to his crying wife.

Vinson cast a condescending glance at Mrs. Hammond before answering. "Driving from Manhattan to Ronkonkoma at this time of day would be more than 90 minutes. We can make it by helicopter much faster."

As Mrs. Hammond continued to sob, Vinson reached over and patted her hand. "I know this is sudden, but you mustn't allow yourself such distress. Cape Verde is much more European than African, and its president is an acquaintance of mine, while others in his administration are good friends. We'll be flying to the island of Santiago, where I have a beautiful complex in the hills. You will be my guests there for as long as you wish. The island is a veritable paradise."

When she spoke, it was to her husband. "I think you should just turn yourself in. I'll be fine."

Hammond caught the momentary look of raw anger that flashed across his host's face before it vanished back into impassive condescension. "I assure you, my dear, that would be most unwise, not to mention ungrateful to our gracious host."

"You will be," Vinson said, "without question the wealthiest couple in the country, and in six months you can apply for permanent residence."

"We don't even have visas," she said, before adding, to her husband, "and you don't even have your passport."

"I have procured visas for you both," Vinson said, "and a new passport for your husband." When Hammond looked shocked, Vinson added, "I have my methods." He glanced out the window. "Ah, excellent. The traffic on the FDR Drive is light."

**

Joanna had already lost ten minutes explaining to her boss, Ed Lyons, what it was all about and another five getting the van and a cameraman. Matt had left Vinson's plane with a near-empty fuel tank, and that would buy them twenty minutes, twenty-five at the most. At least they had early warning, which might give them enough time to be waiting for Hammond when he got there.

With any luck, that is.

Her cell pinged with a text from Kim. *Just heard from the stakeout team. Vinson and Hammond heading downtown, probably for the heliport at the East River piers. Can't get backup in time. Once in the air, they can make it to MacArthur in 22 minutes.*

So much for luck. Shit.

**

The text from the stakeout team was as discouraging as it was terse. *Chopper lifted off just as we got out of the car. Two minutes ago.*

Kim fumed as Bob drove hell-bent-for-leather along the Southern State Parkway, having just broken free of traffic on the Belt near Kennedy Airport. Cord, Tim, and Martin were en route, but they couldn't possibly get there in time. Ken Taylor had alerted the Long Island office of the FBI in Melville, not far from MacArthur, but he was uncertain how quickly they could respond.

She tried to shake off her anger at this latest development and work the problem, instead, but the black cloud provided pressure of a different kind, whispering, "It's all for nothing."

After a moment, she shook herself. "Bob, how fast do those choppers fly?"

"I don't know. Probably somewhere north of a hundred miles per hour, maybe a hundred thirty."

"And how far is it from the East River heliport to Long Island MacArthur?"

"I'd say fifty miles as the chopper flies, more or less."

She did the math. "So, we're talking less than twenty minutes from now for their arrival."

"Sounds right."

This was going to be close.

CHAPTER SEVENTY

The helicopter set down close to the hangar that housed both Hammond's Learjet and Vinson's larger and more luxurious Bombardier 7500. Hammond helped his wife out of the chopper but turned his head when he heard Vinson's voice rise.

"What? I called zhis morning to make sure it was fully refueled."

The mechanic they called Matt was clearly upset. "I'm sorry, sir, but whoever took the call left me a note, which must have been knocked to the floor." He produced a yellow Post-it with a large, greasy footprint on it.

Vinson was not mollified. "How long?"

"The tank was fifteen percent filled," Matt replied. "So, I'd say about twenty-five minutes. Then we'll need to do the usual safety check."

"Be quick about it."

"Yes, sir. In the meantime, you can clear Customs."

"We're not crossing any borders."

And the knot in Hammond's stomach tightened.

***

Kim checked her watch—12:05, just about the time she'd estimated Hammond and Vinson would arrive at the airport. Joanna's friend was no

doubt pumping gas by now. And there was always the possibility...
"What if Vinson goes with less than a full tank?"

"Then, we're fucked." Bob slowed as traffic thickened. "The exit for
Meadowbrook Parkway is next. Beach traffic." He hit the grille lights and
siren, and cars pulled to the right, but slowly.

***

Everything was loaded in the plane. Hammond had given his wife a
Xanax, and she had finally calmed down.

"How's the refueling going?" Vinson asked Matt.

"About halfway there, sir."

"Good, you can stop at seventy percent. That will be much more than
we need. How much longer do you think that will take?"

The mechanic checked his watch. "Should be another five minutes,
then the safety check."

Excellent. Ten minutes at the most, and they'd be airborne.

***

Hey, Kim. This is Matt. Joanna gave me your number. Vinson halting refuel-
ing in 5 minutes. Hammond and wife on board. Vinson says it's a local flight,
but I heard the pilot say they'll have enough to make the Cape Verde Is-
lands. Can't hold them.

Kim read the text to Bob, who'd just turned off Sunrise Highway onto
Lakeland Avenue, and then forwarded the text to Ken Taylor.

Another text from Matt. *Plane has a crew of four, but two guys I've*
never seen before.

"Well, that's great," Kim said. "It sounds like Vinson has a couple of
Gorkov's goons on board." She forwarded the news to Ken Taylor and to
Cord.

Bob kept the accelerator to the floor. "This is gonna be close."

CHAPTER SEVENTY-ONE

Hammond made sure his wife was strapped in as the plane taxied away from the hangar area. "It'll be fine, dear. You'll see." He patted her hand.

But she was staring over at Vinson, who was talking to one of the crew members in Russian.

"Nothing to worry about, my dear, just an extra security precaution." She nodded.

The plane stopped taxiing.

Vinson called out to the pilot. "Why are we stopped?"

"A brief hold by the tower, sir. In-coming flight."

Hammond glanced out his window toward the runway, waiting to see the arriving plane come into view.

***

Bob took the half-right onto Smithtown Road on two wheels. "Sorry, Kim."

"That's okay, I just hope Ken was able to hold up that flight."

"There's the entrance to the hangar area," Bob said. "And, if I remember my aircraft correctly, that's a Bombardier 7500 moving away from it."

A black sedan was coming right at them. "Bob, watch out!"

CHAPTER SEVENTY-TWO

Four minutes had passed, and still no plane had landed. Hammond glanced over at Vinson, whose face remained impassive as he yelled to the pilot. "Ask the tower what the delay is."

***

Bob made a hard right turn as the black sedan clipped the rear quarter panel.

"Gorkov's men?" Kim asked.

"I'm not stopping to ask."

Kim checked the registration number on the tailfin of the waiting jet. "That's Vinson's."

"Hope you have both your Glock and you Chief's Special, 'cause we're gonna need 'em."

***

"The tower only says to continue to hold," the pilot called back. "Maybe the incoming flight has an engine problem."

***

Bob swung the car around to the front of the plane. The black sedan pulled up right in back.

One male in a jacket and tie hopped out of the passenger side. "Are you guys Nolan and Brady?"

"Who wants to know?" Kim yelled back.

"Agent Foerster, FBI, Suffolk County Office. Ken Taylor alerted us."

"We'd love to chat," Kim replied, "but that plane is about to take off with two fugitives from justice on board."

"Our office had the tower order them to hold. We're coming around to your side to block any move. I suggest we wait for additional agents to arrive before we talk these guys off the plane. My superiors also alerted Suffolk County PD."

The driver pulled the black sedan ahead of where Bob had parked.

Another car came onto the field. A moment later, it pulled up behind Bob. Cord, Tim, and Martin deployed with weapons at the ready. All seven took up positions behind the cars and aimed their weapons in the plane's direction.

Agent Foerster pulled out a megaphone. "This is the FBI. This aircraft is grounded. Turn off the engines and prepare to disembark."

***

Vinson unhooked his seatbelt and gestured to the short, heavyset crewman who'd spoken in Russian. The crewman opened a storage locker and pulled out two AK-47s.

Hammond's wife fainted.

"This isn't a 1930s gangster film," Hammond said. "You're not going to shoot your way out."

The short, heavyset Russian glared at him. "Shut up, or you'll be the first." He signaled another crewmen who took up positions on the other side of the doorway. "Open it."

CHAPTER SEVENTY-THREE

As the door opened, Agent Foerster's partner prepared to stand, but Kim pulled him back down by the sleeve. "He won't give up that easily. Let's wait them out."

Foerster nodded. "Definitely. I've called for additional federal units, and here come the first units from the Suffolk police."

Kim didn't see any cars or vans approaching, but two helicopters came into view and then settled into a hovering position overhead. Two more circled at the far end of the field.

Kim took the megaphone Foerster offered. "Fredrick Hammond, this is Detective Brady of the NYPD. You have violated your bail and are now subject to arrest. We know your wife is with you, as is Mr. Conrad Vinson, the pilot, and at least four crew members. Let's not make this worse than it already is. Come down the steps with your hands over your head, one at a time."

With the choppers overhead, Kim moved to the far-right end of the line of cars, from where she could see the open doorway and steps leading to the ground.

"Stay low," Bob said.

As she eased her way a little higher to peer over the hood of the car, a burst of automatic fire erupted from the doorway of the plane.

"I'm okay," she called to the others. "Do not return fire."

***

Mrs. Hammond shrieked at the heavyset Russian. "What is wrong with you?"

"Now, they know we mean business."

Hammond spoke up, more to keep his wife quiet than anything else. "And suppose they return fire with something heavier? You think what we see out there is all we're going to see?"

"Shut up."

Hammond turned to Vinson, who appeared quite passive. "You're the one in charge. Are you going to let him get us all killed?"

Vinson remained calm. "In these tactical matters, I rely on my good friend's judgment."

The short, heavyset Russian grunted, then muttered under his breath, "They are all soft. They do not realize that death is nothing next to the shame of surrender."

CHAPTER SEVENTY-FOUR

A caravan of cars, plus an Emergency Services Truck, came onto the field, and twenty Suffolk County police officers disembarked behind the line of three cars. Kim introduced herself and the others.

"Technically," Agent Foerster said, "I'm in command, but this is really the NYPD's case. Detective Brady is in charge of this operation."

The lieutenant in charge of the Suffolk Emergency Services unit surveyed the scene. "The 7500 has one main exit, plus two emergency exits, one over each wing. We'll leave one patrol car on the starboard side of the aircraft with a crew to cover it, so we'll know in advance if they begin to open either emergency exit. We'll also move the truck into position directly opposite the open hatch."

"I'm going with them," she said.

The lieutenant chuckled. "It's a bit crowded. I suggest you and your guys walk on the side of the truck facing away from the aircraft. And leave one on the far side to cover any escape on that side."

"Bob, you're senior."

He nodded and moved off.

Once the Emergency Services truck was in place, the lieutenant asked Kim, "What's your next move? This has morphed into a hostage situation."

"Which means the first order of business is to get the hostages out." She turned to Cord. "You have his cell number, so get ready to call it on my say so."

She lifted the megaphone. "Mr. Vinson, this is Detective Kim Brady of the NYPD. In a moment your cell phone is going to ring. It will be me. We need to talk, so please answer when I call."

She nodded to Cord, who placed the call and gave the phone back to her. It rang three times and went to voicemail. She ended the call.

"Mr. Vinson, we need to talk. You must know this standoff can't last, and there is no way your plane is going to be allowed to take off. I'm going to try again, and this time, please answer."

***

Hammond watched as the heavyset Russian glared at Vinson, a silent warning against answering the cell when it rang, while his wife's eyes begged him to do something. "For God's sake, Conrad, at least see what she wants."

"She wants us all dead," the heavyset Russian replied.

Vinson's cell phone sounded a few notes from the 1812 Overture. He glared back at the Russian. "They don't need to talk to us to do that." He clicked the phone. "This is Conrad Vinson."

***

She could feel the lieutenant's eyes on her. This had to be done the right way, right from the beginning. "This is Detective Brady…"

"Yes, I know who you are, and I know what you want."

"And I know a good deal about you. But what I want right now is to remove innocent people from this situation."

"There are no innocent people, Detective."

"That is a philosophical argument that you and I can discuss another time. Right now, though, there are people on your aircraft who have done nothing to warrant having their lives at risk, and I would like to see if we can get them to safety."

"And what then, Detective?"

"Then, you and I can have a more substantive conversation. Adele Hammond is aboard, is she not?"

"She is."

"She has no part in this. Perhaps she didn't even want to leave to begin with. Why not let her off the plane?"

A long pause. There was some conversation going on, but she couldn't hear it. He must have his thumb smothering the tiny microphone.

"And what will you give me, in return?"

Inside the truck, officers were preparing a robotic device for maneuvering into position closer to the open door to fire tear gas into the plane.

"In return, I will halt the preparation of a drone to fire tear gas."

A soft chuckle. "You watch too many American action movies."

She turned to the lieutenant. "Please send it ten feet out and back."

The lieutenant answered his men's expressions of alarm by nodding. "Ten feet, and no further."

"Mr. Vinson, in a moment you will see the device moving away from the truck and back."

***

When Hammond saw it, he could no longer contain himself. "They are not bluffing. Don't be a fool."

The Russian took a menacing step toward him. "Shut up, coward."

Vinson gestured to the Russian to stop and spoke into his cell. "Contrary to what you think, Mrs. Hammond is not a hostage. But I will agree to your terms, and she is free to go."

***

A few minutes passed before Adele Hammond appeared in the doorway. Kim called to her, "Walk toward the cluster of cars, Mrs. Hammond."

"I was about to suggest the same thing," the lieutenant said. "Gets her out of the line of fire."

A reminder she didn't need that the situation was still dire.

CHAPTER SEVENTY-FIVE

"Good," Kim said into the cell. "Nice and easy. Now, how about the pilot? There's no harm in letting the pilot go, is there?"

"Not quite the same thing, though. You will wish to question him, no?"

"If you're concerned that we'll ask him where this flight was going, we already know he wanted the plane refueled sufficiently to travel about four thousand miles, but not to capacity. We also assume your destination was a country that does not have an extradition treaty with the United States. My guess is that your flight was headed for the Cape Verde Islands."

***

Vinson didn't hide his astonishment.

"I wonder how much else she knows," Hammond said.

The heavyset Russian's eyes blazed with anger as he growled at Vinson, "Can't anyone who works for you keep their mouths shut?"

Vinson kept his thumb pressed against the microphone of his cell. "That wasn't a guess, it was a cold calculation. I think you have underestimated these people. It's time to see things as they are." He moved his thumb and spoke into the cell. "Very well, Detective. I will release the pilot."

***

She waited until the pilot had reached the group of cars before she spoke to Vinson. "That's fine. Why not send the other crew members while we're at it?"

"That would leave just the principles, would it not?"

"Yes, as it should be."

"And what will you give if I agree?"

The lieutenant's expression changed from concerned to alarmed.

But it was natural that Vinson would feel the need to balk, and she needed to restore the relative calm that they'd enjoyed for the last several minutes. "Appreciation for the good will you've been building since this encounter began. And since I don't believe your intention was ever to hold hostages, you're not really giving up anything."

"In that case, where does the good will come from?"

"From doing the right thing."

A moment later, another man made his way down the stairs from the plane toward the cluster of cars. Kim waited until he was safely behind them. "That's two. The 7500 carries a crew of four."

***

"Two members of the crew didn't want to leave," Vinson said into the phone.

The heavyset Russian sat at the doorway, glaring at the other goon, weapon at the ready, warning him not to make a move or a sound.

"In other words, they weren't regular crew members but employees of yours. And neither wanted to get off the plane and possibly avoid prosecution? I congratulate you on stirring such loyalty, Mr. Vinson."

"Thank you. And now, I take it we've reached the heart of the negotiation."

And he ended the call.

CHAPTER SEVENTY-SIX

"He did what?" Cord was stunned.

"He hung up." But when Cord gestured for her to call him back, she said, "Not yet. Give him some time to stew."

"Or to cook up ridiculous terms," Cord replied.

"I doubt he'll do that. After all, he's out of hostages and we hold all the cards." She thought back over the entire exchange, as well as what Cowens had revealed.

"Well, something about this…" Cord began.

She finished the thought. "Smells like week-old fish. Damned right it does."

***

Hammond couldn't help himself. "What do we do, now?"

The heavyset Russian gestured with his weapon toward Vinson. "Ask the genius. He's the one who just gave our hostages and crew away for nothing."

"One of whom was my wife. Or did you plan on sacrificing her in a stupid attempt to escape from this?"

"Quiet, both of you," Vinson said.

"We're stuck here, thanks to you," the heavyset Russian said. "I told you not to have anything to do with helping him run."

Vinson's cell rang.

"Don't answer it," the heavyset Russian said. "Make her use the megaphone."

***

Kim tried two more calls. Each time, Vinson refused the call.

"I just got a report from my men at the gate," the lieutenant said. "A while ago, a news van tried to get in here. We wouldn't let them in, but they've set up beyond the fence and are filming this from a long distance. I'm afraid if we move them, they'll just set up somewhere else."

"And give the Suffolk police some bad reporting," Kim replied. "I agree, leave them be."

"What next?" the lieutenant asked.

"Back to the megaphone." She thought about what to say, then raised it. "Mr. Vinson, you realize it doesn't stop here. Having started this chess game, we must see it to the end. I'm going to try calling you again. Please pick up."

She repeated the call. Again, he denied it.

Back to the megaphone. "Based on everything I know about you, Mr. Vinson, this is not like you at all. I don't just mean the indecision, which is bad enough and completely out of character for a drug dealer who somehow remade himself into an émigré financial genius. I mean the way each step has gone since Sabrina Dunn's assassination, and even before that, with Mr. Hammond's ham-handed attempt to bribe her. The murder wasn't because of her poll numbers, it was because she'd refused the bribe and could implicate not only Hammond but you as well. But you and I both know you could have easily deflected any blame for the bribe."

She paused and tried his cell again, and again he refused the call.

"Eliminating Koster was smart," Kim continued, "and using Fentanyl caused us no end of conjecture. But see, then Fedorov was eliminated, also with Fentanyl, with Sophie Laguerre's prints on the vial. A totally sloppy move, and way out of character, so much so that I don't believe it was your idea. And then there was the murder of Hammond's employee, Miguel Ramos. Cowens told us all about that. After you'd gone to all the trouble of having Brandon Keifer recruit him as an information source. And shooting Justin Cates? Sheer stupidity, and no doubt sheer emotion."

She tried again. Call denied.

Back to the megaphone. "You're not about emotion, Vinson, and you never were. But someone who is all emotion, someone with a fierce temper, he's the one who's done you down in this deal. He's one of the two crew members who didn't come out when he had the chance, the one who fired that burst at us a while ago. He wants to go out in a blaze of glory, the perfect ending for a fatalistic Russian. The only problem is he wants to take you with him as his revenge."

CHAPTER SEVENTY-SEVEN

Hammond gasped as the heavyset Russian raised the AK-47 and aimed at the distant detective.

"Stop." Vinson's voice was soft but firm, and he had pulled a handgun from his jacket pocket. "Don't even start to turn. Lay the weapon on the floor of the aircraft."

The heavyset Russian spoke over his shoulder to Hammond. "He's pointing the Makarov at me, isn't he?"

"He's pointing a pistol at you, yes." Hammond knew nothing of firearms, let alone Russian-made handguns.

"So, this is how it ends, Conrad? With you selling me out?"

"Everything the detective just said is accurate. You have been my undoing. Lay down the rifle now, please, and stand in the middle of the doorway with your hands up."

"You would shoot me in the back?"

"In a second."

***

"Who the hell is that?" Cord asked.

"The one who's been preventing Vinson from answering the damned phone." Kim tried another call.

"Hello, Detective. I'm sorry I was unavoidably detained. The cause of the delay is standing in the doorway. I know you won't shoot him, but it wouldn't upset me if you did. After you have secured him, I will send out the last crewman. He is a minor participant and will probably cooperate in your investigation. I will then send out Mr. Hammond, and finally myself. Is that agreeable to you?"

"Yes, Mr. Vinson, although why don't you, Mr. Hammond, and the last crewman come out as well?"

"I would think you'd want to proceed in as orderly a fashion as possible. I'll remain on the line until our business is completed."

The man in the doorway with his hands raised didn't move.

"Mr. Vinson, please have him come down, now," Kim said into the phone.

***

"Time to go," Vinson said. "Not one step back."

"Stalin's command to the troops facing the Nazis. A very poor choice of words, Comrade."

"Nevertheless, my command holds."

But he stood motionless in the doorway. "*Nyet.*"

Vinson shot three rounds.

***

As the bulky man tumbled down the steps and landed on the tarmac, dozens of weapons rose to firing positions.

"Hold your fire!" Kim yelled through the megaphone. "Repeat, do not open fire!"

"My apologies for ruining your operation, Detective," Vinson said over the phone. "The man lying on the ground is Vladimir Gorkov. I believe you've been looking for him. I wanted to deliver him into your custody, but, believe me, it is better this way."

By now, Bob, Tim, and Martin had joined her.

"Here comes Hammond," Bob said.

The man looked defeated, worse than he had when his son had been convicted of murdering a firefighter. "Fredrick Hammond, you are under arrest for accessory to murder and violating your bail." To Bob she added, "I'd love to cuff him myself, but we still have…"

From inside the aircraft came the report of one more gunshot.

CHAPTER SEVENTY-EIGHT

"… Joanna Dunbar speaking from Long Island MacArthur Airport where a joint team of New York City police, Suffolk County police, and the FBI, today prevented Vladimir Gorkov, the person believed to be behind the murder of Sabrina Dunn, three other murders, and the attempted murder of an aide to the mayor from leaving the country. Also attempting to flee was financier Fredrick Hammond, who was arrested for violating his bail on a pending fraud charge, and who is also implicated in these murders, and financier Conrad Vinson, both of whom are connected to these crimes. All three were on board Mr. Vinson's private jet and were preparing to leave the country, when they were stopped by law enforcement. As police attempted to talk Vinson and Gorkov off the plane, Vinson shot Gorkov and then himself. Both men were pronounced dead on the scene. Hammond and Vinson were partners in the controversial proposal to privatize a major city housing project in Brownsville and were heavy contributors to the mayor's campaign fund."

***

As the Suffolk County Medical Examiner's Office prepared to take the two bodies away, Kim completed her notes on her cell. Cause of death for both: gunshots with a Soviet made Makarov nine-millimeter.

"Excuse me, Detective," the lieutenant said. "We'll handle the homicides. Obviously, you're going to take Hammond and the kid crewman. Think you'll be able to nail them?"

"I doubt we'll prosecute the kid, but we might use him as a witness. Hammond might take some doing, although trying to run can only make him look guilty. We'll see."

Bob pulled her aside. "Let's get out of here. I'll drop you at home."

"Thanks, but I've got a couple of people to see first. You can come if you like."

CHAPTER SEVENTY-NINE

First stop was a townhouse on East 79th Street. The butler showed her into a sitting room while Bob waited in the car.

Richmond Dunn and his wife were sitting together. He sat silent, ashen-faced, but she looked fresh and alert, the first time Kim had seen her that way. She didn't give Kim a chance to say anything. "We heard the news but thank you for coming by to tell us. Considering the less-than-cordial welcome you've received previously in this house, it's very gracious of you."

Kim took her hand. "Not at all. In my line of work, I find closure is everything it's cracked up to be."

Mrs. Dunn turned serious. "Will you question my husband again?"

Richmond Dunn spoke up. "I didn't know anything. My God, how could I have?"

Kim knelt in front of him. "You have already convinced me you weren't a part of this. We may be back at some point to ask you about the details of your dealings with Hammond and Vinson, but that's all."

Mrs. Hammond touched Kim's shoulder. "I'll walk you out." As they descended the stairs, she said, "I'll eventually forgive him for disowning her, but not yet. And I'm relieved I don't have more to forgive. Thank you, Miss Brady."

Kim held up her left hand, showing her wedding ring. "Ms. Brady."

***

Kim found Felipe Prinz at home, but was not at all surprised he was only partially coherent and the air was heavy with marijuana smoke.

"It's legal," he said with a shrug.

"So you keep saying. We got Sabrina's murderer."

"Thought he was already dead."

"We got the one who ordered it, a Russian mobster. Also, a certain financier of whom you've heard, who was also involved. However, the mobster's dead, along with his muscle man."

His eyes cleared slightly. "Don't tell me. Freddy Hammond. So, this was connected to the Brownsville project after all. How'd Freddy get hooked up with a Russian mobster? Take an ad in the Times?"

"Another member of the group, Vinson. He killed the muscle man and himself."

"You sure you didn't give him a little help?" He broke into a sneer.

"Not my style. You should know that by now. So, what happens to you going forward? I hear Leroy Barnett wants to challenge Mayor Brandt in the primary in three years. Think you might go mainstream?"

The sneer turned to a scowl. "Barnett's a sellout."

"How's that? He got the mayor to agree to most of Sabrina's Law."

"He wasn't supposed to compromise. Never give up anything. And this, with him being black."

"The nerve. Well, I know I'm just a cop, but representative government is supposed to be about compromise. It's the only way it works." His scowl grew deeper. "And that's your problem. You don't want representative government; you want a dictatorship that does only what you want it to do. Well, it's a free country—for now, anyway—so if you want to marginalize yourself instead of doing something constructive, that's your business. Have a pleasant evening."

***

It was well after visiting hours when Kim reached her last destination. Bob had dropped her off and returned to the Castle. Kim got up to Justin

Cates' room using the oldest trick in the book—honesty with the nurse supervisor.

"Just don't be too long," the supervisor said, "or it's my ass."

Justin was awake and reading. "Hey, aren't you breaking the law?"

She kissed him on the cheek. "I'll go now, if you like."

He grabbed her hand. "Hell, no. You did it. I've been listening to Joanna Dunbar sing your praises all evening."

"She wouldn't dare mention my name on the air."

"Nah, she just kept saying stuff like 'diligent police work' and 'dedicated police officers' and such. I was lucky enough to know who she meant."

But she couldn't shake the image of Gorkov lying on the tarmac or of Vinson in a pool of blood on the floor of his own plane. "It wasn't diligent enough to keep two felons alive to stand trial, and that's what we're about."

"They did that, not you. Besides, they saved the taxpayers the cost of a trial."

Bob had said the same thing driving back from Ronkonkoma.

The nurse supervisor entered, looking severe. "Excuse me, but visiting hours are long over."

Kim smirked, pushing the black cloud away. "Sorry, I guess I lost track of the time. Take care, Justin, I'll be back in the next day or two."

CHAPTER EIGHTY

Sunday, August 7th

With the case no longer available as a tool against her depression, Kim poured her energy back into running. She was up at 5:30 and on the road by six, careful not to disturb Jake as he slept. Her first ten-miler would be a perfect tonic to ward off the blues. She pushed the pace, too.

But as she rounded the loop at the top of the greenway, her left hamstring began to bark, and she was forced to walk. After a minute or two, the pain faded, and she pushed to an easy jog. Better.

Another two minutes, and she picked up the pace. Still good, so she pushed to her normal pace.

The sudden stabbing pain in the back of her left leg was like a knife going in. She limped home, having managed just six miles, and was engulfed by a new black cloud of depression.

Jake was waiting when she walked in. "As soon as I woke up and saw you were gone, I figured you'd gone for a run." He handed her an ice block fresh from the freezer and gestured to her leg. "You're limping. Massage it with this for fifteen minutes or until it's completely numb, whichever comes first."

She sat at the dining table, rubbing the ice block against the back of her leg in a steady cadence.

He brought her a fresh bottle of water and sat with her. "Please call Alyssa and make an appointment. See her today if you can manage it. I'll go with you and even take part if you'd like. It's up to you."

Her cell buzzed—a text from Bob. *Cirillo wants us to pick up Keifer for questioning tomorrow morning.*

He gestured to her cell. "If you're thinking you were just saved by the bell, don't. Make the appointment."

He was right. She called the private number Alyssa had given her. The earliest she could manage was Tuesday.

"That'll do," Kim said.

CHAPTER EIGHTY-ONE

Monday, August 8th

Keifer sat in the interrogation room, doubling down on the feigned outrage he'd shown when Kim and Cord had picked him up.

As usual, everyone expected Kim to lead the questioning, but it was as if nothing mattered anymore. She was even considering canceling her appointment with Alyssa Walters for the next day. Only the thought of Jake's anger prevented it.

"Kim," Cord said, "you want to kick this off?"

She nodded but couldn't get her thoughts organized.

Cord turned a fierce face to Keifer, "That's okay, I'm cool with it." He laid out everything Ramos had told them, including their encounters on the express bus and Keifer's requests for information on the case.

"Mere hearsay," Keifer's lawyer said.

"Statement against penal interests," Rick Conti replied.

"I knew he'd been a cop," Keifer said. "I was interested."

"What made you think he'd know about an investigation of a crime committed weeks after he left the department?" Cord asked.

"I figured he still had friends there who'd tell him stuff."

Kim's fog lifted a bit. "You knew he'd left the department on bad terms and played on his resentment. Did he tell you about his girlfriend, too?"

Before Keifer could answer, Cord said, "Did Vinson pay you off before he arranged for you to work for Hammond, or was it all part of the same offer of employment?"

"There was no payoff."

The fog receded further. "You don't think we'd ask if we didn't already know, do you? We've checked your bank records. A $50,000 deposit a week before you started working for Hammond—we checked the employment records, too."

Cord piled on. "And while curiosity about a big criminal case is normal, leaking what you learned about it to the media is not. You be in deep shit, Bro, and I suggest you cop some safety while you still can."

Keifer shook his head. "I never repeated anything…"

"We can do a lineup and have Joanna Dunbar tell us if your voice is the one that divulged case details," Kim said.

Rick spoke up. "I'll make this easy. You're not our primary target. Tell us what your arrangement was with Fredrick Hammond and Conrad Vinson and how you knew the other information you leaked to the press, and I'll knock it down to one count of Obstruction of Governmental Administration, a Class A misdemeanor."

"We also need to know the details of your arrangement with Hammond and Vinson and how it all tied in with their relationship with Kyle Emory," Kim said.

Rick patted her on the arm. "Give us all that, and I'll even make a sentencing recommendation for leniency."

Keifer's lawyer nodded.

"Yeah," Keifer said, "Vinson invited me out to lunch at this real plush restaurant, just him, Hammond, and me. He slid an envelope with fifty grand across the table to me and said there was a cushy job waiting for me at Hammond's company, all in return for me 'misplacing' my findings on his money-laundering scheme. He was screwing the government out of tens of millions in taxes every year."

"What was the cushy job?" Kim asked.

"Senior Consultant, Auditing. The funny part was that although Hammond was paying my salary, almost all my consulting was with Vinson, advising on how to use foreign accounts to launder money from his illegal operations. The only matters I consulted on for Hammond were on ways to route income from his foreign subs back to the parent without paying taxes on them."

"At these lunch meetings," Conti asked, "how were Vinson and Hammond with each other?"

Keifer laughed without humor. "Vinson was the boss."

"What did they talk about?"

"Mostly pressed me for advice, but they did sometimes talk about other things. Whenever Hammond made snide remarks about Mayor Brandt—whom he clearly did not like—Vinson would ask for details and egg him on. But that stopped when Sabrina Dunn entered the gubernatorial race and started making gains in the polls. Hammond said she could derail their big idea for a project."

Kim snapped to attention. "You mean the Brownsville Project?"

"Yeah. Vinson had pressed Hammond to come up with a major real estate project for him to invest in to further cover his illegitimate businesses." He described Hammond's idea for the Brownsville Project. "Vinson wanted in badly, and together they'd convinced Emory to go to the mayor on it."

Kim placed a hand on Conti's arm to keep him from asking the next question. "And?"

"You know the rest," Keifer replied. "Emory went to the mayor, but then Dunn was killed and that seemed to kill Brandt's interest in the project. Vinson couldn't understand it, since the biggest roadblock had just been removed."

"Did you all discuss this after the assassination?"

Keifer froze.

"You want my deal?" Conti said. "I need to know it all."

"A few days before, Vinson made a comment about a plan to deal with the 'Brownsville problem', as he called it. He didn't elaborate. But the morning after the shooting, Vinson called me and said Hammond had recently hired an ex-cop named Ramos who could be very useful, and to get friendly with him. As I got info from Ramos, I passed it on to Vinson."

"Was it Vinson's idea to leak it to the media?" Kim asked.

"I don't know if it was his idea, but Hammond's the one who told me to do it. When I hesitated, he said, 'You wouldn't want to do anything to ruin this great setup you have here.' He sounded just like Vinson when he said it. So, I did."

"Who provided you with the contact numbers at ITN and *City News*?" Rick asked.

"Hammond did. He also told me to dig into Brandt's history before he entered politics, to see if I could dig anything up on him. So, I called them up, spoke to Cappelli, said I was an investigator for a political action committee that was seeking to endorse Brandt for higher office and just needed some background on him. He told me the entire story."

"He told us he didn't remember any details of Brandt's time there," Cord said.

"Everything I told *City News*, I got from Cappelli. I can even show you my notes if you want."

Rick held up a hand. "Not necessary." He turned to Cord. "Of course, Cappelli denied knowing anything. You questioned him after the report was aired on *City News*."

"So," Kim said, "Hammond knew in advance."

"Sure looks that way," Rick replied with a chuckle.

***

"Hey," Rick said to Kim outside the interrogation room, "are you okay? You seem a bit off your game."

The black cloud was closing in. "Just… stuff. I pulled a hamstring running yesterday. I'll be okay. When will you need me for the grand jury?"

"Later this week. I'll open the case with them tomorrow. Let me know when you're ready. But please take care of whatever was bothering you enough to incur an overuse injury."

CHAPTER EIGHTY-TWO

Tuesday, August 16th

Alyssa Walters was only five or six years older than Kim, with blond hair showing signs of premature gray and a manner that had made Kim relax the moment they first met. It had been Alyssa who'd first suggested a getaway for Kim and Jake after the miscarriage, although Jake had come up with Bermuda as the destination.

Kim had just spent three minutes describing their time in what she called paradise, followed by twenty minutes of everything that had happened since she'd returned.

Alyssa allowed her some time to cry it out before saying in a soft voice that somehow softened the words, "You came back too soon."

"I know."

"It was wrong of the mayor to ask you, and it was wrong of your captain to allow you to come back."

"A mayor outranks a captain." But she knew that was only partly true. If Lieutenant Bostwick had still been on the job, he would have put up a stink and that might have made a difference. Or would it?

"I also would have advised you against consulting with your gynecologist about the tests until after your work stress had returned to lower levels."

"I was already feeling the stress, and my depression returning. Jake urged me to call you, but I was so wrapped up in the case…" Kim paused. "Strange how we rationalize things, isn't it?"

"Yes, but we also prioritize, and sometimes we don't do it well, particularly when we are already stressed. The two most damaging words we use are, 'If only'. It's much better to say, 'Next time.' And this is now your next time. Things have calmed down, and you need to decide what your course will be. It's interesting that you initially resisted having children, only to change your mind later."

"A mistake."

"Perhaps, but perhaps not. You told me during our earlier sessions about the factors that influenced your change of heart, the young Mexican girl you'd helped reunite with her parents. That impulse was real."

"But it wasn't possible. And I was just beginning to accept that, to accept that I had my husband and my career and now, my running, and then…" She couldn't go on.

Alyssa gave her a moment. "And then… what?"

No answer.

"Kim, this is the question you need to answer. Take as long as you need but answer it. Here and now."

It came out a whisper. "I'm not as good a cop as I thought I was."

Alyssa waited.

"My judgment on this case was, at times, awful. I kept changing my mind. And then, just when I'd finally focused on the people I needed to bring to justice, two of them ended up dead before I could arrest them. And… it wasn't the first time for that, either."

"Your grandfather's killer."

"Yes."

"You told me about that. I don't see how you could have done anything differently. He was trying to kill you. What choice did you have?"

"That's not it."

"You mean because you felt satisfaction at his death?"

"Yes. I thought nothing of it at the time, but with these two…" Kim let the sentence die.

"Did you feel a sense of satisfaction on Saturday, seeing them both dead."

"No." Kim reflected on it. "No," she said, stronger this time, "I didn't."

"You're a damned good cop. You just need to decide whether to try again to have a baby. If you need to talk more, please call me. And remember, Kim, there is no wrong answer."

CHAPTER EIGHTY-THREE

Tuesday, August 23rd

"A grand jury yesterday handed up indictments in the assassination of Sabrina Dunn and the killings that followed, and the shooting of Justin Cates for Fredrick Hammond, Arthur Cowens, and Sophie Laguerre. Mayor Brandt once again expressed his thanks to the New York City police, particularly the Detective Squad at Police Borough Brooklyn North, as well as the FBI and the Suffolk County Police Department, who assisted in the case. When asked for his reaction to Hammond, a known supporter of his, being involved in the assassination of a political rival, the mayor replied, 'Just because someone supports me, it doesn't mean I approve of him. If he's convicted, I hope he never walks free again.' Separately, developer Kyle Emory has pledged continued support of the mayor. This is Joanna Dunbar for ITN News."

***

Sergeant Dhillon was biting his lip as he greeted Kim.

"What is it?" She didn't need any bullshit the first day back after a brutal case.

"Nothing. Just glad to see you here. And congratulations on your most wonderful conclusion to the Dunn case."

She didn't believe him, but she just said, "Thanks."

Bob was sitting at his desk, where she hadn't seen him since he'd moved into Bostwick's office in the first days of the Dunn case.

"Hey," she said, "what gives? Couldn't take the confines of an office any longer?"

Bob just shrugged.

"No," a voice said from behind, "I just wanted it back."

She wheeled around. "Lt. Bostwick, as I live and breathe. Is this for good, or are you just visiting?"

He was thinner than she'd ever seen him, and his face was gaunt. His scalp showed only a few wisps of hair remaining. "Just a visit since I have another six or seven months of treatment to go. But I heard you two have been rockin' and rollin', and I'm glad see you back, Kim, since I heard the news and wanted to be the one to tell you."

"What news?" She wasn't sure she could take any further upheavals.

"Well, several things. First, you are receiving another decoration for your work on the Dunn case, Meritorious Police Duty. That will go nicely with the two you already have. You'll need a bigger badge holder."

"Thank you, Lieutenant."

"Not done yet. You've also been promoted to Detective, First Grade. Congratulations. It's long overdue."

"Thank you."

"There's more," Bob said. "Not specifically for you, but you'll be interested."

"Captain Cirillo has been promoted to Deputy Inspector and is being transferred down to One-PP," Bostwick said.

"Rumor has it the mayor insisted," Bob added, "I guess to smooth ruffled feathers."

Bostwick cleared his throat. "I don't know what that refers to, but his place here as commander of all PBBN detective squads is being taken by... oh, here he is, now."

Kim turned and saw Steve Colangelo from Internal Affairs approaching, sporting a shiny new captain's badge on his uniform. "Glad to see you, Kim."

"Congratulations on your promotion," she said. "Couldn't take it in IAB any longer?"

"When the Commissioner says he needs you elsewhere, you don't argue. Working with you guys is a bonus." Then he added, "Oh, I've already asked Therese Vargas to withdraw her posting application. I told her that the detectives here had spoken glowingly of her abilities, and I'd like to keep such a great team together. I hope I can count on you."

She glanced from Captain Colangelo to Lieutenant Bostwick to Bob Nolan as Cord, Martin and Tim gathered around. "You sure can."

ACKNOWLEDGMENTS

I began writing *Judgment of Beasts* while preparing the third Kim Brady novel, *Proving a Villain*, for publication and preparing the first Dan Brady novel, *Enemies of All*, for submission to Black Rose Writing. As such, the process was more stop-and-go than any of my previous efforts. And as soon as *Enemies of All* was finalized, I began work on the next Dan Brady novel. My wife, Cindy, asks me if I ever intend on taking a break, but the truth is I waited for 40 years to be able to write for publication, and I don't want to waste a moment or lose an opportunity.

I am truly thankful to Reagan Rothe and his crew at Black Rose. David King, graphic designer extraordinaire, handles the fabulous covers on all my novels as well as preparing the content for publication. Justin Weeks in Sales, Chris Martin in Publicity and Minna Rothe in Marketing round out a great team.

I also thank my intrepid beta readers, Ray Lodato, whom I've known since 1958, and Jan Foley, whom I've known since the late 90s, but have never met in person (the internet can be a truly wonderful thing). Their astute observations have saved me from falling down many a plot hole. And I'm so fortunate that they keep coming back for more.

My good friend, Jim Brady, gets a reprise of his brief role as Kim's cousin. Anyone who would like to be included as a character in a future Kim Brady or Dan Brady novel, please e-mail me at EJL.author@gmail.com.

Finally, my greatest thanks go to my wife, Cindy, the Love of My Life who continues to share this road with me after 46 years. Not only is she my alpha reader, she continues to make sure I don't miss the latest headline-making crimes, prefaced always with, "Here's something you might want to write about."

ABOUT THE AUTHOR

Edward J. Leahy is the author of the Kim Brady Detective Mystery Series and the Dan Brady Detective Mystery Series. He was a finalist for
the 2018 Freddie Award for Excellence. He is a member of the Mystery
Writers of America and the International Thriller Writers and has been
published by New York Teacher Magazine. He's a retired International
Issue Specialist for the IRS with investigative experience and holds a B.
A. and M. A. from St. John's University in Government & Politics. He
served on the Board of Directors of AHRC-NYC from 1998 to 2023.
Born and raised in the New York City Borough of Queens, he lives in
Jackson Heights with his wife, Cindy.

OTHER TITLES BY EDWARD J. LEAHY

NOTE FROM EDWARD J. LEAHY

Word-of-mouth is crucial for any author to succeed. If you enjoyed *Judgment of Beasts*, please leave a review online—anywhere you are able. Even if it's just a sentence or two. It would make all the difference and would be very much appreciated.

Thanks!
Edward J. Leahy

We hope you enjoyed reading this title from:

BLACK ROSE
writing™

www.blackrosewriting.com

Subscribe to our mailing list – *The Rosevine* – and receive **FREE** books, daily
deals, and stay current with news about upcoming
releases and our hottest authors.
Scan the QR code below to sign up.

Already a subscriber? Please accept a sincere thank you for being a fan of
Black Rose Writing authors.

View other Black Rose Writing titles at
www.blackrosewriting.com/books and use promo code
PRINT to receive a **20% discount** when purchasing.